Escape to St Ives

Deborah Fowler

Allison & Busby Limited
11 Wardour Mews
London W1F 8AN
allisonandbusby.com

First published in Great Britain by Allison & Busby in 2026.

A CIP catalogue record for this book is available from the British Library.

First Edition

ISBN 978-0-7490-3397-2

By choosing this product, you help take care of the world's forests. Learn more: www.fsc.org.

Printed and bound in Great Britain by Clays Ltd. Elcograf S.p.A

EU GPSR Authorised Representative
LOGOS EUROPE, 9 rue Nicolas Poussin, 17000, LA ROCHELLE, France
E-mail: Contact@logoseurope.eu

In memory of Tom Parker, who encouraged me to write my first ever short story. He promised me a decent lunch, as a prize, if I could find a publisher. I got my lunch!

PROLOGUE

Chelsea, London

Sir Hubert Eustace opened his eyes to find the sun streaming through his bedroom window. Somewhere nearby, a pigeon was cooing. He shut his eyes again quickly and, just for a moment, he could almost believe he was back home in Devon. Then the reality of his situation smothered all other thoughts, and he turned to his wife for comfort.

She wasn't there, of course. Three days ago, with his blessing, she had set off to stay in their home near Newton Abbot. She'd said she would only be away for a few days, just to catch up with some friends. Sometimes he wondered if she ever met a man on her jaunts. Once, he would have been insanely jealous, but not any more, though he still loved his wife dearly. She was young, healthy and full of life. He was old and ill – it was right she should have some fun.

Of course, he knew he was overindulging her – indeed, he had always done so. He had known her since she was a little girl; her parents had been close friends of Hubert and his first wife Cynthia, and they had been hugely caring and helpful when Cynthia was killed in a hit and run. Then it was Hubert's turn to provide support. When their daughter was just nineteen, her parents had died in a speedboat accident. She was an only child, so he'd acted as her guardian and taken on full responsibility for sorting out her life following her parents' deaths. At some point, during the year that followed, his role as guardian changed to that of lover, and shortly after her twentieth birthday, they married. Hubert was forty-five.

Now, though, their story was nearly at its end. At the Royal Marsden Hospital yesterday, Hubert had been told that he had only two months to live.

CHAPTER ONE

St Ives, Cornwall

Merrin McKenzie was feeling nervous – in fact very nervous, which annoyed her intensely. In her years as a family solicitor, she had battled formidable prosecution lawyers, faced terrifying judges and just last year, she had placed herself between a teenage girl and a loaded gun. This, however, was a different sort of nervous. It was very personal and fuelled, she suspected, by a real sense of impostor syndrome, which, of course, was entirely justified. She had absolutely no experience of running a shop, and here she was, about to do just that. She gazed around her, trying to view the shop objectively, as a customer would do – and failed miserably. She fiddled with a couple of mugs on the shelf in front of her, twisting them at a jaunty angle. Then she put them back as they were, and let out a ragged sigh.

It was now over four years since her policeman husband, Adam, had been stabbed to death on the streets of Bristol. As a result, Merrin had returned to her home town of

St Ives, where she'd not lived for well over thirty years, but where she had expected to find peace and quiet after her terrible loss. However, since her return, she had become involved in a murder, a county line drugs gang, a missing body, a nasty assault, a kidnap and the episode with the loaded gun. If she were being uncharitable, she could say that all of this was due to her association with Chief Inspector Louis Peppiatt, for it was he who had involved her in most of the aforementioned dramas. They had started working together because Merrin had needed a job to keep her occupied while she tried to come to terms with her grief. Louis had offered her pro bono work as a solicitor, representing clients who desperately needed particularly sensitive and compassionate support but couldn't afford to pay for it. Oh yes, Louis had a lot to answer for, but if she was being entirely honest with herself, she knew she should accept responsibility for at least some of the challenges they had faced together. They also shared a common loss. Louis's marriage had broken down some years ago and, like Merrin, he found living alone something of a challenge.

It was the incident with the gun that had made Merrin feel she needed a break from the law. Initially, she had acted instinctively, shielding the young girl who had been kidnapped while temporarily in her care. Immediately after it was all over, everyone kept telling her how brave she'd been, but still nothing registered. It was only when Louis Peppiatt turned to face her, having removed the gun from the perpetrator, that she saw the fear and dread still reflected in his eyes and, at that moment, realised how close she'd come to death.

For the past couple of years, Merrin had been attending pottery classes and absolutely loved them. So, she had taken the plunge, rented a little shop in St Ives's main shopping street and set up a co-operative for creative people. As well as her own ceramics, she was displaying contributions from a sea-glass jeweller, Pippa Meadows; a quirky landscape artist, Joey Moon; and a candlemaker, Lizzie Cambridge – all talented local young people who were hugely excited about the project. They were calling the shop the 'West Cornwall Crafts Co-operative' – not a very original name, but at least it explained what they were doing.

Tonight was the private view; the shop would be formally opened in the morning. Invitations had been distributed, but would anyone actually turn up, let alone buy anything? Far more than for herself, Merrin wanted the shop to succeed for her young colleagues, who had put so much work into creating both the stock and the charming displays of their work. She glanced at her watch – twenty minutes to go until the first guests should arrive. She now felt positively sick with nerves; it was ridiculous.

Merrin climbed the stairs to the first floor, which she had turned into a little pottery studio. Following very close behind her was her dog, William. He had picked up on her mood and was clearly wishing to lend support. She stopped at the top of the stairs and bent down to stroke him.

'Sorry to be so pathetic, William,' she said. 'I'll be OK once someone arrives, assuming anyone does. You're going to have to be good and stay in your basket by the till.'

Dear William was not a thing of beauty, but his understanding of human frailty was quite remarkable. He gave her a kind look and gently wagged his tail. *Don't worry, I've got your back*, he seemed to be saying.

Merrin walked through into the upstairs bathroom and gazed at her reflection in the mirror. She ran her fingers through her hair in an effort to tidy it, but instead she just looked dishevelled – in her own eyes, at any rate. Merrin was not someone who normally gave much thought to her appearance, but this evening she was in uncharted waters. She was short, only just over five feet tall, slim with dark curly hair, big blue eyes and a fresh vivid complexion. She had never been beautiful but she was very pretty, a pleasure to look at, even now in her mid-fifties. However, the woman who scowled back at her from the mirror was not feeling it.

She was still making grizzly faces at herself when she heard the front door of the shop open. 'Pearl, darling, are you there?' It was Clara, Merrin's best girlfriend, who had nicknamed her 'Pearl' since they had been toddlers together.

Merrin felt an instant sense of relief. 'I'm here, Clara,' she shouted. 'Me and William are just coming down.'

Clara was standing in the middle of the shop clutching two huge plates.

'Where shall I put these, Pearl? Tristan has made you some canapés. They're really good, I nicked a few when he wasn't looking.'

'That's so kind of him, but you must let me pay for them,' said Merrin. 'Here, give me a plate, we can put them on this table by the till.'

They put down the plates, and the two women exchanged a hug. Clara Tregonning was the absolute antithesis of

Merrin. She was tall and willowy, with pale blonde hair. She had always been a naughty girl, loved a party, invariably drank too much and was blessed with a wonderful sense of humour. She was also a true friend. While she always professed to being man-mad, it was all talk – she had been faithfully married to Tristan for nearly thirty years and adored him. Together they ran a fish restaurant on the Wharf called Tristan's Fish Plaice.

'Of course you're not paying for the canapés, darling Pearl. They're our present for your shop opening. Now, I'll organise the food and wine. I can see you haven't put out nearly enough glasses. This evening's going to be a wow, the whole town will come out to support you. I've asked Max to bring another couple of cases of wine, because I knew you wouldn't have enough.'

'Clara, I don't want it to turn into a party. It's supposed to be a chance for people to come and see what we have to offer and hopefully buy something.'

'Don't be such a killjoy, darling Pearl. You're thinking like a lawyer – so cautious. Trust me, I know what I'm doing – the more they drink, the more they'll buy.'

Merrin looked at her quizzically but couldn't help laughing. It was true; this was Clara's field of expertise – she'd worked in hospitality all her life, starting as a kitchen porter, aged eleven. 'Just make sure nothing gets broken. A lot of work has gone into all of this,' she said, firmly.

'Pearl, darling, no one is going to get drunk, I'll make sure of that. They'll just be merry enough to spend a little recklessly,' Clara said with a wicked grin. 'Now go away and let me get on with my job, they'll be here in a few minutes.'

As if on cue, Max Richards staggered through the door carrying the promised cases of wine.

'Brilliant, Max darling, well done. Let the party begin,' said Clara, who clearly still had opposing opinions to Merrin as to how a private view should be run.

Max Richards was a Cornishman, through and through. He was also a serious Lothario. He had been at school with both Merrin and Clara and in the same academic year as Jago Tripconey, Merrin's older brother. The four of them had spent much of their time together during their childhood and teenage years. Max called them 'The Posse', clearly having watched too many western movies. Things had changed when Jago went off to Australia and then two years later, Merrin left for Bristol University. Neither brother nor sister had come back to live permanently in St Ives again – until, that is, Merrin returned following her husband's death. As with all true friendships, Max, Merrin and Clara had seamlessly picked up the relationship they'd last enjoyed as teenagers.

Max had never married, although he was good-looking and charming with a marvellous sense of humour. His problem was commitment. The moment a lady started to show interest in a long-term relationship, Max shot off like a frightened rabbit. However, in the last few months, Merrin and Clara had become cautiously optimistic about his current companion. Poppy was nearly twenty years younger than Max and they had been together for over a year – something of a record for Max. Poppy was such a free spirit and she had everyone's full approval – she was friendly, fun and kind. It was just possible that she might be a keeper.

Max and Clara had just finished setting out the glasses and opening some wine, when the first crowd of people arrived bang on six o'clock, immediately filling the shop. Merrin's three other exhibitors, Pippa the jeweller, Joey the painter and Lizzie the candlemaker, were first through the door accompanied by family members. Then Poppy charged into the shop, and having given Max a smacking kiss, began handing round glasses of wine and canapés with Clara. Poppy was followed by Sergeant Jack Eddy, a St Ives local policeman and childhood friend to them all.

'Well, just look at this, little Merrin Trip,' he said. 'It's lovely. You're a clever maid, so many talents.' He gave her a hug.

As a boy, Jack had worked for Merrin's fisherman father, Harry Tripconey. Despite the passage of the years, Merrin would always be 'little Merrin Trip' to Jack.

'Jack!' shouted Max. 'I've got a beer under the counter for you, which I know you'd prefer to wine.'

'God bless you, Max,' said Jack, 'I'm on my way.'

'See, darling Pearl, I told you everything would be alright,' Clara whispered to Merrin as she hurried by with a tray of glasses. 'The artist, Joey, is that his name? He's rather a dish, just my type.'

'Clara,' said Merrin, good-naturedly, 'he's half your age!'

'No harm in window shopping, darling Pearl. Look, you'd better put someone on the till, you're going to make a lot of sales tonight.'

Lizzie Cambridge, the shop's candlemaker, offered to

man the till. Merrin had just finished showing her how it worked when there was a shriek by the door, arms waving above the crowd. It was Merrin's daughter, Isla, who was supposed to be in Guildford, studying law.

Mother and daughter threaded their way through the increasing crowd and embraced.

'Mum, this is fantastic,' said Isla, 'and so much more fun than being a lawyer. Maybe I should give it all up and open a shop in St Ives.'

'Don't you dare, darling,' said Merrin, smiling. 'What are you doing here? Term doesn't end for another week.'

'Mum, I wasn't going to miss this for the world. I got a day off today and then it's the weekend, so I'll be able to stay until Sunday. I'm very excited for you, and Dad would be so proud.'

The evening progressed, people came and went, and the till seemed to be in constant use. Clara was right. It felt like most of the town had turned up, and it wasn't just for the free wine. People were really buying.

'Do you want a break, Lizzie?' Merrin asked.

'No, I'm fine, thanks. Taking all this money is brilliant. Honestly, Merrin, I think our shop is going to be a success.'

'Me too,' said the woman who, only an hour ago, had been convinced the whole project was doomed to be a flop.

Suddenly, near the door, Merrin spotted a familiar face smiling at her. She'd issued him with an invitation but had never expected him to actually turn up. Chief Inspector Louis Peppiatt was always so busy. With him was a young girl whom she recognised as Louis's daughter, Daisy, and also an elderly woman. Could it be his mother? No, Merrin remembered his mother had died when he was young.

Merrin pushed her way through the crowd. 'Louis, Daisy, how kind of you to come,' she said. Normally, Merrin would have given Louis a kiss on the cheek, but in front of his daughter and this unknown woman, she felt inhibited.

'Of course we've come,' said Louis, smiling. 'Merrin, may I introduce you to Sally Baxter, who is my boss's secretary. Without Sally's protection, I would have been sacked years ago.'

Sally and Merrin shook hands. 'He's absolutely right, I'm afraid to say,' said Sally. 'Keeping him out of trouble is almost a full-time job.'

'I can well believe it,' said Merrin. The two women smiled at one another, feeling an instant kinship. Merrin turned to Daisy. 'So, no Ed tonight?' she enquired. Ed was Daisy's younger brother, aged eleven.

'Definitely not,' said Daisy, firmly. 'Dad said you were selling pottery, among other things. Letting Ed loose in here would be asking for trouble – you know what he's like. Oh, is that Isla over there? I must go and talk to her.' Daisy rather idolised Merrin's daughter.

'And I'm going to look at what you have on offer,' said Sally, none too subtly leaving Louis and Merrin alone.

'This looks like a triumph,' said Louis. 'Well done, though I'm rather sad for my sake that it's obviously going to be such a huge success.'

'Why's that?' said Merrin, already knowing the answer.

Louis smiled at her. 'You know very well, Mrs McKenzie! Stop fishing for compliments. I miss you and without being able to pass any pro bono cases your way, goodness knows when I next will have an excuse to see you again.'

'I'm sorry I haven't been in touch, Louis, only getting all this together has been very full-on, and I know how busy you are.'

They were still standing in the doorway of the shop when a young man running down Fore Street suddenly stopped. 'Mrs Mac, how are you?' The diminutive figure of Billy Carew stood in front of Merrin, a huge grin on his face.

'Billy, how lovely to see you. How's college?' Merrin asked.

'Everything's fine – I love college and the family are good too, thanks to you.' Billy turned to Louis. 'I don't know who you are, sir, but Mrs Mac saved me, saved my whole family. I owe her so much.'

'Billy, this gentleman is Chief Inspector Louis Peppiatt, and it was he who told me about your case and suggested I should try to help you,' said Merrin.

Billy smiled a little nervously at Louis. 'Well, thank you for telling Mrs Mac about me. I don't know what I'd have done without her.'

Louis and Billy solemnly shook hands. 'I know how you feel,' said Louis, gruffly.

'I must go,' said Billy, 'I'm painting a holiday cottage up Bailey's Lane and it must be finished tonight, as the next lot of guests are coming in tomorrow afternoon. Good luck, Mrs Mac.' And in a moment he was gone.

'It's nice to have actually met Billy in person, at last – I only ever saw him at a distance in court,' said Louis. 'He looks like he's turned his life round after that nonsense of being charged with carrying a knife. And he's right, of course, you've pretty much saved him and his family. I understand you're still helping them.'

'Not so much now, really, I just check up on them from time to time. Louis . . .' Merrin hesitated and made an issue of looking round the shop to avoid eye contact. 'I miss you, too,' she said.

Louis smiled at her. 'Then we'd better do something about that, hadn't we?'

After the guests had left, the floor had been swept, the glasses washed and the stock replenished, the four creators of the West Cornwall Crafts Co-operative stood and stared at one another, unable to believe what had just happened.

'How much did we take?' Merrin croaked at Lizzie, her voice hoarse from all the talking.

'Over three thousand pounds altogether,' Lizzie replied.

There was a stunned silence, broken at last by Isla, who had stayed behind to help clear up. 'Wow!' was all she could manage, on behalf of them all.

'Upstairs in my studio,' said Merrin, 'there are three bottles of champagne. I put them there not really daring to believe we'd be celebrating – and certainly, never for one moment did I think we would take that much money.' She looked at her watch. 'It's only just nine, and I assume we're all too wired to go home yet. Shall we turn out the shop lights and go upstairs, to address the problem of the champagne that's cluttering up my fridge and definitely in the way?'

'Yes!' shouted everyone. 'Absolutely, yes,' said Joey Moon, making them all laugh.

They all sat down on the floor as Isla served the champagne. 'The canapés were eaten ages ago, but someone must've brought some cheese straws, so we can eat those.' Isla placed them in the middle of the floor within everyone's reach.

Meanwhile, William had taken a fancy to Pippa and was sitting on her lap, giving Merrin baleful looks to make sure she was feeling jealous. 'Yes, I am jealous, William,' Merrin conceded.

'Me too,' said Isla, 'traitor!'

They munched and drank in silence for a few minutes, and Isla topped up glasses. 'How much money did each of us take?' Pippa asked at last.

'As you know, you've each got your own button on the till,' said Lizzie. 'So I've cashed up the subtotals to show each person's sales. The till roll is downstairs but basically, Joey took the most, then Pippa, and the rest was split pretty evenly between me and Merrin.'

'If this goes on, I could give up bar work and paint full-time,' said Joey, his face alight with excitement.

'We need to be very cautious about making those sorts of decisions,' said Merrin, very aware that her three colleagues were all in their early twenties. 'We can't expect to take anything like that amount every day. Free wine and a night out for the locals, before the season kicks in, must have been a major factor in our success tonight.'

'Some of the schools up-country break up today,' said Lizzie, 'so the season's almost begun – the traffic this evening was horrendous coming into town.'

'And the punters who came tonight didn't just eat and drink,' said Isla, 'they bought as well. Some who bought this evening were locals, who, on the whole, don't have much money. Once we get the visitors down in force, I bet they'll go mad for this shop. Well done, you lot.'

They then discussed who would be manning the shop and when. Pippa offered to do three days a week because she could work on her jewellery beside the till, while everyone else needed a separate space in which to work. They had agreed that initially they would draw no wages for running the shop, but hoped this would change as the business grew. It suddenly all felt very exciting. Merrin's main aim, when she had first thought up the idea of a co-operative, was to help creative young people establish an outlet for their work – an outlet which wasn't going to cost them a great deal. Her plan was that hopefully the sale of her ceramics would cover the cost of the rent, and if this evening was anything to go by, it certainly would.

When everyone had left, Merrin locked up the shop and she and Isla walked home along the Wharf, with William beside them. It was a warm early July night, the tide was almost full, and the lights of the town were reflected in the gentle waves as they swept into the harbour.

'How was Cip?' Isla asked. Cip was her nickname for Louis. She maintained Chief Inspector Peppiatt was too much of a mouthful.

'I wish you wouldn't call him that, darling,' said Merrin.

'He doesn't mind,' said Isla. 'I spoke to Daisy but didn't get a chance to speak to Cip. I saw you two in earnest conversation – is he OK?'

'He's fine, I think. We haven't really seen each other for months, what with me involved in setting up the shop and him trying to keep West Cornwall a safe place in which to live. Of course, we used to meet regularly when I was doing pro bono work, but he understands I needed a break from that after Emily's kidnap.'

'You could meet without it being associated with work,' Isla suggested.

'Maybe,' said Merrin.

'Look, Mum, I'm not trying to set him up as your boyfriend. It's just that as much as I love Clara, Tristan and Max, Louis is different. He understands your world, yours and Dad's. You have a lot of shared knowledge and experience, and he would make a great friend – someone who, like you, knows about life beyond the confines of our dear little town. Cip's marriage broke up, you lost Dad . . . You must both get lonely. It's time you guys had some fun.' Isla smiled. 'And he's a good man in a crisis.'

Merrin smiled back. 'I certainly can't deny that. Actually, we did talk about meeting up if either of us can find the time. Oh, Isla, look at that.'

The light of the moon had cut a path across the harbour and into it came a stunning yacht, chugging slowly in on its motor. It was an old clinker-built sailing boat, full of character – the likes of which were not often seen in the modern world of fibreglass. A figure climbed onto the yacht's prow, the motor was cut, and they watched entranced as an anchor was thrown overboard and the yacht settled onto its mooring.

'What a beauty,' said Merrin. 'I wish more boats were still made of wood.'

'She's lovely,' Isla agreed. 'I wonder where she's come from.'

'No doubt we'll know soon enough. It will be all round

the town by morning,' said Merrin. 'Come on, darling. You must be exhausted after your drive, and I've got a busy day tomorrow with the shop opening. We need some sleep.'

They turned their back on the harbour and began climbing up the hill to Merrin's cottage. After a moment, Merrin stopped and looked back at the beautiful yacht. For some reason, it made her feel uneasy.

CHAPTER TWO

Retail sales on Saturdays during the season were always somewhat unpredictable in Cornwall. It being the main changeover day, visitors were either coming or going which meant, even on a lovely sunny day, the beaches were often very quiet as visitors packed or unpacked. That didn't mean, however, that the beaches were instantly filled with locals. Most of the indigenous population were heavily involved in hospitality and retail, so there was no time for fun – maximising the season was all-important.

This being the case, the opening day of the West Cornwall Crafts Co-operative was not the grand affair they had expected. As inexperienced retailers, Merrin, Pippa, Joey and Lizzie waited in vain for customers. The few that did appear had just arrived in town, so they had a quick look round and said they would be back later in the week. By lunchtime, they had taken just twenty-three pounds.

'It seems you were right, Merrin,' said Joey, glumly. 'It doesn't look as if I'll be a full-time painter any time soon.'

'You can't make a judgement on the strength of one morning's trade, Joey,' said Merrin, firmly. 'Look, why don't the three of you go out and get some lunch. I've brought a sandwich so I'm fine. It's a lovely day – go and sit on the beach for a bit, that'll cheer you all up.'

Left alone, Merrin ate her sandwich and gave William some treats. She knew it was stupid, but she always felt uncomfortable about eating in front of William unless he had something to eat as well. She was just about to call Isla to suggest they went out for dinner that evening, when the door was flung open and an impossibly glamorous woman walked into the shop. She looked as if she had just stepped out of one of the pages of a fashion magazine. Her smooth, glossy dark hair was expensively cut to jaw length, which somehow accentuated her incredible cheekbones and startling blue eyes. She was simply dressed in a cream linen shirt and blue linen trousers. On her feet were some crazy-looking sandals in all colours of the rainbow. She carried a handbag, perfectly matching the colour of her trousers and which Merrin suspected was probably Hermès.

'Hello,' she said, 'what a wonderful little shop. Do you mind if I look round?'

'Of course not,' said Merrin, trying hard not to look awestruck by the woman's appearance.

'I take it you don't make all this marvellous stuff yourself?' she asked.

'No, there's a merry band of us,' said Merrin. 'I just make the ceramics and I have three fellow associates, all young people hoping to get their skills recognised. We've formed a sort of co-operative. They'll be back soon, they're just having some lunch.'

'I love these paintings. They're interesting, sort of abstract and yet not. I'm probably talking nonsense.'

'The artist is a young man named Joey Moon,' said Merrin. 'He uses a drone to get a bird's-eye view of the Cornish landscape. His absolute hero is the artist Peter Lanyon. Do you know his work?' The woman shook her head. 'Some of his paintings are usually on display in the Tate, in the gallery's permanent collection, if you're interested in having a look.'

'You sound as if you really care about these young people. My name is Roxanne Barrow, by the way, though everyone calls me Roxy.'

'I'm Merrin McKenzie.' The two women shook hands. 'The thing is,' Merrin continued, 'I know the appreciation of artistic endeavour is a very subjective thing, and the three young people I chose to give space to in this shop produce work that I love. It might not be the right approach commercially – I should perhaps be impartial and have chosen people whose work I thought would sell best. However, in the end, the only way I could make a choice was to fill the shop with items I love.'

'I totally get that. I think if I were in your shoes, it would be the only way I could run this place,' said Roxy.

At that moment, Joey came through the open door, carrying a coffee. 'I've brought you a proper coffee, Merrin – Americano with hot milk, right?'

'Perfect, Joey, thank you. This lady is showing an interest in your paintings.'

'Hello,' said Joey, 'my name's Joey Moon. Can I help you in any way?'

'How do you do, Joey Moon – great name, by the way. My name's Roxy.'

They shook hands and began talking avidly about Joey's work. While they were busy, Merrin hurried upstairs and dialled Pippa's number.

'Pippa,' Merrin said in hushed tones, 'there's a woman in the shop who apparently loves what we're doing here, and she looks like she might be loaded. Can you and Lizzie hurry back. I think Joey is going to make a sale and I think you two might do as well.'

'On the way,' said Pippa.

Merrin was not wrong. Roxy spent an extraordinary amount of money buying two paintings from Joey, a brooch and necklace made with sea glass from Pippa, a variety of candles from Lizzie, and plates and bowls from Merrin. Towards the end of the spending spree, her husband arrived, whom Roxy introduced as Tony Barrow. He was a good-looking man, about the same age as Roxy, which Merrin judged to be mid-thirties. Unlike his wife, Tony was dressed in a pair of salt-stained jeans, a faded T-shirt and equally faded espadrilles. He seemed completely unfazed by the amount of money his wife was spending, uninterested really, except to mention that the parcels would take up a lot of room on the boat.

'Boat?' said Merrin. 'Was it, by any chance, your wonderful clinker-built sailing yacht that came in on the tide last night?'

'Yes, we arrived about ten o'clock, and I don't think we're now in a hurry to leave, are we?' Tony looked across at Roxy for confirmation.

'No,' she gushed. 'I've never been to St Ives before. In fact, I've never even been to Cornwall. I've immediately fallen in love with your fabulous little town. I hope you guys realise just how lucky you are to live here.'

'We do,' they all chorused, dutifully. It was a question they were used to answering.

'What's the name of your yacht?' Merrin asked. 'She's a wonderful old girl.'

Tony smirked. 'She's called *Llamedos*, spelt with two *L*s.'

'Was she built in Wales then?' Merrin asked.

'He's teasing you,' said Roxy. 'Tell the story, Tony.'

'No, you tell it,' said Tony, clearly a man of few words.

'The boat was a wreck when he bought it, so he had to pretty much rebuild it from scratch. When he came to registering her, he found it very difficult. Every name he came up with, someone else had already taken. He got so fed up, he dreamt up the name *Llamedos*, which is *Sod-em-all* backwards. It was accepted immediately, apparently, with no problem!'

Everyone laughed. 'I really like that,' said Joey.

'Talking of names,' said Roxy, 'Joey, you ought to make better use of your surname. On every one of your paintings, you ought to paint a little moon – different moons for the different moods of each painting – full, half, new, even a harvest moon. It could become a sort of trademark for you and would help get your name known. Potential customers would ask the significance of the moon, and whoever is selling your work could then tell them your name.'

'Actually, Roxy, that's a really great idea,' said Joey. 'Thanks so much.'

In preparation for leaving, Tony went to the till to pick

up Roxy's numerous bags, and from behind the counter came a low growl. 'Who's that?' said Tony, peering over.

At the sight of Tony, William's growl became louder and he displayed a not very attractive set of yellowing teeth.

'I'm sorry,' said Merrin, hurriedly, 'that's William – he's a rescue dog and he has issues, but he never actually bites anyone.'

'Looking like that, I'm not surprised he has issues. It seems as if two completely different dogs have been stuck together – his front half is totally different from his rear end,' jeered Tony.

Normally, Merrin would have responded none too favourably to such an insulting description of William, particularly as it was entirely true. Instead, she smiled through gritted teeth, trying to focus on what good customers the Barrows had been.

'Well, thank you very much,' she said, 'I hope we'll see you again before you leave St Ives.'

'You certainly will,' said Roxy. 'Hey, Joey, paint a moon on one of your paintings and I'll buy it. And before we leave, maybe you'd all like to come aboard *Llamedos*. Bye, guys.' And with that, they swept out of the shop.

'Goodness,' said Pippa, 'she must be seriously rich. Odd though that her husband didn't seem involved. I understand why he wasn't interested in my jewellery and maybe the candles, more a girly thing, but you would have thought he'd want to be involved in choosing Joey's paintings and Merrin's ceramics.'

'I noticed that,' said Merrin, 'and I didn't especially like the way Roxy seemed to be flaunting the fact that she was the one with the money. I felt a bit sorry for Tony – at least, I did until he started being insulting about William's looks. William certainly didn't like him.'

'Well, I hope they come back,' said Joey, grinning, 'and I'd better start practising my moon painting.'

CHAPTER THREE

Chief Inspector Louis Peppiatt burst into Sally Baxter's office, hot and dishevelled, like a boy who was late for school.

'So sorry to be late, Sal dear, the traffic was awful and yet the season's hardly begun.' He glanced towards the open door of the office belonging to Chief Superintendent John Dent. The room was obviously empty. 'Have I missed sir?' He glanced at his watch. 'I'm not that late.'

'The summons came from me, not from sir, although the instructions are his and his alone.'

'Goodness,' said Louis, smiling. 'I'm late for a summons from the power behind the throne, now that is truly terrifying.'

'Enough of your nonsense. Would you like a coffee?'

Coffee dispensed, Louis drew up a chair beside Sally's desk. 'So, what can I do for you, fair lady?'

'You're not going to like it, which is why sir left me to break the news. He wants you to go to St Ives to investigate the theft from an art gallery.'

'That's a job for Jack Eddy, surely,' said Louis. 'I'm trying to sort out who's who in that nasty GBH over in St Austell. Jack always deals with petty pilfering in the St Ives shops. He's really good at it, because the shopkeepers know and love him and work hard with him to help track down the culprits. I'd just be in the way.'

'It's not petty pilfering. I gather it's a very valuable painting. I'm not sure how much it's worth, but certainly many thousands,' said Sally.

'There's a young man in hospital from last weekend's altercation and there is a strong possibility that he won't survive,' said Louis, gravely. 'If the poor chap doesn't make it, we're certainly looking at a manslaughter charge, maybe even murder. I think that takes precedence over a stolen painting.'

'Louis, I've already made that argument on your behalf,' said Sally, wearily. 'Sir is not to be swayed. He thinks it might be the beginning of a spate of art thefts, and let's face it, there's plenty of opportunity at this time of year with the galleries full of stock.'

'Alright, Sal, I'll dash over there now and debrief Eddy – but I need to be back in St Austell by four when I'm interviewing the suspects, who are currently being rounded up.'

'You're making a fuss, Louis. You'll have plenty of time, in fact even time enough to pop in to see Mrs McKenzie and find out how her shop is doing today.' At this point, Sally could not contain a rather sly grin.

'Stop it, Sally, we've been through all this. I am a huge admirer of Mrs McKenzie, but that's it. I'm sure her shop will be a great success, but I can't help wishing she hadn't given up her pro bono work, she's so good at it. Incidentally, I met Billy Carew last night. Do you remember that case?' Sally nodded. 'Merrin and Billy's uncle have turned Billy into a fine young man, in my opinion. She's brilliant at dealing with these sensitive cases, and she really cares. To be honest, she's wasted as a shopkeeper.'

'She's rather more than that,' Sally said indignantly. 'As well as making her own ceramics, as I understand it, she is providing three talented young people with a showcase for their work. She's charging them no rent, you know. It's just a different way of helping out. It's so hard for creative young people to get established. They usually need a job to support themselves and end up being too tired to work on the thing they really want to do. Mrs McKenzie is giving her three a real chance to follow their dreams. I think it's wonderful.'

'How do you know all this, Sally?' said Louis, frowning. 'I thought they were all just sharing a shop together and presumably saving money by splitting the costs.'

'I had a long chat with her daughter, Isla, and Daisy too, last night. Isla told us all about what her mother is trying to achieve. All the young people have to do is take it in turns to man the shop, and keep it stocked, of course. Mrs McKenzie does everything else and pays the bills. She's a lovely woman, Louis – kind, talented and, for some inexplicable reason, obviously very fond of you.'

'Thanks for the vote of confidence, Sally. Look, I know I've told you I met Merrin's husband once. He was an extraordinary man, so impressive. Merrin adored him and is still grief-stricken at her loss. She and I have been through a lot together in the last few years, and it's true, we're fond of each other, but that's as far as it goes, as far as it will ever go. Enough now, please.'

'Alright, I will never mention the subject again, except to say this – you're lonely, she's lonely, you share many of the same ideas and interests, and I believe you both care deeply for one another. You really need to pull yourself together. It's such a bloody waste, dear boy.'

'I must go,' said Louis, standing up.

Sally came out from behind her desk and, uncharacteristically, gave Louis a hug. 'Sometimes you should really listen to your elders and betters. If you were mine, I think I'd send you to bed with no supper for being so stubborn.'

Louis kissed her on the cheek. 'Elders and betters?' He grinned. 'I'll take the elders but certainly not the betters!'

'And you're also very rude – be off with you, and don't come back here until you've found the art thief. Sir expects nothing less.'

CHAPTER FOUR

The gallery owner, Jeremy Murdoch, was clearly distraught as he regaled Louis and Jack Eddy with details of the theft.

'Honestly, Chief Inspector, I just don't know how he managed to do it.'

'Or she?' suggested Louis.

'Maybe, I suppose. The painting was in the window, so the theft was – well, so audacious. Not only was there a good chance of someone seeing the painting being taken from inside the gallery, but it happened on Friday afternoon when Fore Street was packed. Someone could also have seen it being taken out of the window from outside the shop.'

'I suppose the thief could have been mistaken for a member of your staff, particularly anyone looking in from outside,' suggested Louis.

'How big was the painting, sir?' Jack asked.

'Not big,' said Jeremy, 'not much bigger than A4. It was

in the window because the subject was obviously going to be a popular one.'

'How come, sir?' Jack asked.

'It's a charming painting of a seal, its head popping out of the sea. It's a dull day but the colours are beautiful – greys, silver and just a tiny hint of pale blue. Exquisite, actually.'

'Who's the artist?' Louis asked.

'P. Kernow,' Jeremy replied.

'Ah, no wonder you think the painting's exquisite. Peter Carew is a wonderful artist.'

'I-I couldn't possibly comment about that,' said Jeremy, looking awkward.

Louis smiled. 'It's OK, Mr Murdoch. I know Peter and I appreciate what a private man he is, and how he likes to hide behind his pseudonym.'

Jeremy stared at Louis for a moment. 'Were you the policeman who was involved in saving that young girl, who was kept captive up in a stable on Peter's farm?'

'Yes, that was me,' said Louis, 'which is how I came to know Peter, although I'd been an admirer of his work for years.'

'I was there, too,' said Jack, obviously anxious not to be left out.

'I absolutely hate the idea of such a lovely painting being in the hands of a crook,' said Jeremy. 'Do you think there is any chance of getting it back?'

Louis hesitated. 'When you think back to yesterday afternoon, did any of the visitors to your shop stand out in any way? I gather from Sergeant Eddy that you have no cameras inside the gallery. Isn't that rather rash, sir?'

'Now this has happened, yes, possibly it is, but we've never had any trouble before. I've always worked on the principle that it would be very difficult to steal the average painting because the size would be hard to conceal. It would be different if we were selling jewellery, or something small.'

'Not so difficult if it's A4 size,' said Jack. 'It would fit in a carrier bag, no problem.'

'Which is why the thief went for that particular painting, I suppose,' said Jeremy. 'And to answer your question, I can't remember anyone in particular standing out yesterday, but I will think about it.'

'Wait a minute,' said Louis. He went outside and was back in seconds. 'Mr Murdoch, there's a council CCTV camera just across from your shop, and from the angle, it looks like it will pick up your gallery window. Has anything been done about this, Sergeant?'

'No, boss. I only learnt just now that the painting was taken from the window display,' said Jack, looking aggrieved.

'Well, get on to the control centre right away. It amazes me that you haven't followed this up already, Sergeant.'

'Right, boss,' said Eddy.

'It wasn't his fault,' said Jeremy, as soon as Jack hurried out of the shop. 'He came to see me yesterday afternoon. The gallery was very busy and a policeman hanging about is not good for trade. I'm fairly certain I didn't mention that the painting was taken from the window – I was anxious to get rid of him, to be honest.'

'Thank you for sparing Sergeant Eddy too much grief from me,' said Louis, privately thinking Eddy should have checked for a camera anyway. 'Have you informed Peter Carew about the theft?'

'Yes, I called him yesterday evening. He was very upset. I'm not surprised, I thought it was one of his best works. How he got the sea to look translucent using watercolours, I just do not know.'

'Do you paint yourself, Mr Murdoch?' Louis asked.

Jeremy smiled. 'A little, just for pleasure really – but my daubs are useful in that they make me appreciate just how talented the artists are whose work I sell.'

'I can see you love your work. You're a lucky man,' said Louis, smiling.

'You're right, Chief Inspector, and tell me, do you love your work?' Jeremy asked.

Louis laughed. 'A fair question, I suppose!' He thought for a moment. 'I think the answer is probably *now and again*. We'll see if the camera shows up anything useful and either I or Sergeant Eddy will let you know the results, one way or the other. I understand Eddy has talked to the shops either side and opposite you, but no one saw anything useful. It's really difficult to know where to go from here – but let's not despair, Mr Murdoch, until we learn what the camera throws up.'

As soon as Louis left the gallery, he called Jack Eddy, who sounded decidedly grumpy. 'They've got the coverage for Friday, boss. I'm here now and we're running through the tape.'

'Does the camera cover the gallery window?' Louis asked.

'Yes, boss,' said Jack.

'Well, you'll be glad to hear that Jeremy Murdoch has come to your rescue and says he neglected to tell you about the painting being in the window display. However, Eddy, surely you should have thought about checking for a camera, in any event. We need to see who went in and out of that gallery, and whether they were carrying anything which could have concealed the painting. This is a chance to cover yourself in glory. Got that?'

'Yes, boss,' said Jack, sounding a little more cheerful.

'I'm off to St Austell shortly. Contact me if you find anything interesting.'

Louis cut the call. Jack Eddy was a good man, with a quite extraordinary degree of local knowledge, but the word *ponderous* did come into Louis's mind when thinking about his sergeant. On impulse, he walked through to the Wharf, and sitting down on a bench overlooking the harbour, he called Peter Carew.

Peter answered almost immediately. 'Peter, it's Louis Peppiatt. I'm calling about your missing painting, I am so sorry.'

'Thank you, it is a bugger. I'm not often pleased with my work, but that one was a rare exception. Still, I'm very happy to have a chief inspector on the job – though it's a bit over the top, isn't it, for a straightforward theft?'

'You're a very important artist, Peter, but I must admit that my boss has got it into his head that this could be the beginning of someone, or even a gang, having a bit of a spree where art theft is concerned.'

'Well, Louis, you're clearly the man for the job. If you can find a kidnapped girl, I feel sure you can find a missing painting.'

'Can I remind you, Peter, that it was you and Merrin who found Emily, not me. I was just involved in the clear-up operation.'

'True,' said Peter, laughing. 'Perhaps we should put Merrin up for the job of finding my seal painting! Where are you at the moment?'

'I'm in St Ives, sitting on the Wharf, admiring the view. However, I've shortly got to go back to St Austell to interview some nasty, vicious youths, who are going to deny everything.'

'What a thrilling life you lead, Louis. Have you time to pop into Merrin's shop?'

'Briefly, I suppose. Why?'

'I want to ask you and Merrin to come to mine for lunch, maybe at a weekend – in fact, what about tomorrow? I know Merrin wants to see my studio and I thought, rather pompously, you might like to see it, too. What do you say, are you free tomorrow? Surely chief inspectors get Sundays off occasionally? Actually, it's not even a day off, is it? You can interview me on my views as to who stole my painting.'

'Have you got views on that, then?' Louis asked.

'You're going to have to prise the information out of me. You can practise on the nasty, vicious youths this afternoon. So, you'll come?'

'I would love to,' said Louis, 'and yes, I am free. I'll go in to see Merrin now and find out how she's fixed for tomorrow. Thank you so much, I'll come back to you.'

* * *

The founding members of the West Cornwall Crafts Co-operative were sitting around drinking cups of tea when Louis arrived.

'What's all this then? It doesn't look much like work to me.' At the sound of his voice, William came rushing out from behind the counter, tail wagging with excitement. He loved Louis.

A lot of fussing and tummy rubbing went on, until Merrin said, 'So, are you going to say hello to the rest of us, or did you just come to see William?'

Louis straightened up. 'Mostly William, of course,' he said, smiling. 'You must be aware that William and I haven't seen one another for a long time. We have a lot of catching up to do.'

'Did you meet this lot the other night?' Merrin asked, waving in the direction of her colleagues.

'I think so – Pippa, Joey and Lizzie. Is that right?'

'That's brilliant,' said Pippa. 'How on earth did you remember us all in that scrum?'

'Because he's a policeman,' said Merrin. 'He never forgets a face, so you lot better watch it. May I introduce Chief Inspector Louis Peppiatt.'

'Goodness,' said Joey, 'a chief inspector. We really better be on our best behaviour.'

'So why are you all sitting about drinking tea and looking pleased with yourselves?' Louis asked.

'At lunchtime, we sold a massive amount of stuff to just one woman,' said Merrin. 'She bought items from all of us and she's threatening to buy another of Joey's paintings. It was really quiet and then she came in and spent, spent, spent. It was amazing.'

'I'm very pleased for you all,' said Louis. 'Merrin, are you by any chance free for lunch tomorrow? Peter Carew has invited us both and after lunch has promised to show us his studio.'

'Actually, that would be lovely,' said Merrin. 'Isla's leaving at about ten tomorrow morning to go back to Guildford, so I will be feeling a bit lonely.'

'Great,' said Louis. 'I'll let Peter know you can come and I'll pick you up at midday. Will that suit?'

'Perfect,' said Merrin.

'He's nice. Is he your boyfriend?' Pippa asked, after Louis had looked at his watch and dashed out of the shop, heading for St Austell.

'No,' said Merrin, firmly, 'just a good friend.'

Chief Inspector Louis Peppiatt spent the rest of the afternoon and evening conducting a frustrating series of interviews with the three young men he knew, from witnesses, were responsible for the awful injuries inflicted on a fourth young man, who was still in intensive care. None of this was helped by their legal representative, who was well known to the police, but not in a good way. Martin Geeson saw it as his job to keep his clients, largely serious villains, out of prison. He did this by schooling them in how to lie effectively, and when they couldn't think how to wriggle out of a question, to just utter the immortal words 'no comment'.

One of the young thugs, named Chris Pirie, Louis identified as being the most likely one to crack. For a start, he was only nineteen, and twice during the interviews he had asked how the victim of the attack was doing. Louis was quick to emphasise that the victim was at death's door, and if he died, a murder charge was likely. This clearly frightened Chris, but Louis felt he had a genuine concern for the victim. Clearly, there was some decency in the boy, whereas the other two, in their late twenties, were already hardened criminals, confident and rude – thoroughly nasty individuals who already had a history of violence.

By seven in the evening, everyone was tired, and the odious Martin Geeson said his clients needed a rest. In a last-ditch attempt to get a confession, Louis took Chris into the interview room once more. 'Tell him nothing, Chris,' Martin advised.

'Chris, I think you're a decent person, despite your involvement in what's happened. You've asked how the victim is doing, you seem genuinely distressed to hear how badly he has been injured. Your companions are well known to the police and have been put away several times already in their young lives. This is your first offence. If you tell me exactly what happened, who did what to whom, and why, I will make sure that when the case comes to court, the judge will be well aware of your help and, I suspect, the minor role you played in the attack.'

'I said to say nothing, Chris. Not a word,' said Martin. It sounded more like a threat than advice.

'Be quiet, Mr Geeson, you're really not helping your client.' Louis looked at Chris across the desk and smiled gently. 'We'll look after you – witness protection, the full works. Just tell me what really happened, please.'

There was a long silence and then Chris began to sob. 'I never touched him, but I watched while they kicked him and punched him, and I did nothing, nothing at all to help him. He was so badly hurt and we just walked away and left him.'

Martin Geeson put his head in his hands. 'Stupid, so stupid,' he murmured. 'I think you've done enough for tonight, Peppiatt. You're taking advantage of my client's youth and inexperience.'

'You mean you haven't had the chance to coach him in the ways of making things as difficult as possible to seek justice. I'm going to take Chris's statement now, and all three of your clients will be remanded in custody.'

'You can't hold them in custody, not without charging them,' said Martin, clearly outraged.

'I absolutely agree with you, Mr Geeson, which is why it is my intention to charge them with grievous bodily harm,' said Louis. 'You'll just have to hope and pray the victim doesn't die.'

While Chris was having a break before making his statement, Louis made sure that he would be safe in the cells, well away from his companions. He was just going back into the interview room when a young WPC called out. 'Chief Inspector, we decided it was important not to interrupt you, but we've had Sergeant Eddy from St Ives call asking for you several times. He says it's urgent.'

Louis had forgotten all about the stolen painting in the intervening hours. 'I'll give him a call now. I'll go outside for a breath of air, so show Chris into the interview room. I won't be long.'

'Hello, boss, good to get you,' said Jack. 'You just won't believe what we've seen on the tape.'

'Eddy, I'm short of time. What did you see? Just spit it out.'

Louis heard Jack take a deep breath. 'The person who took the painting out of the window was a little girl.'

'When you say a little girl, how old are we talking? Also, did you see her come out of the gallery with the painting, and was she with anyone?' said Louis, impatiently.

'We all think she is about eight or nine years old. She's a pretty little maid. Boss, if you remember, the entrance into the gallery is on the left, if you're facing out onto the street. Unfortunately, this means that we could see no one coming in or out of the gallery, because the camera bypasses the gallery doorway. It's at the wrong angle.'

'Have you checked to see if she passed in front of the gallery window, either coming or going?' said Louis.

'Yes, boss. When she entered and left the gallery, she must have gone in the opposite direction to the gallery window. We checked very carefully. There is absolutely no sighting of her. We're now checking all the council cameras in St Ives to see if she appears anywhere else. If she's still in town, she shouldn't be too difficult to spot.'

'Good work, Eddy. When she took the painting out of the window, could you see anyone beside or behind her, another child or an adult?'

'No, boss, the camera can't penetrate to any depth into the gallery. It just shows shadows.'

'Right, Eddy – get a few stills of the child, for you to show around the town, and I'll meet you at the station at say, ten-thirty tomorrow morning.'

'It's Sunday, boss, and Mrs Eddy is cooking a special roast, because our son and his wife are coming down to stay for a few days.'

'It won't take long, Sergeant. You tell Mrs Eddy you'll

be home well in time for lunch – say by eleven-thirty at the latest. Will that pacify her, do you think?'

'It should do the trick, boss, thanks. A little girl, it's hard to believe!'

'It is,' agreed Louis. 'Taking a packet of sweets or a chocolate bar is one thing, but a painting worth thousands of pounds, it does beggar belief. I suppose what we have to consider is whether she took the painting because she likes seals, or whether it's more sinister than that and she's being controlled by a Fagin of the art world.'

CHAPTER FIVE

When Louis arrived at the station the following morning, Jack Eddy was already in residence and very pleased with himself.

'We found her, boss, on another camera at the Malakoff. She was with a woman, who looked like she was her mother. They were holding hands and the little girl was carrying a tote bag, quite large enough to contain the painting.'

'So what have you done about it, Eddy?' Louis asked.

'Well nothing, boss, as yet. It was quite late last night that we found her.'

'And the footage took place after the incident at the gallery?'

'Oh yes, it was 5.14 p.m. on Friday. We haven't had time to go through Saturday's cameras as yet, but someone is on it today.'

'Of course, the significance of the Malakoff could be

that mother and daughter, if that's what they are, were about to catch a bus, which is not good news. Alternatively, they may be staying somewhere nearby. Get someone out searching today with a photograph, Eddy. Start with the Pedn-Olva Hotel – they could have been about to walk down the steps near it. Then check all the B&Bs in the area. Can I see the photograph, please?'

Jack placed two photographs in front of Louis. 'That's the one of the little girl taking the painting, and there she is with her mother and the bag.'

Louis studied them in silence for a moment. 'They genuinely look like a loving mother and daughter,' he said at last. 'Yet look at the child taking the painting from its hook on the wall – she doesn't appear either scared or furtive. It's all very odd. One thing's for sure: that gallery owner, Murdoch, is decidedly flaky. If he's going to continue displaying valuable paintings by putting them in the window like that, it's madness. He needs to sort out his security, big time. A child shouldn't have been able to take a painting off the wall so easily.'

'He's a nice enough chap, but away with the fairies,' Jack agreed.

'I'll go round to the gallery now,' said Louis, 'and try and convince him of the error of his ways. In the meantime, you organise the search so you can get off in time for your lunch. We don't want Mrs Eddy upset, now do we?'

'We certainly don't, boss,' said Jack, with much feeling. 'Should I see if Sergeant Satchel is free? He'd be kind and tender with the little maid, if he does find her.'

'Excellent idea. If he's free, tell him to call me direct, rather than trouble you. I'm having lunch with Peter

Carew, as it happens. The signal's not great at his place, so tell Ben Satchel to keep trying if he can't reach me immediately.'

Louis arrived at the West Cornwall Crafts Co-operative just before midday, having failed to introduce any real sense of urgency so far as Jeremy Murdoch was concerned.

'It's a wicked world out there, Mr Murdoch, and you're carrying some very valuable stock. You do need to upgrade your security – to see who is coming in and out of your gallery, and also invest in a very prominent camera within the gallery, so it's obvious to your customers that their every movement is being recorded.'

'I don't like the sound of that, my customers aren't those sort of people. I appreciate that in your job, Chief Inspector, you see people at their worst, but not in my gallery – oh no, definitely not in my gallery. They just love art.'

'Yet the potential art-loving customer who entered your gallery on Friday allowed a child to steal a valuable painting,' said Louis, not unreasonably.

'There must be some mistake,' replied Jeremy. 'I think you've got it wrong.'

There was no reasoning with the man, but Louis's frustrations faded somewhat when he found the inmates of West Cornwall Crafts positively buzzing with excitement again.

'Now what's happened?' he asked, amused by their general enthusiasm.

'That woman, Roxy's her name, came back and bought a whole lot more,' said Merrin.

'This time, she bought loads of my scented candles,' said Lizzie, 'and some more jewellery and some of Merrin's ceramics.'

'And,' said Joey, 'she bought two more of my paintings because I'd painted a moon on them.'

'I've no idea what that means,' said Louis, laughing, 'but come on, Merrin, we don't want to be late for Peter. You can explain about the moon in the car.'

Peter Carew seemed very pleased to see them both. The three of them had not met since the kidnap trial, when they'd all had to give evidence. After the event, they'd had dinner together but it had been rather a subdued affair, given they'd been forced to relive the details of those terrifying events. Now, all they had to do was enjoy the day and each other's company.

'Having thought about it,' said Peter, 'I've decided I would like the visit to my studio to come before lunch to get it out of the way. Jenny is waiting to show you round and while you're doing that, I'm going to finish preparing the meal.'

'Who's Jenny?' asked Louis.

'His Labrador,' said Merrin, with a smile. 'Are you really not going to come into the studio with us, Peter?'

He shook his head. 'Definitely not. As you know, my dear, no one except Jenny has ever been in there. While I'm making an exception for you two, because of my high regard for you both, I can't bear to witness what, for me, will be something of an intrusion.'

'Peter, we don't have to see your studio at all, if it makes you feel uncomfortable,' said Louis.

'Not uncomfortable, and I wouldn't have asked you over if the invitation had not been a genuine one. It's not so easy these days to justify my status as a recluse, since my nephews are regular visitors now. However, when it comes to my art, it's still a very private thing. Come on, I'll take you to the door, and please bring Jenny back to the kitchen with you when you've had a look round.'

It was the most superb artist's studio. Louis gasped as Peter closed the door behind them. Paint was splattered over a wooden floor. Three canvases stood on easels; none of the paintings were finished, and all were quite different but already showing evidence of Peter's iconic style. Round the walls hung marvellous paintings of Cornish scenes at various different times of year. There were often animals and birds included in the paintings, but not a human to be seen. After the explosion of colour, the next sensation was that of smell: of linseed oil, of turpentine and through an open window, the scent of honeysuckle. There was a log-burning stove, on which sat a kettle and two battered leather armchairs, in one of which sat Jenny, who wagged her tail as soon as she saw Merrin. The two large windows on either side of the studio made the room feel bright and airy, and on either side of each window hung faded curtains in Cornish tartan. The building itself was made of granite and must once have been an animal shed of some sort. A large trestle table, which ran the length of the room, was covered in the tools of Peter's trade – brushes, palettes, a huge pan set of watercolour paints, an array of tubes, a collection of jam jars, rags and boxes full of oddments. It was all surprisingly neat.

Merrin looked at Louis, who appeared to have gone

into a trance, and she could see he was close to tears. She knew he loved watercolours, and Peter's paintings in particular, but was unprepared for seeing how moved he was. Quietly, so as not to disturb him, she sat down in the chair beside Jenny and gently stroked her head while looking around. The room was warm and welcoming with the myriad colours bouncing off the walls, and she could suddenly see how relatively easy it must have been for Peter to become a recluse in this place. He really needed nothing and no one, except for the company of his old dog, his amazing talent and all of this.

Slowly, Louis walked around the walls, looking at each painting in turn. Merrin watched him, recognising that in the turmoil of the life he led, he had found something special. No, from the look on his face, something quite wonderful. She knew he was a deep thinker and very well read; a surprisingly compassionate man, given his job, and very astute when it came to recognising and sympathising with human frailties. This, though, was altogether different, another dimension to his character, and she could see it ran deep, very deep indeed.

At last he turned to her and now he was excited, almost jubilant. 'This is the most marvellous place I've ever seen, truly. Do you feel it, too?' he asked.

'I feel it through you,' Merrin said. 'I can see it's wonderful, but to you it's much more than that, and it makes me very happy to see you like this, so entranced.'

'Entranced, exactly, that's the very word!' Louis held out his hand and pulled her out of the chair. He put his hands on her shoulders and gently kissed her on the lips, then pulled her close into a warm embrace.

'Sorry,' he said, against her hair. 'I shouldn't have done that.'

After a few moments, she disentangled herself from his arms. 'It's quite alright, just a reaction to all of this. I totally understand.' She took his hand. 'Come on, we better go and find Peter, he'll be wondering what's become of us. You, me and also Jenny.'

'Died and gone to heaven, that's what I feel like,' said Louis, still caught up in the moment.

'Come on!' said Merrin, sternly. 'I'm sure Peter will let you come back again sometime.'

'I'm not sure I'll ever want to,' said Louis, quietly, stopping in the doorway to look back at the studio. 'Everything – the studio, the paintings, you – it's all been just perfect.'

As Louis and Merrin entered his kitchen, Peter looked up from the range, studied them for a moment and then grinned. 'What have you two been up to then?' he asked.

'Nothing,' they chorused.

This made Peter smile some more. 'Thanks for bringing the wine, Louis. Muscadet, perfect as I've made a fish pie. I assume you'd both like a glass?'

'Just half a glass for me, please,' said Louis, 'as I'm driving. Peter, your studio is wonderful. I don't think I've ever been anywhere which felt more life-enhancing – yes, that's it, a sort of *carpe diem* moment. It made me, well, us, I think,' he said, turning to Merrin, 'glad to be alive. And your paintings, the detail, it's like you've painted individually every blade of grass, every leaf, every feather on a bird's wing. I just can't imagine how you achieve that.'

'Well, there is a trick to it,' said Peter, 'but, of course, I'm not going to share it with you.'

'I should hope not,' said Louis, smiling, 'it would spoil the magic.'

'And what about you, Merrin?' Peter asked.

'I love your paintings, Peter, and I love your studio, it's an extraordinary place. I also loved seeing how much it all meant to Louis – the policeman completely vanished.'

Peter nodded in Louis's direction. 'From the look of him, I reckon he's still absent without leave!'

'Then I'd better prove you wrong,' said Louis. 'As I mentioned on the phone, my boss has put me in charge of finding out who's stolen your seal painting.'

'One of Peter's paintings has been stolen, that's awful!' said Merrin. 'Sorry, I won't interrupt again.'

'The odd thing is that the CCTV camera outside the gallery shows the painting being taken off the wall by a little girl, about eight or nine, they reckon,' said Louis. 'Checking all the cameras in St Ives, we found her again at the Malakoff with a woman who looks like her mother. My sergeant in Truro, Ben Satchel, is over in St Ives at the moment trying to track down the pair. I just hope the fact they were seen at the Malakoff doesn't mean they've left town.'

'In your capable hands, Chief Inspector, I'm sure the painting will be found, and I can assure you that if it has been taken by a child, I will not be pressing charges. Enough now, you're off duty.'

The fish pie was delicious, the conversation flowed, and Peter and Merrin finished off the bottle of wine. Over coffee, Merrin raised the subject of Joey Moon, having explained to Peter all about her co-operative.

'I first heard about Joey from a fisherman friend of my dad's,' she said. 'Apparently, even as a young child, Joey used to ask the fisherman working out of Hayle to let him come aboard when they went to sea. He would help sort the crab and lobster pots and then on the way home, he would draw the approaching landscape. His idea is that most people view the sea from the land. His paintings show the land from the sea.'

'Interesting,' said Peter.

'Joey paints in oils and his absolute hero is Peter Lanyon. Like you, he loves nature and the countryside but, like Peter Lanyon, his work tends to be abstract. He has managed to save up enough money to buy a drone and now sends it out to sea to collect images. He's very friendly and good with customers, but where his work is concerned he's very much a loner.' Merrin smiled at Peter. 'Not unlike someone we know!'

'How old is he?' Peter asked.

'He's twenty-two. He still lives at home and works in his bedroom. He augments his income by working in a bar, but over the last few days, he's sold four paintings.'

'Four! That's bloody good going,' said Peter.

'Look, I know you're very busy and now, of course, you have your nephews to think about, but I just wondered if you could drop into our shop incognito and then tell us what you think of Joey and his work. If you could give him some advice, I am sure he would be grateful, but you can pass it on to him through me, if that would be easier for you. I just think he's really got something and he's so dedicated and hard-working.'

'Yes, of course I'll do that. Which days does he work in the shop?' Peter asked.

'Thursdays and Saturdays mostly,' said Merrin.

'I'll pop in this Thursday, if you like. Could you just confirm that he will be there before I come?'

'Yes, of course,' said Merrin, 'that's so kind of you, Peter.'

'I'm a great admirer of Peter Lanyon's work, too,' said Peter. 'Of course, he was friends with the other great artists of the time, like Barbara Hepworth and Ben Nicholson, and he was born in St Ives, like me. He died far too young in a gliding accident. I will be very interested to see your boy's work. Is he a local lad?'

'Born and bred,' said Merrin.

They left Peter after Merrin had first insisted on helping with the washing-up, and also taken time to make a serious fuss of Jenny.

'It's been an enormous privilege to come here today,' said Louis, as the two men shook hands, 'and I'll keep you up to date on the missing painting.'

'Today is all due to your friend Merrin,' said Peter. 'She prised me out of my shell, none too gently, I might add. Who would have thought a year ago that I would let anyone near my studio, never mind a member of His Majesty's constabulary.'

They drove through Trevega and up onto the Zennor road. The moment they did so, Louis's phone started chirping away. 'I'm sorry,' he said, 'but I'd better stop, I might have to write something down.'

Surreptitiously, Merrin watched him as he took the call, firing questions, agreeing, disagreeing and finally arranging a meeting in fifteen minutes' time. The policeman was back, the mad joy of their moment in the studio quite gone. She didn't know whether to be sad or relieved.

'I've got to interview someone at Pedn-Olva. I'll drop you home first,' Louis said.

'No need for that,' said Merrin, 'just leave me at the Market Place and I'll walk from there. I have to pick up William from the shop in any event, and I'd like to see how they've got on this afternoon.'

'You probably gathered that was Ben Satchel on the phone. He has found mother and daughter, they're staying for a few days at the Pedn-Olva Hotel. Ben asked about the painting and the little girl, whose name is Jessie Young, showed him straight away where she was keeping it. Ben says unless the mother is a consummate actress, she was greatly shocked. He's ordering them some tea and cake while they wait for me – typical Ben, an excellent idea.'

'When was the painting stolen?' Merrin asked.

'Friday, the day of your private view.'

'Then surely it can't have been a planned theft. If it was, they wouldn't have stayed in town, would they?'

'I agree,' he said, 'and at least we can be absolutely sure that the painter of the picture will not be howling for their blood! Bless him.'

Just before they reached the Market Place, Louis stopped the car. 'I'm so sorry, Merrin – in the studio, I was out of order. I was just so caught up in the moment. I hope you will forgive me.' The anxiety in his face was plain to see.

Merrin put her hand on his arm. 'I understand completely, there is nothing to apologise for. As you say, you were caught up in the moment. Given how much Peter's paintings mean to you, it was hardly surprising.'

'Thank you for your understanding,' said Louis. 'I'll see you soon.'

'Good luck with the interview, not an easy one I imagine,' said Merrin.

Back in his farmhouse, Peter Carew put another log in the range, sat down in his chair and took his time lighting his pipe. Then he looked across at Jenny, who was watching him from her chair.

'I suppose you're not going to tell me what went on in the studio, are you?' Jenny thumped her tail in agreement. 'Well, I'll tell you what I think, old girl. I think we have a matching pair in those two, though I very much doubt they know it yet.'

CHAPTER SIX

A little group was waiting for Louis in the lounge of the hotel when he arrived at Pedn-Olva. Ben introduced him to Jessie, her mother Samantha, and a WPC, Mary Jones, who had joined them to chaperone Jessie, if necessary.

'Where is the painting now, Jessie?' Louis asked, gently.

'Upstairs in me and Mummy's bedroom. You can come and see it, if you want.'

'Yes please, if that's OK with Mummy.' Louis looked at Samantha. 'Would it be alright if we all went upstairs? I'm sorry about the intrusion into your bedroom.'

'Of course it's alright, Chief Inspector,' said Samantha. 'I'm so sorry about all this, but I can explain—'

'In a moment, Mrs Young,' said Louis. 'Let's all go and see the painting first.'

Mother and daughter had a lovely room looking out to sea. Jessie ran to her bed and carefully pulled the painting from her tote bag. Louis stared at it in silence for some moments. It was, without doubt, one of Peter's finest paintings. The detail of the seal's head; the swirl of sea around it, suggesting that the seal had just broken the surface of the water; and, as Jeremy Murdoch had indicated, the colours were exquisite.

'It's a lovely painting, isn't it, Jessie?' said Louis.

'Yes,' agreed Jessie, 'Leo loved seals, he would have liked this picture very much.'

Louis noticed the use of the past tense and decided not to pursue a discussion about Leo with Jessie. This could wait until he could talk alone with her mother.

'I know the artist who painted this picture,' Louis said. 'He paints lots of pictures of Cornwall, often with animals and birds, too.'

Jessie looked up at Louis. 'He must be a very clever man,' she said.

'You're absolutely right, Jessie, he is,' said Louis. 'I wonder whether you would mind staying in your room for a little while and looking after the painting. Ben and Mary will stay here with you to keep you company while I have a talk with Mummy. I promise not to be long. Maybe you'd like to watch some television?'

'OK,' said Jessie, 'but I don't want to watch telly.' She looked up at Mary. 'If we look out of the window, we might see some seals.'

Samantha gave her daughter a kiss. 'I won't be long, darling,' she promised, but her daughter was already absorbed looking out to sea.

Louis found a quiet corner in the bar, and he and Samantha Young settled down.

'I could make this a formal interview,' said Louis, 'but maybe it would be easier for you if you just told me about

Leo and seals. Am I right in assuming they are at the heart of this matter?' Samantha nodded. 'Take your time, please.'

As Samantha composed herself, Louis watched her. He judged her to be in her early forties, a nice-looking woman, but careworn and, at this moment, very nervous. 'Come on,' he said smiling, 'I don't bite!'

She smiled back and began. 'Leo was Jessie's older brother by three years. They were very close and Jessie adored him. Three years ago, we came on holiday to St Ives as a family – Leo, then aged nine, Jessie who was six, me, and my husband Francis. We had a lovely holiday and during it, Leo joined the local children in pier jumping. I was nervous because of the seals in the harbour, but they seemed used to the children and Leo absolutely loved them. Jessie sat on the pier watching her brother and the seals.'

She paused. 'Could I possibly have a glass of water?' she asked.

Louis fetched her water, and after a few minutes, she continued. 'We went home – we live in Surrey – and the new autumn term began. Leo was rugby-mad, which pleased his father a great deal. Towards the end of the term, just a few weeks before Christmas, Francis went to collect Leo from an after-school rugby practice. You know how dark it gets in the evenings at that time of year?' Louis nodded. 'Well, driving home, Francis took a corner too fast. There was a cyclist who he had to swerve to avoid, and he lost control of the car. The car came off the road and hit a tree. Francis suffered a broken collarbone and some lacerations. Leo was killed outright – *dead at the scene*, I think you call it.'

'I'm so terribly sorry,' said Louis. 'I have an eleven-year-old son, I can't imagine . . .'

There was silence for a moment and then Samantha rallied. 'Francis and I tried, we both really tried to stay together for Jessie's sake, but we couldn't – his guilt, my fury, his depression and the fact that, if I'm honest, immediately after the accident I hated him, I couldn't bear to be in the same room as him. There were no charges brought against him, though he must have been driving too fast. He lost his job, he started drinking heavily, so we split up. Jessie and I go to see him about once a month. Obviously, I won't let him drive her anywhere, which he understands. He's a shadow of the man he once was, and I'm ashamed to say I have absolutely no desire to help him, even for Jessie's sake. You probably think I'm an awful person.'

'Actually, I don't,' said Louis, 'but in any event, what right have I to judge you?'

'Jessie has been very brave and we have looked after one another. When I asked where she'd like to go on holiday this summer, she immediately said St Ives to see the seals. I thought it was a very bad idea but she begged me, and I thought maybe it made sense for us to go somewhere where the four of us had been so happy. In fact, I don't know if it was a good idea to come back. There have been a lot of tears since we arrived. Maybe that's good, cathartic perhaps – there is no rule book in our situation, is there?'

'No, there isn't,' Louis agreed.

'I didn't see her take the painting. We had just bought her a surfing T-shirt and the shopkeeper had presented her with a free tote bag. She must have slipped the painting in there, and she obviously was aware she had done something wrong, because she told me nothing about it. It wasn't until your sergeant found us and asked her if she had taken the painting, that I found out what she'd done. It's a beautiful thing. I expect it's worth a great deal of money.'

'Your daughter has excellent taste,' said Louis, tactfully.

'What happens now?' Samantha asked. 'If there is going to be a charge of theft, can you charge me? Let's face it, I should have seen what she was doing, and she's never stolen anything in her life before. Her school will confirm she is a good, honest child, I'm sure.'

'You go back up to your room now and wait with the others,' said Louis. 'I'm just going to call the artist. Try not to worry, we'll sort something out, and I'm so very sorry about what has happened to your family.'

Peter Carew answered his phone immediately. 'I've stayed close by, Louis, I thought you might call me. Did you find the child?'

So, Louis told Peter Samantha's story. He concluded by saying, 'Honestly, Peter, I believe every word she told me was the truth. Over the years, I've become a right old cynic. I'm so tired of the excuses and lies I have to listen to day after day. But Samantha Young isn't one of those, I am absolutely certain.'

'And I absolutely respect your judgement, Louis, of course I do. Obviously, I'm not going to press charges. No money has changed hands between me and the gallery. Jeremy had the painting on loan, until he's sold it and claimed his commission, so he's not involved in any decision. Let me think a moment, would you?' There was silence on the line for some moments. 'Tell me,' Peter continued, 'is little Jessie an intelligent child?'

'I only met her for a few minutes, but yes, I would say she's a bright little spark, and her mother's an articulate and intelligent person,' said Louis. 'I also don't believe they have any money problems, although the father lost his job. Presumably, Samantha must have some private money. I am certain the theft wasn't for financial gain.'

'Why didn't Jessie tell her mother what she'd done?'

'I'm no psychiatrist, but I would say the theft of the painting was an emotional reaction to losing her brother. Ben, my sergeant, said Jessie seemed relieved to be able to tell him she had the painting. There was no hesitation in admitting to him she had taken it, and her mother says she's an honest child, though what mother wouldn't say that in the circumstances?'

'So, you wouldn't think I would be corrupting her into believing stealing is acceptable, if I gave Jessie the painting?' asked Peter.

'You're going to give that marvellous painting to Jessie?' said Louis, astounded.

'No, you are,' said Peter. 'Your friend Merrin may have made a good fist of getting me to join the real world. However, that doesn't include meeting a bereaved family I don't know and making an embarrassingly large gesture. That's your job, boy – just don't cock it up. Make it a memorial to her brother. Why am I telling you all this? You'll know what to say.' The line went dead.

For a few minutes, Louis continued to sit in the bar,

wondering just what to say and how to say it. Finally, he stood up and climbed the stairs to the Youngs' bedroom. As he entered the room, the chatter stopped instantly and the tension was palpable. Samantha stood up, her face white as a sheet.

'The artist does not wish to press charges,' said Louis. Samantha gasped and sat down on the bed. 'Jessie, come here.' He beckoned to the child, who came and stood before him – nervous but bravely.

'Do you know why you took the painting?' he asked.

'No,' said Jessie in a small voice. 'I just saw it and loved it so much, and I knew Leo would have loved it too. I know it was wrong.'

'When the artist was a young man, he fell in love with a beautiful girl and they were going to be married,' said Louis. 'Sadly, she had a poorly heart and quite suddenly died. The artist was so sad, he became a recluse. Do you know what that means?'

Jessie shook her head. 'No, but it's a very sad story.'

'It means he shut himself away from the world, he didn't want to see anyone. Now, though, he is starting to feel better, but he knows how it feels to lose someone very precious, just as you and your mummy have lost Leo. Because he knows how you feel, he wants you to keep the painting as a memorial to Leo and his love of seals. The painting is yours to keep for ever, Jessie.'

Everyone was stunned. 'Goodness,' said Ben, 'that's so kind.'

'Can we go and thank him?' said Jessie. 'Can we go now?'

'No,' said Louis, 'he still doesn't see many people, but

maybe by the time you're grown up and he's an old man, he'll let you come and thank him then. He's getting better all the time.'

'I'd like that,' said Jessie.

'I have an idea,' said Ben. 'It's my day off tomorrow. Why don't I take Jessie and Samantha to Hell's Mouth? I've just checked – it will be low tide by early afternoon.'

'What happens at Hell's Mouth?' asked Samantha.

'The seals go there to rest. No one can reach the beach. There are high cliffs all round, but we can look down at them and the seals feel safe. It's not far, just beyond Gwithian,' said Ben.

'Can we, Mummy, can we?' said Jessie.

Ben looked at Louis. 'That'll be alright, won't it, sir?'

'I don't see why not,' said Louis, smiling.

Samantha came up to Louis. 'Thank you so much, Chief Inspector. I am so grateful. Like Jessie, I wish we could thank the artist – at least we know his name,' she said, pointing to the signature *P. Kernow*. 'I just want him to know how much we shall treasure it.'

'That's not actually his name, he still hides his identity,' said Louis.

'Then as you said, maybe we can meet him one day,' said Samantha.

'Yes, maybe one day,' agreed Louis.

CHAPTER SEVEN

A summons to his boss's office had been issued first thing, so Louis Peppiatt arrived at ten o'clock sharp. Sally was waiting for him.

'I'm glad you're on time, dear boy. Sir is not in the best of moods. There are all sorts of rumours flying about with regard to the art theft, and Ben Satchel is saying nothing.'

'I'll tell you all about it when I come out, if I survive, but I'd probably better go straight in now to calm sir's nerves. What am I saying, you'll be listening at the door anyway, won't you, darling Sal?'

'As if I would,' said Sally, though her expression defied her words.

As always, the mood of Chief Superintendent John Dent could always be judged by the state of his eyebrows. This particular morning, they were bristling alarmingly. There was no question of a greeting.

'What's all this I hear about you giving the thief the stolen painting? Tell me the rumours are not true, Peppiatt.'

Louis couldn't resist it. 'The rumours are entirely true, sir,' he said.

'What!' shouted John Dent. 'Have you gone completely mad, Peppiatt? Who do you think you are – Father Christmas? Thieves will now be rushing into Cornwall in the certain knowledge that if they are caught stealing something, our kindly police force will tell them to keep it. What in God's name is going on?'

Louis was aware that he'd probably overdone the teasing. 'Please, sir, let me tell you the full story and I think you'll then understand.'

John Dent remained silent while Louis told him the tragic history of the Young family. The eyebrows subsided. 'I still think it would have been better,' he said, 'if the artist had given Jessie the painting himself, not a senior police officer. However sad the circumstances, that little girl still stole the painting and you, Peppiatt, are supposed to be upholding the law.'

'The artist and I did discuss the whole matter, sir, but we both felt, and I know Ben Satchel agrees, that Jessie only took the painting as an emotional reaction to the loss of her brother. She knows it was wrong, I just don't think she could help herself.' Louis paused. 'And as for me giving Jessie the painting, it was the only way it would work. The artist is a recluse. He can't easily mix with people, so he asked me to present it to Jessie on his behalf – which I did. As far as I am concerned, the case is closed.'

'In that respect only, I couldn't agree with you more. The sooner we sweep this sorry tale under the carpet, the better. I just hope the press don't get hold of the story.'

'Moving swiftly on, sir,' said Louis, hoping to God his

boss wouldn't find out that the recently appointed Sergeant Satchel had taken mother and daughter to see the seals at Hell's Mouth. 'I don't know if you've heard, but we've had a breakthrough on the St Austell thuggery.'

'That hasn't filtered through yet,' said John Dent.

'We have three men in custody, one of whom has told us what happened. He was there but maintains he didn't join in the attack, and I believe he's genuinely very ashamed about not trying to stop the beating or attending to the victim afterwards. The victim is still in intensive care. At the moment the three are charged with GBH, but it could turn into either manslaughter or a murder charge, if he dies. We are going to offer witness protection to the young man who is prepared to give evidence. We have taken his statement, which is very comprehensive.'

'You're getting soft, Peppiatt – giving a thief back what she's stolen, giving a vicious youth police protection. Do you need a holiday?'

'No, sir,' said Louis firmly. 'The young man in question is our only hope of nailing the other two, unless the victim survives and is well enough to testify. The remaining two are hard nuts and unfortunately are being represented by Martin Geeson.'

'I see,' said John Dent. 'Well, I suppose we'll have to protect this lad if he's our only witness. You need to toughen up though, Peppiatt. The younger officers look up to you, they admire you, and some of your antics seem to have turned you into something of a hero. Therefore, your position carries responsibilities. Do try and live up to them.'

'You do realise that sir actually paid you a compliment

for once, Louis,' said Sally, as Louis slunk back into her office.

'I think I missed that one, Sally,' said Louis. 'I was thinking it was more like newspaper down the back of the trousers time!' His grin suggested he didn't much care either way.

'That was a terribly sad story about little Jessie and family, and what a nice man the artist must be to give her the painting. Is it very valuable?'

'Yes, it is. He's a fine artist and a fine man.'

Merrin was cashing up the till at the end of the day, and feeling exhausted. *We've only had the shop open for four days and I'm already knackered*, she thought. *What on earth am I going to be like by the end of the season?* Louis had called earlier in the day to tell her that the theft of the painting had been resolved, and that Peter had actually given the painting to the little girl, Jessie.

'I can't say I'm surprised,' Merrin had said, and Louis had agreed. Their conversation was very short and a little stilted – an awkwardness seemed to have developed between them. Merrin wasn't sure if she'd imagined it and wondered if Louis was still embarrassed by their moment in Peter's studio. Also, he hadn't suggested another meeting, but then neither had she.

Merrin collected her bag, put the lead on William and was about to leave the shop when there was a knock on the door. Her heart sank. She knew she should be grateful for any custom, even if it was after closing time, but she'd had enough for one day. She opened the door to find Roxy standing outside.

'Oh, I'm so glad I caught you, Merrin. Can I come in, just for a moment? This won't take a second. I expect you are dying to go home.'

Merrin plastered on a smile. 'Yes, of course, come in.'

'I've just spent part of the afternoon in the estate agent's. I'm thinking we might buy a cottage down here, and dear Max has been so helpful. I believe he's a friend of yours – Max Richards, that's right, isn't it?'

'Yes,' said Merrin, 'we were at school together. He's one of my dearest friends.'

'Lucky you,' said Roxy. 'He's so good-looking and very charming. I bet he's really good at his job, too.'

'Yes, he is and he's very reliable. You can trust him completely.'

'Merrin, I was wondering whether you and Max would join Tony and me for dinner on Wednesday. It's probably going to be our last evening in St Ives, as we're planning to leave on Thursday or early Friday morning. Max has already accepted and it would be lovely if you could join us, too.'

'That's very kind of you, thank you, I'd love that,' said Merrin, wondering whether she actually would enjoy it.

'Max has agreed to book us somewhere nice for eight o'clock, and I've suggested we all meet at the Sloop at seven-thirty for a drink first. What do you say?'

'That sounds fine, thank you,' said Merrin.

'I've asked Max to come and pick you up on his way to the pub,' said Roxy.

'Honestly, there is absolutely no need for that,' said Merrin, feeling over-managed. 'I only live just round the corner.'

'Well, I've arranged it now. I'm sure you won't mind being escorted by such a handsome man. See you then, if not before.'

As Roxy walked off down Fore Street, Merrin looked at William, who had stood close beside her during the conversation. He hadn't growled at Roxy, as he had at her husband, but he was wearing his cross face – which meant there was a tiny show of bared teeth, if you looked closely.

'I know she's been a very good customer, but I don't like her much either, William,' Merrin confided, 'and why's she making such a fuss of Max, when she already has a perfectly good husband?'

Merrin closed and locked the shop door, and she and William started for home. *This is what comes of living alone*, Merrin thought. *I'm discussing human relationships with my dog – that can't be right.*

CHAPTER EIGHT

Tuesday morning had been a busy one for Louis. There was the paperwork and a court appearance involved in the charging of the young men responsible for the St Austell mugging – the victim was still in intensive care. Louis had studied again the statement made by Chris Pirie. It was detailed and believable, but at the end of the day, it was one man's word against the other two. It wasn't enough, particularly when dealing with a slippery lawyer like Martin Geeson.

Mid-morning, he received a call from Samantha Young. She and Jessie had enjoyed their day with Ben and luckily, there had to have been at least a hundred seals on the beach at Hell's Mouth, she told Louis.

'We're leaving to go home today,' she said. 'I just wanted to thank you again for your understanding and help. I am so grateful. What happened, in the wrong hands, could have escalated into a real trauma for Jessie, on top of everything else. You and Ben have been so marvellously kind.'

'Only doing our job, Mrs Young,' said Louis. 'I do wish you and your daughter well. Maybe this holiday in St Ives, despite the drama, may prove helpful for Jessie.'

'I think you could be right,' said Samantha. 'Jessie has written a letter to the artist thanking him for the wonderful painting. I've given it to Ben, who says he will pass it on to you to give to the artist. Is that OK?'

'Perfectly fine, Mrs Young. I hope you'll come back and see us again.'

By mid-afternoon, Louis had beaten the paperwork into submission. On and off during the day, the death of Leo Young played on his mind. How could a father ever cope with being responsible for his son's death? Louis thought of his own son, Edward – and imagining the same thing happening to him was unbearable.

On impulse, he called his ex-wife, Stephanie. 'Hi, Steph, how are things?' he asked.

'Fairly hard work,' she began. 'No, that's not right. Everything's fine, really. It's just that the term ends on Friday and the children are demob-happy – overexcited while actually being very tired. Not a good combo.'

'No, indeed,' said Louis. 'I was just calling to see if I could take the children out for supper this evening. You and Andrew too, if you would like to come, though by the sound of things, you'd probably like a break from the kids.'

'Actually, Louis, I've just bought a whole heap of barbeque stuff. It's a beautiful afternoon and the pool's in action. Why not come over, bring your swimmers if you want, and we'll just have a relaxed evening here. What do you say?'

'That sounds marvellous. What time shall I come?' Louis asked.

'Come as soon as you can. The children will be home at any moment.'

'Bless you, I'll bring a bottle.'

It was a scene of domestic bliss. The children were jumping in and out of the pool, with accompanied happy screams. Andrew, Stephanie's husband, was sitting in a deckchair reading the paper, and Stephanie was sitting at a table in the shade, chopping up the ingredients for making a salad. Hearing the noise in the garden, Louis had walked round the side of the house and let himself in by the garden gate. His presence as yet undetected, he stood for a moment, quietly watching. This had once been his home, and although he and Stephanie had separated nearly seven years ago, he still felt the pang of loss when visiting. It wasn't about Stephanie – any bitterness surrounding their divorce had long gone – and nor was it the house. It was the loss of family life he so keenly missed. His little terraced house in Truro was home, after a fashion, but he never seemed able to shrug off the loneliness he felt living there.

Edward spotted him first. 'Dad!' he shouted, jumping out of the pool and running across the lawn towards his father.

'Edward, a towel before you hug your father,' Stephanie shouted in vain.

Edward threw himself into his father's arms. Looking over the top of their son's head, Louis smiled at Stephanie and shrugged his shoulders. 'I'll dry out soon enough,' he said. 'It was worth it for the hug.'

The lovely afternoon slipped seamlessly into a beautiful evening. Andrew abandoned his paper and began cooking on the barbeque and Louis brought them both a glass of wine. The two men got along well enough; indeed it was impossible to imagine anyone not getting on with Andrew. If Louis was honest, he found him deadly dull, but he appeared to be making Stephanie happy and the children seemed to like him.

'I feel a bit awkward, cooking the barbeque when I presume this used to be your role.' Andrew said. He was a kind and thoughtful man, Louis acknowledged.

'No need,' said Louis, handing him his glass. 'When I was here, we didn't have a barbeque. I'm not sure why. I suppose they weren't so popular then, and of course, they're not ideal with very small children around, especially Ed.' The two men exchanged a smile in recognition of Edward's legendary ability to be seriously accident-prone.

After supper, while they were all still sitting round the table, Daisy came up to her father. 'Have you dried out yet, Dad? Is it safe to sit on your lap?'

Louis pushed back his chair and patted his knee. 'Yep, safe for you, darling, but I'm not sure about it being safe for me. Snuggling up to your old dad only means one thing – you're after something.'

'Dad, that is so cynical. I suppose it's because you're a policeman,' said Daisy, pretending to look seriously aggrieved.

'He's right though, isn't he?' said Edward. 'And I know what it is you want.'

'Shut up, Ed,' said Daisy. 'I was wondering whether I could spend a couple of days in St Ives and go bodyboarding with Isla? She asked me the other day at Merrin's shop party. There's a spare bed in her room and she says I could stay.'

'Hey, that's not fair,' said Edward. 'What about me?'

'Isla didn't ask you, Ed. Not everything is about you,' said Daisy.

'Let me think for a moment,' said Louis. 'I have in mind a diplomatic compromise.'

'Why a compromise? This is nothing to do with Ed. He's just sticking his nose in as usual,' said Daisy.

'Daisy, just listen to your father, please,' said Stephanie, wearily.

'Right, this is what's going to happen, if Isla is willing,' said Louis, firmly. 'Steph, if you wouldn't mind dropping them into St Ives on Day One. Ed can join the girls for a surf in the morning and I will pick him up at lunchtime. He can come back to Truro with me. We'll do boys' stuff and he can stay with me overnight, while Daisy stays with Isla. On Day Two, Ed and I will come over in the afternoon, so Ed can have another surf, and then I will drive our lucky but undeserving children back to Falmouth. If your mother agrees, there is no room for argument.'

'Agreed,' said Stephanie, immediately. 'It's a fine plan. Daisy, you sort out with Isla when it would suit her for you to go to St Ives, and then tell Dad promptly, so he can get the time off.'

'I still don't see why Ed has to be involved at all,' said Daisy, removing herself from her father's lap and glaring at Edward.

'Enough!' chorused Louis and Stephanie.

The children were despatched to bed, as next day was

still a school day, and Andrew insisted on handling the clearing up. The sun was low in the sky by the time Louis and Stephanie settled down in the garden with a coffee.

'You've been very quiet this evening, Louis. Anything wrong?' Stephanie asked.

'Just tired, sorry,' said Louis.

'How many years have we known each other? On second thoughts, let's not count them. Something's on your mind.' She smiled. 'It's good to share.'

So, Louis told her about the Young family, of the car crash and its consequences.

'You weren't involved in the investigation into the car crash, though, were you?' Stephanie asked.

'No, that happened somewhere up-country about three years ago. I just got involved because of the little sister, Jessie, taking the painting. What upset me, I suppose, was the idea of a father killing his son. How he must have longed for it to have been him who died, not his boy. It made me think about Ed and how unbearable it would be for the whole family. The boy, Leo, would have been about Ed's age now at the time of the crash. I can't stop thinking about it.'

'Policemen are not supposed to become personally involved in their cases,' said Stephanie, gently, 'and at least the artist made things right for Jessie by not pressing charges and even giving her the painting. That was kind.'

'His name's Peter. He was the man who, with Merrin McKenzie, found Emily, the girl who was kidnapped last summer,' said Louis.

'I thought it was you who rescued Emily? That's what the papers said at the time,' said Stephanie.

'I took the gun off the kidnapper, but I couldn't have done it without Peter and Merrin.'

'How is Merrin, or should I ask how are you and Merrin?' said Stephanie.

'Please, Steph, not you as well. I've had Sally lecturing me about Merrin, and it's just not appropriate.'

'Sally? What, Sally Baxter? She must be as old as the hills! She's not still working, is she?' said Stephanie.

Louis smiled. 'Very much so. Devon and Cornwall Constabulary would fall apart without her. She's got me out of so many scrapes over the years, she absolutely cannot retire until I do.'

'Louis, I know Sally is very fond of you, and I'm very fond of you, too. Since we both clearly feel the same about Merrin being perfect for you, why are you so reluctant to even talk about her?'

'Because our relationship is private, and it is also platonic and always will be.' The moment of madness in Peter's studio flashed into his mind. He instantly dismissed it. 'As you know, she was married to Adam McKenzie for well over thirty years and she's nowhere near getting over his loss. I respect her for that. We're friends and I hope always will be, but nothing more. I'd really like to drop the subject, please, Steph, I mean permanently.'

'I did ask last summer whether Merrin would like to come to ours for Sunday lunch, but what with one thing and another, I've never followed it up. So, can I at least ask her again, now it appears she's going to be playing host to our daughter?'

'By all means,' said Louis, 'but I won't be there.'

CHAPTER NINE

Wednesday proved to be a frustrating day for Merrin. She was running low on her stock of ceramics and knew she needed to spend several days in her studio. Obviously, the shop looked its best when it was full of product. However, this meant leaving Horatio alone again – it felt as if she had hardly been at home at all during the last few weeks. She was sure it wasn't her imagination that he was becoming increasingly grumpy and sad.

The other concern was with regard to the stock check, which Merrin had offered to do for all four businesses. When comparing sales with current stock, it appeared that several items were unaccounted for. She double- and triple-checked her figures but it definitely looked as if three items had gone missing, including one of her own mugs.

She felt rather embarrassed raising the matter with her three colleagues, fearing they might think she was accusing them of stealing from one another – but she needn't have worried.

'I'm so glad you mentioned it. I've been wondering how to tell you all that one of my little brooches has gone missing,' said Pippa.

'And I'm missing one of my candles,' said Lizzie.

'Well, I'm missing nothing,' said Joey, 'which presumably means my paintings aren't good enough to steal.'

The joke was not universally well received.

'I'm missing a mug. It rather looks like we may have a thief in town,' said Merrin. Immediately, she thought about little Jessie. Had her stealing gone beyond a love of seals? Had she managed to deceive both Louis and Ben Satchel into believing the theft of the painting was a one-off? It seemed unlikely but it was definitely possible. 'Joey,' she said, 'why don't you have a wander up and down Fore Street and see if there are any other shops that have anything missing. If so, we had better get hold of Jack Eddy.'

Joey returned surprisingly quickly. 'You're right, Merrin,' he said. 'The fudge shop is missing quite a few items, a couple of surf shops have realised some small items of clothing have disappeared, and a few toys have gone from the Wharf Post Office.'

'That's awful,' said Merrin. 'None of us can afford to lose stock. I'll just go upstairs and make a couple of phone calls.'

Before talking to Jack, Merrin decided to call Louis. If there was a chance that Jessie was a serial thief, it was important Louis knew before she and her mother left town. He was not in his office, but she reached him on his mobile.

'Louis, have Jessie and her mother left town yet?' she asked.

'They left this morning, I believe. Why?' He sounded flustered and none too friendly.

'I'm sorry to trouble you,' said Merrin, 'I can hear you're busy. It's just that there have been a number of thefts in Fore Street in the last few days, and I just wondered if they were connected to the theft of Peter's painting.'

'Of course they're not,' said Louis, briskly. 'Jessie only took the painting because of her brother. I thought I'd explained that.'

'You did,' said Merrin, feeling her patience ebbing away, 'but I just thought it was somewhat of a coincidence that all these items have gone missing at the same time as the painting. As you know, we don't have much theft in St Ives, apart from at the very height of the season. It just seemed odd – a significant number of shops have lost stock, including mine.'

'Whoever has been stealing items in Fore Street in the last few days, I can assure you it wasn't Jessie Young. Money is very tight for a lot of people these days, which probably accounts for the increase in crime. Eddy is the man you should be talking to. I must go. It's a very busy day.' The line went dead.

Merrin stared at her mobile. During the time she and Louis had known one another, they had fallen out on several occasions over cases in which they were both involved. However, their misunderstandings had dwindled over the last year or so; in fact she couldn't remember when there had last been a cross word between them. Their relationship had become caring and supportive, or so she'd thought. Just now, though, the coldness of his tone, the apparent lack of interest in the thefts and the abrupt ending of the call were completely out of character. She was surprised at how hurt and upset she felt. With a sigh, she dialled Jack Eddy's number.

Jack Eddy was in his element. He arrived at the West Cornwall Crafts Co-operative and was immediately given a mug of tea and a muffin, which pleased him greatly. Lizzie was at home making candles, but Jack took a great interest in Joey and Pippa's work, and, of course, once again admired Merrin's ceramics. Eventually, he was persuaded to consider the thefts and so he got out his notebook and faithfully recorded each item they suspected had been stolen from the shop. Joey then gave him a list of the other shops that appeared to have fallen victim to the thief. At no point did Jack mention Jessie Young, and after her terse conversation with Louis, Merrin decided not to mention her either.

'Well, I best be going if I'm to catch all the other shops before closing time,' Jack said at last. 'Well done again, little Merrin Trip. There really is no end to your talents, my maid.'

'It's no good,' said Joey, grinning, as Jack set off up Fore Street. 'What's with this "little Merrin Trip"? I just have to ask.'

Merrin smiled back. 'It's not as peculiar as it sounds, Joey. Growing up, Jack was good friends with my older brother, Jago, and he alleges he remembers the day I was born. He also saved me from a seal when I was pier jumping, much too young. Anyway, my maiden name is Tripconey. My father, Harry Tripconey, was a fisherman –

in fact that's how I heard about you and your painting, from one of my dad's friends. Anyway, bizarre as it sounds, although I am now in my late fifties, I think Jack still thinks of me as a child. "Little Merrin Trip" is what he used to call me when I was small, and it's what he still calls me now.'

'I understand,' said Joey, smiling, 'and I know about your father, he was a legend. What's your brother do? Does he live locally?'

'Sadly, no, he lives in Australia, just outside Sydney. He married a local St Ives girl and they emigrated together. Jago and his business partner developed a chain of shops selling surfing equipment. Now, they've been joined by his business partner's girlfriend and both Jago's son and brother-in-law. Together, they've developed a clothing brand, which is suddenly doing terribly well.'

'Not JAGO'S Clothing? I love that stuff,' said Joey.

'Yes, it was only launched in the UK earlier this year, but I think Jago gets a real kick out of the fact that his brand is now being sold in his home town.'

'That's amazing,' said Pippa. 'Does that mean we will be trading in reverse soon, with the West Cornwall Crafts Co-operative taking Sydney by storm?'

Merrin laughed. 'A nice idea,' she said. 'I'm going to leave you now. I'm having dinner with Roxy and Tony tonight, along with a friend of mine. To be honest, I'm not looking forward to it very much, though I really don't know why.'

'I must admit that I don't like them particularly, despite them being such good customers,' said Joey, 'and I don't know why either.' He hesitated. 'No, scrub that, I know exactly why I'm not sure about them. It's because William doesn't approve of them, particularly Tony.'

'Sound thinking,' said Merrin, and at the mention of his name, William wagged his tail in apparent agreement.

CHAPTER TEN

Max arrived at Merrin's cottage shortly before seven-thirty. He'd changed out of his work suit and was now wearing a beautifully cut blazer, an open-necked shirt and some very stylish cream chinos. It looked as if he'd just had a haircut, too.

'You're looking very dashing,' said Merrin, a little sourly.

'Hey, what's wrong with you, lovely lady? You've managed to make a compliment sound like a criticism.'

'I'm just concerned for your virtue, Max dear,' she said. 'Roxy already has the hots for you and that, presumably, was when you were wearing your boring-but-reliable estate agent's uniform. This get-up is going to send her wild. Actually, now I come to think about it, I don't care about you and your virtue, I'm just concerned for Poppy, who loves you dearly. You behave yourself this evening, please.'

'I can't do much else, can I, with her husband present? What's he like, the husband?' Max asked.

'He's good-looking, but he doesn't say much. Obviously, Roxy holds the purse strings – oh, and William doesn't like him. Actually, William doesn't really like either of them.'

'Obviously, a major consideration,' said Max, giving William a pat on the head just to demonstrate that he, unlike Roxy and her husband, was very much in favour. 'Have we time for a quick stiffener? Surely we deserve one if we have to face a rich, sex-mad woman and her monosyllabic husband, both of whom are despised by William?'

Merrin poured two glasses of white wine, and they sat down round the kitchen table. Horatio flew down from his perch on the wine rack and landed on the table between them. He eyed Max for a moment and then shouted, 'Nuts!'

'Is your bloody bird saying I'm bonkers?' said Max who, although he was a huge success with women and owned a thriving business, was possessed of a self-esteem that could be easily dented – even by a parrot.

'No,' said Merrin, laughing. 'We're having a drink and therefore Horatio is expecting accompanying nibbles, nuts being his favourite. I'll get him a couple.'

Drinks dispatched, Horatio put back in his cage and William placated with a treat and the promise they would not be long, Merrin and Max walked round the corner to the Sloop Inn.

'I told Roxy that we'd meet them in the little bar, and I've booked Porthminster Kitchen for eight o'clock,' said Max. 'Oh look, they're sitting outside.'

Roxy leapt to her feet, dashed over and kissed them both on the cheek. 'Max, you haven't met my husband, Tony.'

Tony, rather reluctantly, got to his feet, shook Max's hand and nodded at Merrin. 'You're late,' he said. 'Still, I guess there's time for another drink, if we hurry. What do you guys want?'

'Dry white wine for us both, I think,' said Max.

'I'll get the drinks. Darling, you talk to Merrin and Max,' said Roxy.

'So, Tony, I believe you're leaving St Ives tomorrow?' asked Max.

'Probably very early on Friday morning with the tide,' mumbled Tony.

'And where are you heading next?' said Merrin.

'The jury's out on that one. We're still trying to agree where to go. I want to go to the Scillies, but Roxy's not so keen.'

There then followed a long awkward silence, during which neither Max nor Merrin could think of anything to say and Tony seemed totally uninterested in making any attempt at conversation. They were saved by Roxy arriving with the drinks.

The meal proved equally tricky. Roxy flirted outrageously with Max throughout and Max, being Max, couldn't help but respond with obvious enthusiasm. Tony didn't appear to mind but that might have been because he drank continuously, switching from beer to wine, then back again to beer, before ordering several double brandies in quick succession. Initially, Merrin tried to engage Tony in conversation, but as his drinking began to take effect, there was very little point. All she did discover was it appeared he didn't have a job, as such. Presumably, Roxy's money made it unnecessary – but being a kept man certainly wasn't making Tony happy, by the look of things, Merrin surmised.

Having finished her coffee, Merrin could stand it no longer and said she really needed to go home, as she had a very early start in the morning. Much to her surprise, Max said he had to go too, which clearly disappointed Roxy.

'Max, darling, I'll see you tomorrow morning,' said Roxy. 'I'll pop into your office so we can talk some more about that lovely little cottage.'

Having made their goodbyes and thank-yous, Max and Merrin climbed down the steps from the restaurant and both took a great gulp of sea air.

'What an evening,' said Max. 'Thank God that's over.'

'It's hardly fair of you to moan about the evening. You were having a lovely time with Roxy, while I was stuck with Tony, who could barely speak a word for most of the meal.'

'I know, I'm sorry. Look, could we go back to yours for one more coffee? I need advice as to how to rid myself of Roxy.'

'Yes, do come back for coffee, but my advice only requires one sentence. *Just don't encourage her, Max.* I love you dearly, but you are absolutely hopeless where women are concerned – absolutely no self-control.'

While Merrin brewed the coffee, Max sat in an armchair by the fireplace and William immediately jumped on his lap. 'Despite what you say, I can't be that bad a person,' said Max, pointing at William, snuggled up on his knees. 'I'm sorry, I've just realised I'm sitting in Adam's chair. Shall I move?'

'Absolutely not,' said Merrin. 'It's reserved for the special people in my life, and you're definitely one of them, despite your wicked ways.'

'Tell me,' said Max, with a grin, 'does Chief Inspector Louis Peppiatt get to sit in Adam's chair?'

'Occasionally,' said Merrin, immediately looking uncomfortable.

'How are things going between you and him?' Max asked.

'I don't know what you mean,' said Merrin, defensively. 'We're just friends and sometimes colleagues, when I do pro bono work for him.'

'If you say so,' said Max, 'but seeing you together at your private view, it was obvious you were both delighted to be in each other's company. I want you to be happy again, darling girl, and honestly, I believe you and Louis are made for one another.'

Merrin turned her back on Max and made a fuss of pouring their coffees. Being reminded of Louis at the private view felt both poignant and painful. It was only five days ago. What had gone wrong between them in that time? The cause had to be linked to the kiss in the studio, but why? Suddenly she felt as if she might cry. Hurriedly, she rubbed her eyes and put the coffees on the little table beside Max.

'Let's not talk about Louis any more, Max,' she said, firmly.

Approximately thirty miles away, Louis sat in his armchair in his bleak little sitting room, a whisky in hand. He'd tried to think about his work, he'd tried to think about his children, but his thoughts kept straying back to Merrin, and to his crass behaviour on the phone. What had he been trying to do? Destroy their friendship? And if so, why? He knew his feelings for her ran deep, but they were also very muddled. He thought back to the evening of the private view. They had been so happy to be together again, and had both admitted they'd missed each other. *I'm behaving like some bloody teenager*, he thought. He knew from her voice on the phone that he had hurt her feelings, and that was the last thing he ever wanted to do.

Maybe things would seem clearer in the morning.

CHAPTER ELEVEN

Roxy had been in Max's office for over two hours. Other potential customers had been in and out, looking for properties and asking questions, but Max found it difficult to concentrate. She was sitting by his desk, watching him all the time, sometimes interrupting a conversation to tell a prospective customer what a wonderful estate agent he was.

'Honestly, Roxy, it's really not helpful singing my praises to customers. It's weird, quite off-putting for them, I'm sure,' Max said, when the office had temporarily emptied and they were alone.

Roxy was unrepentant. 'Darling Max, surely you know the difference between advertising and PR. Advertising is simply you telling the world what a great estate agent you are. Public relations involve someone else sending out the same message. The latter is infinitely more powerful and far more likely to bring in the punters.'

'I'm sure you're right, but I find it embarrassing and I

do need to get on with some work now. I have a huge pile of paperwork to sort out, surveyors to book, solicitors to contact. Do you really want this cottage, Roxy?'

'Of course I do, darling. I'll get together all the information you need and let's meet for a drink this evening to finalise the arrangements,' said Roxy, with a disarming smile. Standing up, she gave him a prolonged kiss on the cheek.

'So, what time are you actually leaving tomorrow?' asked Max.

'We decided to leave in the early hours of the morning to catch the tide. We'll have a late supper on board tonight, stow everything away and then be good to go. So, an early evening drink would be good. What time do you finish work, darling?'

'About five-thirty. I could meet you in the Sloop at, say, six,' suggested Max, realising she was not going to take no for an answer.

'Why don't I come back here and we can have a drink in your flat?' said Roxy. 'You mentioned last night that you live above the shop. I'll bring a bottle of champagne so we can celebrate the purchase of my cottage.'

'We've a long way to go before we can say it's your cottage,' said Max.

'Don't be silly, darling. I'm prepared to pay the asking price, I'm a cash buyer, and I'm sure you won't allow any gazumping to go on. I don't need a survey. You say the owners are desperate to sell. Let's try to set an all-time record for the purchase of a freehold property.'

'Conveyancing solicitors are not known for their speed,' Max remarked.

'Don't be so negative, darling. You can rush this through for me, I know you can. See you at five-thirty.' And with that Roxy swept out of the door.

Max let out a sigh. He had to admit he was enormously attracted to Roxy. She was his sort of woman – beautiful, demanding, poised, confident, certainly someone used to getting her own way, and clearly very wealthy. For a moment, his thoughts strayed to Poppy. She was lovely, kind, caring, fun and clearly adored him. She was a charming Cornish girl, but she wasn't exciting – at least not in the same way as Roxy.

He mentally chastised himself for such thoughts. In any case, Roxy had a husband and was sailing off to heaven knew where in the morning. Maybe that was part of her charm, for Max knew about women. All his instincts told him that Roxy was his for the asking; she had invited herself to his flat this evening but would be gone on the morning tide. No strings, just how he liked his relationships.

Jack Eddy had completed his investigation into the thefts that had taken place up and down Fore Street. They had begun on Friday lunchtime, as far as he could tell, and the last recorded theft had taken place on Sunday. Several shopkeepers, including Merrin, conceded that the timing of the thefts was somewhat vague because they had not noticed immediately when items went missing, as they weren't of great value.

'It's a rum situation,' he told Merrin. 'Quite a lot of items have been stolen but none of them expensive. It makes no sense. Why risk being prosecuted for theft when the items are of such low value?'

'Unless the person concerned is really poor,' Merrin suggested.

'Maybe,' agreed Jack. 'The other odd thing is that no one has the slightest idea who the thief could be. Over the years, working with the shopkeepers, we've usually managed to spot the probable culprit pretty quickly. Then it's simply a question of waiting until he or she goes to steal something again, and then I nab them.' Dear old Jack puffed out his chest, with obvious pride. 'We've had a very high success rate over the years, so the boss says.'

'Well certainly, none of us have the slightest idea who can be doing this. How many items altogether are missing, Jack?' Merrin asked.

'I haven't totted it up yet, but it must be nearly twenty,' said Jack. 'That's an awful lot of stealing to go undetected, which makes me think you could be right – there's more than one person involved. Maybe it's even a gang.'

It was on his way back to the station that Jack had his lightbulb moment. Jessie and her mother were two people. The timing was right too. Without even waiting to get back to his desk, he called Louis on his mobile.

'What is it, Eddy?' said Louis, who, to Jack's ears, sounded very grumpy. It seemed like the perfect opportunity to cheer him up, as Jack was sure he had stumbled on the solution to the thefts. He explained the details and volume of thieving that had taken place, and then triumphantly divulged his theory.

'Don't be ridiculous, Eddy,' said Louis. 'Of course it's not Jessie and Samantha Young who are responsible for these thefts. I can't imagine what makes you think they're involved.'

'Well, I was talking to little Merrin, and in view of the high number of thefts, she suggested it could be the work of more than one person. That thought coupled with the timing of the stealing – to my mind, boss, it all adds up.'

'Oh, so it was Mrs McKenzie who put you up to this idea, was it?' said Louis.

'No, it wasn't her, boss,' said Jack, now genuinely baffled by his boss's reaction. 'I got the idea on the way back to the station, just now.'

There was a protracted silence. At last Louis spoke. 'I'm sorry, Eddy, I was out of order. It was a good idea of yours, but I am absolutely certain that Jessie and her mother are not involved in any way. The seal painting was a one-off. Back to the drawing board for you, I'm afraid.'

Having ended the call with his sergeant, Louis sat slumped in his chair. Poor Jack – he was only doing his job, and having never met the Youngs, how could he possibly be expected to know that they couldn't have been involved in this new spate of thieving? All Louis's instincts suggested that both mother and daughter had told him the absolute truth. His ugly mood, of course, was entirely due to his confusion regarding his relationship with Merrin, but to take it out on poor old Jack Eddy was unforgivable.

The only sensible thing to do was to go and see Merrin to clear the air, but since the confusion was self-induced, he realised he first needed to work out what his feelings were and why they were causing him so much unhappiness. Only then would he be able to explain them to Merrin.

CHAPTER TWELVE

Friday morning found Merrin and William wandering about on the harbour beach. It was just after eight o'clock and the tide was well on its way out, having clearly taken with it the lovely yacht *Llamedos*. Merrin could not avoid feeling immensely relieved to see that Roxy and Tony Barrow had left St Ives. Of course, if Roxy was seriously going to buy a cottage in town, they would be back. However, Merrin had the feeling that Roxy was a woman given to wild enthusiasms which often did not come to fruition. Against this, of course, buying a cottage in St Ives would give her the excuse to spend time with Max, which she certainly seemed anxious to do. Roxy's massive spending spree in the shop had been a huge bonus, but even this, Merrin felt, she would not miss. Roxy's spending had been almost frenzied and in many respects nonsensical – who on earth would want to buy four paintings in one go from the same artist? Merrin felt that if she and her colleagues were to truly judge the success, or otherwise, of the shop going forward, Roxy's purchases should be ignored – they were somehow unreal, far from normal trading.

Merrin also felt protective towards Max – he was such a weird mixture. With her brother Jago living so far away, Max was very much like a second brother to Merrin. He was caring, kind and reliable. He always had her and Isla's best interests at heart and would help them in any way he could. However, where his love life was concerned, he appeared to have fewer scruples, and Merrin was well aware that Roxy was very much his sort of woman. She was very relieved that Roxy had gone; hopefully, if Poppy suspected Max's interest in Roxy, she would forgive him.

William was pleased with himself because he had found a dead fish. Even from several metres away, Merrin could smell it. 'Drop it,' she demanded. William stood his ground, fish in mouth, both triumphant and defiant. Unlike most dogs, William enjoyed eye contact with his trusted humans. He and Merrin stared each other out, but after several moments, Merrin won: William dropped his gaze and the fish. 'Good boy, come on then, time to go.'

They turned round and started back towards the cottage. There were always a number of dead fish in the harbour, and Merrin could never understand why the seagulls didn't touch them. *Maybe because they're not covered in batter, salt and vinegar*, she considered. At the top of the slipway, she turned and gazed out across the harbour. *Home*, she thought, wondering, not for the first time, how it had ever been possible to leave this lovely place.

* * *

Merrin spent the morning on paperwork; there seemed to be an awful lot of it for one small shop. She then attacked Isla's bedroom. Isla would be home tomorrow and as far as Merrin was aware, she would be in St Ives for the whole summer. During her university years, Isla had tended to go travelling during the summer months, so to have her home was a real treat for Merrin.

Paperwork neatly filed and the cottage clean and tidy, Merrin clipped on William's lead and decided they should take in a visit to the shop and see how sales were doing. She was halfway up Fore Street when she heard a voice calling her name. She turned round and for a moment did not recognise the woman coming towards her.

'Merrin, I'm so glad to find you. I've just been to see Max and he's fixing up somewhere for me to stay.'

It was Roxy, but barely recognisable from her normal chic self. Her lovely hair was damp and dishevelled, and she was wearing a waterproof jacket, jeans and a worn T-shirt several sizes too large. However, it was not just the lack of her normal stylish appearance that concerned Merrin; it was the expression on Roxy's face. She looked distraught, her eyes were wild – something was clearly very wrong.

'Roxy!' said Merrin. 'What on earth's happened? You look,' she hesitated, 'very distressed. And why are you here? I saw your yacht had gone this morning.'

'Oh, Merrin, I'm so pleased to see you. I need your help. I've done such a stupid thing,' she wailed. For a moment, Merrin thought she was about to cry, but then she seemed to pull herself together. 'Could we go upstairs to your studio? I need to ask you something.'

'Of course,' said Merrin. 'Come with me and I'll get you a cup of tea – you look like you need it.'

'I'd prefer a gin and tonic,' said Roxy.

'A little early, I think, considering it's only four o'clock,' said Merrin. 'Come on, let's see if we can sort you out.'

Joey was alone in the shop when they arrived. 'Roxy?' he said, obviously taking in her unusual appearance.

'Don't ask, Joey,' said Roxy, shortly. 'We're going upstairs to talk.'

Joey raised his eyebrows at Merrin as she began to follow Roxy up the stairs. Merrin shrugged her shoulders in response.

A cup of tea in hand, Roxy began. 'Tony and I could not agree as to where we should go next. I need to get back to London, and he wanted to go to the Scillies to meet up with some friends. In the end we decided that he would go to Scilly and I would get the train back to London.' Roxy drank her tea in silence for a moment and Merrin thought it best to remain silent. Eventually, she started again. 'We – well, we had a bit of a row on board. I thought Tony was being very selfish. I was looking forward to sailing back to St Katharine Docks, and he knew I had commitments in London that meant there wasn't time to take in the Scillies as well. We'd had a very late supper and argued throughout. I admit I was furious so in the end I abandoned the meal, shouted goodbye and climbed down into the tender. I rowed ashore and left the tender tied up. It was late, certainly after midnight, I think, so I decided I'd better find a hotel. It was only when I was walking out of St Ives towards the hotels that I suddenly realised I had left my backpack on board, which contained my phone, my purse, my laptop, all my credit cards and a change of clothes for the journey back to London – in other words, my whole life.'

'Oh my God!' said Merrin. 'So, what did you do then?'

'I ran back down to the Wharf, just in time to see *Llamedos* chugging out of the harbour into the open sea. And, of course, I had absolutely no means of contacting Tony.'

'Surely, though, he'll find your backpack and realise what's happened?' suggested Merrin.

'He'd been moaning about the amount of things I'd bought, like Joey's paintings, which were cluttering up the cabin, so I put my backpack in one of the kitchen cupboards we weren't using. There is virtually no chance of him looking in there. Why would he?'

'If he's heading for Scilly, you need to contact the harbour master at St Mary's, and get him to look out for *Llamedos* and have someone tell Tony what's happened.'

'I suppose so,' said Roxy, seeming oddly reluctant.

'Let's call the harbour master right away,' said Merrin. 'I'll find his number – though I expect Tony has arrived by now, if he left so early this morning. Which island do you think he was going to visit?'

Roxy shrugged her shoulders. 'I don't know. I was so angry with him, I didn't think to ask – actually, I didn't care much where he was going. Wherever his friends are staying, I presume.'

The conversation with the St Mary's harbour master proved helpful but inconclusive. No one had seen *Llamedos*, but he took Merrin's mobile number and said he would ask around to see if there had been a sighting and if so, would get in touch.

'So what have you been doing today?' Merrin asked.

'When I realised I had no money, I knocked on Max's door. It was a bit awkward because his girlfriend was staying. Anyway, I got a few hours' sleep on the sofa and Max has since found me a B&B in Fish Street.'

'But what are you going to do about money?' Merrin asked.

'That's where you come in, Merrin. Could you possibly lend me some money just for a few days? I thought you might not mind as I've spent so much in your shop and I'll need cash, obviously.'

'How much?' Merrin asked.

'I was thinking five hundred pounds should cover it,' said Roxy. 'I'll have to get some clothes, a toothbrush and some make-up, pay for the B&B and have enough money to get myself up to London.'

'You could still get the evening train up to Paddington today,' Merrin said. 'I'll give you the money for the fare and drop you at the station. How does that sound?'

'No, I need to stay around St Ives for a few days to try to get my stuff back from Tony,' said Roxy.

'OK,' said Merrin reluctantly, wondering what Poppy felt about Roxy sleeping on Max's sofa. 'There should be some cash in the till, as I haven't done the bankings for a couple of days. However, I will have to ask Joey and the others for their blessing.'

'I don't like the sound of that, I'd be so embarrassed. Do you have to tell them?' Roxy hesitated. 'Maybe you could lend me the money personally, rather than through the shop. It really will only be for a few days.'

'Alright, I suppose I could do that,' Merrin said, somewhat hesitantly. 'Come with me to the Wharf Post Office now. I can only take out three hundred pounds at a time, but I can draw out the balance tomorrow. Will that do?'

Having given Roxy the money and parted company, Merrin chided herself as she walked back towards the shop. Why had she been so reluctant to help the poor woman when she had been such a generous customer and had played hostess to a delicious dinner just two nights ago? Her story was plausible enough, so why, Merrin wondered, did it leave her feeling uneasy?

As soon as Merrin entered the shop, Joey was full of questions – why was Roxy still in town, why did she look so awful, what did she want? Merrin related Roxy's sorry tale, leaving out the fact that she had lent her money.

'How were sales today?' Merrin asked.

'Not bad, I think. I'm only working this afternoon because Pippa has a dentist appointment. Yesterday was very interesting though. Such a nice guy came in and appeared to be very interested in my paintings. He didn't buy anything, but he was very encouraging. He's a fan of Peter Lanyon, too, so we had a lot to talk about.'

Peter Carew, of course, thought Merrin, who'd temporarily forgotten his promise to have a look at Joey's work. 'Did he give you any advice?' she asked.

'Yes,' said Joey, laughing. 'He told me to go wild! He said I had something very original and that I should not be constrained by my admiration for other artists. "Develop your own style," he said. "I want to be able to walk into a gallery one day soon, and say, instantly, that's the work of Joey Moon."'

Merrin and William walked down onto Porthmeor Beach. She stood for a moment looking up at the Tate Gallery. Maybe one day, Joey Moon would be displayed there, in which case all the hassle involved in setting up their little co-operative would have been worthwhile.

As soon as she reached home, she called Peter Carew. 'You made quite an impression on young Joey Moon,' said Merrin. 'Thank you so much, you've really fired him up.'

'Good,' said Peter. 'Honestly, Merrin, in my view he's really talented, and charming too. Unlike me, once he gets his break, he'll be able to help sell his paintings, not run a mile from any prospective buyer, as I do.'

'I understand you told him to go wild!' said Merrin. 'I'll be intrigued to see how that pans out.'

'He's obsessed with Peter Lanyon. Being influenced by great painters is all well and good, but it can end up being restrictive. In the case of Joey, he's more than halfway towards creating his own style, his own visual language. Truly, I believe he could achieve great success, and I told him so.'

'It's a shame you didn't tell him who you were. He would have been truly made up to have known that.'

'Come on now, Merrin,' said Peter. 'You've dusted down this weary old recluse and brought him out into the sunshine, but there are limits. One step at a time. Our tame policeman wanted me to present the seal painting to little Jessie. Now that really was going too far.'

Merrin laughed. 'In your defence, I can see that wouldn't have been your thing. Still, I'm sure Louis made a good job of it.'

'Of course he did,' said Peter. 'How is he anyway? Has he recovered from his visit to my studio? I do hope not!'

'I don't know,' said Merrin. 'I haven't seen him since our visit to you.'

Peter immediately noticed that Merrin's voice had gone very flat, and instinct told him not to pursue the subject.

'It's Billy's birthday in a couple of weeks and I thought I might throw a modest party. You and the chief inspector would be most welcome.'

'Blimey, Peter, a party – that really is progress,' said Merrin, genuinely impressed.

'Don't get overexcited. It would just be Billy and his brothers, and you and Louis to provide me with moral support.'

'Can I bring Joey?'

'No, you absolutely cannot. No one knows who I am and where I live, and I don't believe a young whippersnapper like Joey can be trusted to keep his mouth shut.'

'Spoilsport,' said Merrin, smiling to herself.

'Bully,' retorted Peter.

Merrin's next call was to Max. It went to voicemail, but a few minutes later, Max rang her back.

'Sorry,' he said. 'I was with a client. How are you? How's the shop going?'

'A neat attempt at a side-step, Max, but completely futile. As you well know, I am calling about Roxy. What's going on, do you think?'

'It all sounds pretty straightforward to me. I presume she's told you what happened. Roxy had a row with her awful husband, and exited the boat, leaving her entire world behind her. I've fixed her up with temporary accommodation while she sorts things out.'

Merrin noted Max's obvious enthusiasm. 'But why doesn't she just go straight back to London where, for some reason, she has to be? Does she have a job?' Merrin asked.

'I don't know about a job, but I think she's staying in St Ives because she's desperate to get her stuff back. She's worried her bloody husband might make free with her credit cards, I imagine. He clearly has no money of his own – that was obvious at dinner the other night, wasn't it? I feel really sorry for her. She seems very tense and stressed.'

A thought suddenly struck Merrin. 'Max, as you feel so sorry for Roxy, how much money did you lend her?'

'What makes you think I lent her anything?' said Max, defensively.

'Because she's borrowed some from me,' said Merrin.

'How much?'

'She wants five hundred pounds, but so far I've only given her three hundred,' said Merrin.

'Well, you got off lightly,' said Max. He was silent for a moment. 'I might as well tell you, Roxy borrowed a thousand from me.'

'Why does she need all this money? It makes no sense.'

'To fund her lifestyle while she's still staying in St Ives trying to track down Tony, I suppose. I don't know, Merrin, but her distress is real,' said Max.

'I can't imagine why she's distressed, with thirteen hundred pounds of other people's money in her pocket. I might have promised her five hundred, but in view of your contribution, she's getting no more out of me.'

'I'm sure Roxy's not a bad person. She's just used to a different standard of living from the rest of us.'

'It won't do Roxy any harm to learn how it feels not to be rolling in money. Please, Max, don't get involved with her. I don't know why I'm saying this but I'm sure she's bad news.'

'It's a bit late for that,' said Max.

'What do you mean?' Merrin said. 'I know you're a fast worker where women are concerned, but surely there's been no time for you to become involved with her?' Max remained silent. 'Oh God, Max, when?'

'She came to my flat early yesterday evening, before they were due to sail. We were supposed to be tying up the details for her cottage purchase, but we never got round to that, I'm afraid,' he said, a little sheepishly.

'You idiot,' said Merrin, 'what about Poppy? I gather Poppy was staying with you the night Roxy rocked up in the small hours and slept on your sofa. For God's sake, Max, what are you like?'

'Poppy doesn't know about Roxy. You won't tell her, will you?'

'No,' said Merrin wearily. 'How many times have we had this exact same conversation?'

'Don't let's go there,' said Max. 'You're a true friend, dear Merrin.'

'Heaven only knows why, I must be off my head,' Merrin replied.

CHAPTER THIRTEEN

Isla arrived home in time for lunch on Saturday, to a riotous welcome from her mother, William and, of course, Horatio. A delicious bottle of white wine was uncorked to accompany one of Merrin's legendary lasagnes.

'I quite thought you'd go travelling this summer, but I'm so glad you've decided not to,' said Merrin.

'I've got a lot of studying to do. This conversion course is a lot harder than uni. Also, I thought I could probably pick up a job in one of the restaurants or bars for August to help with finances. Then, of course, there is the other thing,' said Isla.

'What other thing?' Merrin asked.

'The chance to spend some time with my dear old mum, of course.'

'I definitely don't approve of the use of the word *old*, with reference to me. In any event, I think you speak with forked tongue. I think you may have another motive for wanting to spend your summer in St Ives in the form of young Joey Moon.'

'Mother, how could you possibly say such a thing?' said Isla, failing to hide the fact that she was blushing. 'I've only met him a couple of times.'

'The jungle drums have already told me you two hit it off immediately you met. In fairness, I can see why. He's pretty gorgeous and if I was twenty-three, I'd certainly give you a run for your money, young lady!'

'So was it Pippa who told you about me and Joey?' Isla asked.

'I'm afraid I'm not at liberty to disclose my sources,' said Merrin, primly.

They both laughed and Merrin topped up their wine. 'As I strongly believe in supporting all family ventures,' said Isla, 'I may pop into your shop from time to time during the summer just to see how the sales of Joey's paintings are progressing – for no other reason, obviously.'

'Obviously!' said Merrin.

'Actually, Mum, while I think about it, I have invited Daisy Peppiatt to come over on Tuesday for two days of surfing, and have suggested she stays here on Tuesday night. Is that OK with you?'

'Yes, of course,' said Merrin, 'but what about her brother, Edward? He'll be mad at not being included.'

'He's catered for. I thought you'd know all about it from Cip. The plan is that Stephanie is going to drop over both kids on Tuesday morning, and at lunchtime, Cip is going to pick up Ed and take him to stay overnight in Truro. He's then going to return him to St Ives on Wednesday afternoon, so Ed can have another surf, and then he will take them both back to Falmouth.'

'It's very kind of you to spend so much time with Daisy,' said Merrin.

'She's really nice, and funny too. Also, the poor thing is fifteen – a ghastly age, neither one thing nor the other,' said Isla, sounding decidedly middle-aged. 'Oh, and the other thing is that Stephanie has invited us to Sunday lunch. She wanted to make it this Sunday, but I explained it was my first proper day back at home, so she's suggested next Sunday. Are you up for that, Mum?'

'Is Louis going to be there?' Merrin asked, trying to sound casual.

'I don't know, I presume so. As I've said, I thought you'd know all about this.' Isla studied her mother for a moment. 'Are you and Cip OK?' she asked.

'Of course we are,' said Merrin, brusquely. 'It's just that we don't see each other very often these days.'

At the same time as Merrin and Isla were discussing arrangements regarding his children, Chief Inspector Louis Peppiatt was at home, sitting at his desk and staring at the note Ben Satchel had left him. Apparently, Sir Hubert Eustace had called the Truro station a couple of times on Friday and needed to talk to Louis personally, as a matter of some urgency. Louis remembered Sir Hubert only too well. It was a tragic case. Lady Cynthia Eustace had been walking along the pavement, hand in hand with her six-year-old son, Jeremy, whom she had just collected from his primary school in Newton Abbot. A car on the opposite side of the road, coming towards them, took the corner too fast and swerved across the road towards the pair. Seeing what was happening, Lady Cynthia managed to push her son out of the path of the oncoming car but in doing so, took the full impact herself. She died instantly. Jeremy was unhurt but, of course, deeply traumatised.

The driver left the scene and, in the rush to help mother and child, none of the witnesses could give a description, not even as to whether the driver was male or female. The car had been stolen; the general feeling was that it had been taken by some young hooligan. However, when the abandoned vehicle was found, there were no fingerprint matches to the police database. Eventually, Sergeant Louis Peppiatt was told to drop the case, but he couldn't. He'd been the first policeman on the scene and had sat holding the trembling, terrified little boy until help came.

It took him five months but in the end Louis tracked down the culprit, a seventeen-year-old boy, who was rightly treated harshly by the courts. Sir Hubert had been deeply grateful, but that had to be over twenty years ago, so Louis couldn't imagine what he wanted now.

The phone was answered almost immediately. 'It's Louis Peppiatt, Sir Hubert – I gather you have been trying to get hold of me.'

'Yes, indeed,' said Sir Hubert, 'and a merry dance you've led me. So, I gather you are now based in Truro and have risen to the dizzy heights of chief inspector. Is that so? If it is, from personal experience I'm sure your promotion is well deserved.'

'Thank you, sir,' said Louis. 'What can I do for you?'

'My wife's gone missing and I want you to find her,' Sir Hubert said, without preamble. 'You may think it careless of me, having lost one wife to then lose another.' Louis couldn't think of an appropriate reply, so remained silent. 'We have a house in London, and also a small estate just outside Newton Abbot – oh, but you know that, of course, it was where we were living when Cynthia died.'

'Yes, sir, I remember it well,' said Louis.

'My wife went down to Devon to see some friends and said she would be back in a few days. That was over two weeks ago. I rang the house but our housekeeper said she had only stayed one night and then left without saying where she was going. I've tried her mobile, over and over again, but it's not working. I'm worried sick. I'm a wealthy man – maybe she's been kidnapped.'

'Have you received any ransom demands?' Louis asked.

'No,' said Sir Hubert, 'but that doesn't mean someone hasn't taken her.'

'Have you contacted the police?' Louis asked.

'Don't be ridiculous, man, of course I have. I'm talking to you, aren't I?'

It was then that Louis remembered how aggressive Sir Hubert could be. It was part of the reason the hit and run case had been dropped, in his view. His governor at the time had received such a barrage of insults from Sir Hubert that he'd eventually had enough.

'I meant have you contacted the Met, sir?' said Louis, patiently. 'As you are currently based in London, it's their responsibility to handle the case.'

'Were you even listening to me, Peppiatt? My wife went missing in Devon and unless I am very much mistaken, you are a member of Devon and Cornwall Constabulary.'

'I agree,' said Louis, 'but I'm based in Cornwall. I think

the Met is your best bet initially, but if you want to report her as a missing person, close to where she disappeared, then you could contact the Newton Abbot police station. There's a good man there at the moment – Inspector William Westbury. He should be able to help you.'

'So what you're saying, Peppiatt, is that you're refusing to help me?' Sir Hubert was shouting now.

'I can't, sir, I'm very sorry.'

'Can't or won't, Peppiatt?'

Louis considered the question. 'Well, both really, sir. I can't take on your case as I'm based in West Cornwall, and therefore I won't be able to help you.'

'Well, you certainly haven't improved with age, Peppiatt. Promotion has clearly turned you into a pompous arse. Good day to you.'

Louis put his mobile back on his desk and stared at it for a moment. He had mixed feelings about Sir Hubert, despite his rudeness. The man sounded desperate, his voice was reedy and thin – he sounded like a man at the end of his tether. How old was he? Louis wondered. He did the sum; Sir Hubert couldn't be more than in his early sixties. Over the years, Louis had often seen his name in the press. He was a popular figure, having built a huge company specialising in producing eco-friendly products. Somewhere Louis was sure he had read that the company had been very successfully floated on the stock exchange. Just now, though, the man had not sounded like a highly successful businessman – he'd come across to Louis as being scared and oddly vulnerable.

Nonetheless, there was nothing Louis could sensibly do to help.

CHAPTER FOURTEEN

By the following Tuesday morning, Jack Eddy reported to Merrin that another three items had been confirmed as having gone missing from Fore Street shops. 'It could be quite a bit more than that, my little maid. I've only checked one side of the street. Have you lost anything else?'

'I don't think so, Jack – we're being very careful, though when the shop's full, it's difficult to keep an eye on everyone. Have you any idea yet as to who it might be?'

'Not a one, little Merrin Trip,' Jack said, shaking his head. 'I've never known anything like it. I'm used to the odd thing going missing, but nothing on this scale. I don't mind telling you, it's keeping me awake at night.'

'That's a shame, Jack, poor you,' said Merrin.

'There is an upside though – Mrs Eddy is always complaining about me snoring. It's normally our main topic of conversation at breakfast, so the last few days have been very peaceful.'

'So what have you talked about instead, Jack?' Merrin asked, intrigued.

'Nothing at all,' said Jack with a grin. 'That's why it's so peaceful. You know, I think you might be right – it has to be more than one person doing this.'

'Have you spoken to the boss about it?' Merrin asked.

'I tried to but he's very teasy at the moment. However, if the thefts continue at this rate, I'm going to have to talk to him again.'

'Actually, he's going to be in St Ives both today and tomorrow. His children are going surfing with Isla. He'll probably pop in to see you, I imagine.'

'Let's hope so,' said Jack.

Pippa arrived as Jack was leaving. It was one of her days for manning the shop. Merrin watched, fascinated, as she assembled a pile of sea glass ready for polishing. They were a mix of shapes and sizes and a variety of colours. Although as a child Merrin had collected odd pieces of sea glass on the beach, seeing them in such profusion was startlingly beautiful.

'I know sea glass comes in a number of colours, but down here I've only ever seen blues and greens, and white occasionally,' Merrin said. 'Where do you get these lovely reds and browns? Do you buy them in?'

'Certainly not. The very idea, that would be cheating!' said Pippa, smiling. 'I have a friend, a fellow jeweller, who I met at art college. She lives up north where there are more reds and browns on the beaches for some reason. So, periodically, we swap colours, also sometimes shapes if one of us is looking for a particular shape for a piece of jewellery.'

'William and I spend a lot of time wandering about on the beaches. Do you want us to keep a lookout for any sea glass?' Merrin asked.

'All volunteers gratefully accepted,' said Pippa. 'The harbour beach is a good spot.'

'It's our go-to evening walk when the tide's low,' said Merrin. 'We'll see what we can find. I'm off now but I will be home most of the day, if you have any problems or need a break.'

'I'll be fine and I have plenty of polishing to do. I think people seeing me at work actually helps sell my jewellery.'

'I bet it does,' said Merrin.

Merrin was anxious to get home because Stephanie was shortly dropping off her children. Isla was at the cottage waiting for them, but Merrin wanted to see Stephanie in person to thank her for the lunch invitation. As it happened, she was just in time – she was just climbing the stone steps up to her cottage when Stephanie appeared at the front door.

'Oh, Merrin, I'm so glad to see you,' said Stephanie. 'Are you sure you don't mind having my crew? It doesn't look as if Louis will be able to pick Ed up until about two o'clock, so I've given them some lunch money.'

'No need for that,' said Merrin. 'I have some pasta standing by. Thank you for your Sunday lunch invitation. It is this coming Sunday, isn't it?'

'Absolutely, I hope you both can come – about twelve-thirty, would that suit? I've given Isla directions as to how to find us.'

'Perfect,' said Merrin. 'See you then.'

'Bye,' said Stephanie as she started to walk towards the Wharf. Then she stopped and called out. 'Merrin, Louis doesn't know if he can make it for Sunday lunch, due to the pressure of work. Try to persuade him to come when he collects Ed this afternoon.'

Fat chance of that in his current mood, Merrin thought as she let herself into her cottage, awash with children and wetsuits.

Despite assurances to the contrary, the surfing party was late back for lunch, because apparently *the surf was wicked*. So, they had only just started eating the pasta when Louis arrived to collect Edward.

Louis Peppiatt did not look happy and there was no friendly greeting. Merrin would have been angry at his apparent rudeness, except for the fact that she could see he was miserable.

'I need to collect Ed and get back to the Truro station. There's something I need to do first before I can take the rest of the day off,' he said, staring at the children rather than at Merrin.

'Whatever you've got to do, it can surely wait ten minutes so Ed can finish his meal. Surfing always makes everyone so hungry. Look, I've just boiled the kettle – I'll make us a coffee and we can drink it on the balcony upstairs. There's something I want to talk to you about.'

Cornered, Louis nodded agreement.

'Hello, Cip,' said Isla, 'you look a bit grim. Are you OK?'

'Fine, thank you, Isla,' said Louis. 'Ed, I need to get to Truro, so eat up as quick as you can.'

‘There’s ice cream in the freezer, Isla,’ Merrin called as she headed up the stairs, Louis following reluctantly in her wake.

The view from Merrin’s balcony was particularly spectacular. The tide was in, the boats in the harbour riding at anchor. The sea swirling round the harbour walls was a gorgeous combination of azure blue and green, reminding Merrin of Pippa’s sea glass.

The atmosphere was tense and it appeared that Louis wasn’t going to say anything, so Merrin ploughed in. ‘I don’t know what’s gone wrong between us, Louis, but it’s making me very unhappy. Your friendship means a great deal to me. We’ve been through so much together and I think you owe me an explanation as to why you’re being so . . . well, so peculiar.’

‘There’s nothing to tell,’ said Louis, concentrating hard on his coffee.

‘Louis, that’s simply not true,’ said Merrin, exasperated.

There was silence. Then Louis looked up from his coffee and met her eye. ‘You’re right, of course, it’s not true and I owe you an explanation for being so, what you call, peculiar.’ For the first time he smiled.

‘So, are you going to tell me what’s up?’ Merrin asked, gently.

‘It’s too long a story to start now,’ he said.

‘You’re dropping Ed over tomorrow afternoon. If the young are out surfing, we can talk here, or if not, we can go for a walk. How does that sound?’

‘It sounds good,’ said Louis, ‘thank you.’

Merrin searched his face. ‘You look slightly less gruesome already,’ she said, smiling.

'Gruesome and peculiar – I don't know why you bother with me.'

'Good point,' said Merrin, cheerfully.

CHAPTER FIFTEEN

Merrin didn't sleep well. By five o'clock in the morning, she gave up trying, got dressed and took a very pleased William out for his morning walk before even the sun was up. Watching the sunrise from the top of the Island made Merrin wonder why she didn't do this every morning. It was stunning, the dawn of a new day, but what would it bring? she wondered. In her heart she knew that her sleeplessness was due to Louis and trying to anticipate what he might be going to say.

The previous evening, Merrin and Isla had taken Daisy out for supper to a new pizza restaurant. They'd all had a good time. Isla was right – Daisy was charming, excellent company, funny and surprisingly confident for her age. She was also sports-mad, hockey being her true love, and she was hoping to qualify for the junior county team. Merrin loved her enthusiasm and could quite see why Isla enjoyed her company, despite the age gap. The Peppiatts seemed to be a lovely family, despite the marriage break-up. All

Merrin could hope was that, whatever Louis had to say, it would not ruin the growing friendship between their two families.

After a hasty breakfast, Merrin had spent a busy morning potting in her studio. She left for home just before midday with a view to having a shower and a change of clothes before Louis turned up. She had just stepped out of the shower when the doorbell rang. Still in her towel, Merrin rushed downstairs to find Clara in the kitchen, having let herself in.

Clara looked her up and down. 'Really, Pearl, have you only just got out of bed? I know you're sort of retired, but this is the height of laziness!'

'I got up before dawn, walked William and have just completed over four hours of potting – not exactly lazy, I think you would agree.'

'So why the shower?' said Clara with a wicked grin.

'Because I was covered in the combination of sand from my walk and clay from my potting. What is this inquisition in aid of, may I ask?' said Merrin, clearly exasperated.

'Don't get huffy, darling Pearl. It's just that Jack tells me your lovely policeman is in town today, so I thought you might be making yourself fragrant for him.'

'I'm not going to dignify that remark with an answer. I just wish you'd all leave the subject of Louis and me alone. Make yourself useful and brew some coffee while I get dressed, and then you can tell me about the real reason for you invading my space.'

'Which is?' said Clara, raising an eyebrow.

'The latest gossip on Roxy and Max, of course,' said Merrin, running up the stairs.

Coffee made, the two women sat down at the kitchen table. Clara wasted no time. 'Roxy has really got her claws into Max, hasn't she?'

'I'm rather afraid she has,' Merrin agreed, 'and I'm so sad for Poppy. I just wish she'd go home – Roxy I mean, not dear Poppy, of course.'

'Poppy is bound to find out,' said Clara, 'ours is such a small town, if you ignore the visitors. I saw them going into Max's office last night, but they didn't even attempt to turn on the lights, they just went straight upstairs to his flat. Then they were seen kissing up the top end of Porthminster Beach. To be honest, I expect Poppy knows already. Let's face it, Roxy is not exactly the most discreet person.'

'We just need Tony to come back and whisk her away – fast,' said Merrin.

'That's the other thing I need to talk to you about,' said Clara. 'Darling Roxy is lying through her teeth about what happened the night they were intending to leave St Ives.'

'What do you mean?'

'That night the restaurant was a bit stuffy. It was a warm day but we couldn't open the doors because of the wind. So, Tristan kindly offered to finish clearing up at the end of the evening, so I could get some fresh air.'

'He's a good man,' said Merrin.

'He is,' Clara agreed. 'Anyway, I walked along the Wharf and saw *Llamedos* chugging out of the harbour, but the yacht was towing its tender, quite definitely.'

'It would seem I'm being very stupid here,' said Merrin. 'I don't get the significance.'

'Oh, come, darling Pearl, keep up. Max told me that

Tony and Roxy had supper together on board but had a flaming row as to where they should be sailing next. Roxy got in such a rage, she left the boat and rowed the tender back to the shore. Max says it was on her way to find a hotel that she remembered all her stuff was still on board. She dashed back to the Wharf in time to see the yacht leave the harbour. If that's what really happened, *Llamedos* should not have been towing the tender. Got it?'

'Got it,' said Merrin. 'What time did you see the yacht leave, Clara?'

'It must have been after midnight. I know we'd thrown everyone out by then.'

'That's about the time Roxy says she ran back to the Wharf and saw for herself that the yacht was leaving the harbour. Maybe, while she was looking for a hotel, Tony collected the tender from where Roxy had left it.'

'How?' asked Clara. 'He'd have had to swim for it.'

'That's not impossible,' said Merrin.

'It is impossible, because I've checked and Roxy's bloody tender is neatly tied up close to the slipway. It's definitely the right one, it has *Llamedos* painted on it. Also, when I saw the yacht leave the harbour, there was no one else on the Wharf. The town was deserted.'

'Your eyes could have been deceiving you about the tender being towed away,' suggested Merrin.

'Not a chance,' said Clara. 'Truly, Pearl, I'm absolutely certain about what I saw.'

'Have you told Max any of this?' Merrin asked.

'Of course not. For a start, he wouldn't believe me – he's well and truly besotted, in my view. Also, I'm not sure of the implications. Why did Roxy lie and what does it mean?'

'It means that Roxy must have been on the yacht as well as Tony when *Llamedos* sailed out of St Ives.' Merrin stood up abruptly and began pacing up and down her kitchen. Then she turned and faced Clara. 'And the problem with that scenario is that it's impossible, because the wretched woman is here in town – and so is the tender.'

Luckily, having shared her thoughts on Max and Roxy, Clara was due back at the restaurant for the lunchtime shift. This meant Merrin didn't have to explain that, indeed, she was expecting a visit from Louis, and therefore suffer yet more innuendos about their relationship. She dressed and tidied the cottage, and was just settling down with another coffee to check her emails when her phone pinged an incoming text message. She saw it was from Louis and her heart immediately sank, so sure was she that he was going to cancel.

Instead, he had been super-efficient. He had arranged with Isla that the children would have pasties on the beach for lunch. He had given Edward the lunch money and having dropped him off at Porthmeor, he'd made sure Edward found Isla and Daisy, before leaving him. Louis expected to be at the cottage in about ten minutes.

True to his word, Louis arrived at Merrin's front door bang on time.

'I've an idea,' he said, looking and sounding flustered. 'The children may well come back here around lunchtime to change, and the town is absolutely heaving with people. I've got the car down on the Wharf – why don't we drive out to Trencrom and climb the Hill, where we'll definitely have some peace.'

'That's a lovely idea,' said Merrin. 'Is William allowed to come?'

'Most definitely,' said Louis, 'he can pretend to chase rabbits while we talk.'

The brief journey to Trencrom was not nearly as awkward as they had both feared.

'Daisy is amazing,' said Merrin, as they drove out of town. 'Quite extraordinary for fifteen – good company and so confident. Smart too, I bet, and so driven when it comes to sport.'

'Yes, you're right, we've never had to chase her to do her homework, or anything else, really. She's very self-motivated – in fact, no one is harder on Daisy than Daisy herself. She's very strong-willed, mind you, but I suppose that goes with the territory. It's lovely to see such passion and commitment. I have to admit to being very proud of her.'

'I'm not surprised,' said Merrin. 'Did your divorce affect her? She seems so together.'

'Up to a point – she was eight and old enough to understand what was going on. She minded me moving out, but Steph and I made sure we never argued in front of the children, so I don't think Daisy blamed either of us, but she was very sad. Ed, of course, was young enough to apparently take it all in his stride – he just went with the flow. Sometimes though, I do wonder if it has affected him more than we realise.'

'In what way?' Merrin asked.

'He's very chaotic and can't organise himself. I suppose I sometimes wonder whether that easy-going little boy worked out that the best thing to do during the break-up period was to let everyone else decide what was happening, and just tag along. Maybe, as a result, he learnt very few organisational skills. Who knows? Now, enough about my children – it's very kind of Isla to get Daisy into bodyboarding. Daisy thinks your daughter is marvellous, which, of course, she is.'

'Even when she calls you Cip?'

'I don't mind. As you can imagine, over the years, I've been called a great deal worse!' said Louis, smiling.

Talk of children and families kept them busy until they were climbing up Trencrom Hill, when exclaiming over the view took over. From the very top, the sight of both coasts was stunning; to the north, they could see as far as Padstow, and to the south to Mousehole. The whole of Mounts Bay was laid out before them, St Michael's Mount, of course, being the jewel in the crown.

'You can quite see why this made an ideal Iron Age fort,' said Merrin. 'They had a three-sixty-degree lookout for oncoming enemies, who would be very out of puff by the time they climbed up the Hill and negotiated the battlements.'

'Come on,' said Louis, 'let's go and sit over on the rocks in the sun, the view will still be splendid there.'

'Do you know the story of the Trencrom giant called Trecobben?' Merrin began as they settled down on the rocks.

'We're not here to talk about giants,' said Louis, smiling slightly but looking as nervous as Merrin felt.

'No,' she agreed.

Louis took a deep breath. 'I'll start with the easy bit. This is very presumptuous of me, but are you being hassled by friends and family who think we should be, well . . .' He hesitated.

'A couple, an item, whatever you want to call it – partners, maybe,' suggested Merrin. 'The answer is *all the time* – Clara, Tristan and Max, of course, long-distance enquiries from Jago, and even the odd double entendre from Peter Carew.'

'Stephanie, various colleagues, including hints from my boss, the chief super, would you believe? Then there's dear Sally, who you met the other evening, who never gives it a rest – she thinks you're marvellous – and, yes, I've picked up Peter's odd remarks, too.'

'So, that was the easy bit, which I think we both find annoying and intrusive,' said Merrin, gently. 'Now tell me the difficult bit.'

'The kiss in the studio, of course. You were sitting there, stroking the dog, looking lovely, and then you said something along the lines that you found pleasure in my pleasure at being in that marvellous studio. So, in that moment, it seemed like we were one person and I just couldn't help myself. But, of course, it was wrong and I'm deeply sorry and very embarrassed.'

'You have no need to feel either sorry or embarrassed. I completely understand how it happened.' Merrin hesitated. 'In my view, there is only one person who has voiced an opinion about you and me which makes any sense,' she added.

'Really, who's that?'

'Isla. She said that she thought it very important for us to be friends, that we have a lot in common – my understanding of your job because of Adam, and both of us believing in the importance of upholding the law. She said we had both suffered personal loss, and were probably lonely at times. She also said we have the same sense of humour and should be having lots of fun together, but she stressed she wasn't suggesting that we had to be a couple to achieve all that.'

'She's a marvel, your daughter,' said Louis. 'You see – oh, how do I explain?' He was silent, clearly struggling for words.

'Go on, please, Louis.'

'I know you're still grieving for Adam. You know he was my hero. The idea of me making advances to his widow feels terribly wrong – not when I kissed you, I'll admit, I was caught up in the moment – but afterwards, I just felt I was letting both of you down. Also, you really don't need another policeman in your life. I appreciate West Cornwall is nothing like Bristol so far as crime is concerned, but look at what we've had to cope with in the last few years. We've had more than our fair share of violence and danger, haven't we?'

'It was you who got stabbed,' said Merrin.

'It was you who stood in front of a loaded gun,' said Louis.

They looked at one another and began to laugh. They were back.

At that moment, William dashed past them barking madly. Ahead of him was a rabbit who was easily outrunning him and then sensibly darted down a hole. William immediately turned round and trotted back towards them.

'He doesn't look too sad,' said Louis, 'more relieved at not catching the rabbit, I think.'

'That's because he has such a sweet soul,' said Merrin, firmly.

'Come on, up you get,' said Louis, holding out his hand. 'The kids will be out of the water by now, I should think.'

They were starting off down the Hill when Merrin suddenly stopped.

'Look,' she said. 'I'm not very experienced in such matters, having lived a rather sheltered life, but I thought it was a pretty decent kiss, Chief Inspector. It's also another reason for not needing to apologise. Just saying.'

Louis turned and grinned at her. 'That's most gracious of you, Mrs McKenzie. You've made my old heart glad.'

They climbed into the car.

'There's just one thing, Louis. I have a bit of a mystery going on which I think I'm going to need your help to unravel.'

'No, no, please no,' said Louis in mock horror, dropping his head onto the steering wheel.

Ignoring him, Merrin began. 'You remember that woman called Roxy, who spent a great deal of money in our shop? Well . . .'

CHAPTER SIXTEEN

Chelsea, London

Jeremy Eustace had last seen his father only two weeks previously but the change in him was truly shocking. Hubert was sitting in his usual chair, facing the magnificent view of the River Thames through a large picture window. Otherwise, everything was different. His face was gaunt, his complexion grey, and in the short space of time since they'd last met, he had lost a huge amount of weight. He was on a drip and a young nurse was in attendance.

'Hello, Father, how are you doing?' Jeremy asked.

'This is my son, Jeremy,' Hubert said to the nurse. 'Could you leave us alone for a few minutes, please.'

The nurse withdrew with a kindly smile in Jeremy's direction.

'Come and sit down, my boy,' said Hubert, patting the arm of the chair placed beside him. 'In answer to your question, no, I'm not alright. I'm afraid I have to tell you that I'm dying.'

'What!' said Jeremy. 'You can't be, you're only sixty-two.

Surely the doctors can't have got it right. What's wrong with you?'

'My old friend cancer, of course. As you know, I've had it for several years but now it's suddenly bolted. It's spread just about everywhere and it's no fun, I can tell you. It's not the reason I asked you to come and see me.'

'It's certainly reason enough,' Jeremy replied. 'I'm so, so sorry, Father.'

'Apparently, I only have about five weeks to live, and I need Annie back here, but she seems to have disappeared. That's why I need your help.'

Jeremy was fond of his stepmother and seeing the vulnerable state of his father made him anxious to help.

'How long has she been away this time?' he asked. 'And does she know how ill you are?'

'She knows I have cancer, but I told her I was in remission, which was apparently true at the time. I only found out about my death sentence after she'd left,' said Hubert. 'She went down to Newton Abbot to stay for a few days to see some local friends, but she only stayed one night and that was two weeks ago. She's not answering her phone, either. I want to see her again before I die, Jeremy, and I know she would want to be here if she knew how ill I was.'

'Have you contacted the police?' Jeremy asked.

'I tried to get Louis Peppiatt involved. I don't know if you remember him.'

'Of course I do, Father,' said Jeremy. 'He was very kind to me, and it was him who finally tracked down the man who killed Mother – that's right, isn't it?'

'Yes, but since then he's been made up to chief inspector

and is far too busy and important to help us, the sod. He gave me the name of an inspector in Newton Abbot but he's really not interested. Annie's been listed as a missing person, but I suspect that's all they've done. A beautiful young wife leaving a sick old husband – it's not much of a mystery, is it? It must happen all the time.'

'I do find Annie's jaunts rather odd, as you know,' said Jeremy, 'but you're right, she'd certainly never leave you if she knew you were seriously ill, let alone dying. What about contacting the Met?'

'Peppiatt suggested that, but I want to keep the whole matter very low-key. I'm very anxious that the share price shouldn't be affected.'

'Bugger the share price, Father. This is your life we're talking about,' said Jeremy.

'Don't you dare talk like that, Jeremy!' said Hubert. 'I've spent my entire working life building my company. I don't want to leave this earth with all I've worked for crumbling to dust. You know how volatile the stock market can be, and should Annie be involved in any kind of scandal, it could be disastrous for the company.'

'It's a great company, Father, and I'm sure it would take more than a misbehaving wife to damage it.'

'Well, I'm not prepared to take the risk, so I want you to find me a private detective who is prepared to act very privately indeed. Will you fix that for me, my boy?'

'Yes, of course, Father, I'll get on it straight away. One thing that's making me sad is that if the doctors are right, you're not going to see your grandchild. Sophie isn't due for another four months, but we now know it's a boy, so we can call him Hubert.'

'Don't call him that, it's a godawful name.' Hubert's voice sounded strained; he was obviously becoming very tired. Jeremy realised he'd have to ask quickly the question foremost in his mind.

He hesitated, feeling awkward, but he'd promised his wife he would raise the matter. 'Father, I do realise this is an awful and tactless moment to raise the matter of your will. I believe I will inherit your shareholding in the business. Annie is inheriting both houses and any money floating about in banks and stocks and shares is going to be divided equally between Annie and me. Is that right?'

'You know it is,' said Hubert. 'We've discussed it often enough.'

'The thing is, Father, bearing in mind that we have a child on the way, Sophie and I were wondering if you would consider giving us this house, which as I know from personal experience is a great place to bring up a child. Our flat has no garden and only two small bedrooms. I'm sure Annie doesn't want or need two houses.'

'Out of the question,' said Hubert, breathing heavily. 'I started with nothing, nothing at all. As well as receiving a huge shareholding, you draw a significant salary. So get a mortgage and buy your wife and son a decent house instead of whinging at me on my deathbed. You're well provided for, and Annie has been a good wife – she deserves the houses. Now get out of my sight and set up that private detective today. I'd like to brief someone tomorrow at the latest. Call the nurse as you leave.'

Jeremy walked up to the King's Road and hailed a cab to take him to the company's London headquarters. He'd get his PA working on finding a private detective as soon as he reached his office. Finding Annie was important for his father, but it also occurred to Jeremy that she might be persuaded to ask Hubert to change his will in favour of giving him the London house. He could perhaps offer her more than her half-share of the liquid assets, which would probably appeal to her. Annie had the old man wrapped round her little finger. He'd always given her everything she wanted. It wasn't greed that had made him ask for the Chelsea house; it was because the house was the most memorable link to his mother. Jeremy had been born in London and he and his mother had spent most of their time there until he started school. Even then, although they spent the term time in Newton Abbot, the holidays largely took place in London. Hubert's business was based in Newton Abbot, so mother and son had often been alone when in London, which Jeremy had loved. In truth, he had always been afraid of his father. The house in Chelsea held all the most precious memories of his lost mother, but Jeremy knew his father would only see this as pathetic sentimentality.

CHAPTER SEVENTEEN

Merrin had overslept because she'd just had her first decent night's sleep in some days. She attempted to pretend to herself that her lack of sleep was unconnected to Chief Inspector Louis Peppiatt. However, as she and William walked across Porthgwidden Beach, she had to admit that her friendship with Louis, now fully restored, made all the difference to her sense of well-being. She even realised she was smiling to herself, which was somewhat embarrassing.

She'd just finished breakfast when there was a knock on the door. It was Roxy. Seeing the remains of Merrin's breakfast on the kitchen table, she was full of apologies.

'I'm so sorry to disturb you. I should have sent you a message rather than barging in like this,' she said.

'It's no problem,' said Merrin, starting to clear the table. 'Would you like a coffee?'

'No thanks,' said Roxy, 'I don't want to take up any more of your time than necessary. I just wondered if I could have the balance of the loan you promised, the two hundred pounds.'

Merrin stopped her clearing. 'Roxy, I just don't understand what's going on. I know Max has already lent you a thousand pounds, and I've lent you three hundred. Why on earth do you want or need any more?'

Roxy sat down heavily on a kitchen chair. Merrin studied her in silence for a moment. She was back to her former well-groomed self but there was still a great deal of tension about her, an unease, and she looked exhausted.

'Merrin, you know why I need the money,' Roxy began. 'Tony has my entire world on the yacht – bank cards, laptop, phone – and he doesn't even know it, in all probability. I need the money to stay here for a few days and then, if necessary, have enough money for the return fare to London.'

'I still don't understand. All you have to do is call your bank and credit card companies and stop all payments. You can borrow my phone if you want. Then you can jump on a train home. Why are you hanging about in St Ives? Is it because of Max?'

Roxy had the grace to look somewhat embarrassed. 'Why would I be staying in St Ives because of Max?' she asked.

Merrin was becoming increasingly irritated. 'Oh, for heaven's sake, Roxy, the whole town knows about you and Max. You've hardly been discreet, either of you. It's absolutely none of my business what you get up to, but it seems a bit hard on your husband and it's certainly hard on Max's girlfriend Poppy, who is the best thing to have happened to Max in a long time.'

Roxy looked genuinely shocked. 'The whole town knows about me and Max? Are you sure?'

'Certain,' said Merrin, grimly.

'Then that explains why Poppy hasn't been answering Max's calls.'

'You amaze me. How on earth did you work out that one?' said Merrin, sarcastically.

'I'm sorry about Poppy, of course, but I've fallen in love with Max, and he with me. I can't just walk out of his life, not yet anyway.'

'Two thoughts,' said Merrin. 'Firstly, I've known Max all my life. On average, he falls in love about once a month. His feelings for you won't last and that's no reflection on you and your charms, it's just how Max is. Secondly, what about your husband – are you really going to abandon him for Max?'

'Tony's not my husband. I'm not married,' Roxy murmured.

There was a long pause while neither of them spoke. Horatio, however, shouted, 'Nuts!', which seemed rather appropriate. Neither of the women took the slightest notice of him so he turned his back on them, fluffed up his feathers and sulked. At last, into the silence, Roxy spoke.

'I don't love Tony. He's a bit of an oaf, isn't he? But he's a very attractive man, when sober, so we had a fling. His other attraction is his beautiful yacht and I love sailing. When he offered me the chance to sail down to Cornwall with him, I just couldn't resist. We fell out because I'd frankly had enough of him and wanted to go home. He wanted us to go to the Scillies to join up with some of his friends, who are probably ghastly. You have to be very,

very fond of someone to spend any length of time with them in the confines of a smallish boat. I just couldn't face it. There was no love lost, it was just a passing fancy. I want to stay in St Ives a little longer – primarily, I'll admit, because of Max, but also I think Tony will be back here in a day or two.'

'Why would he do that?' Merrin asked.

'Because he'll have run out of money and he'll be hoping we can make it up and that I will fund the rest of his trip. He's wrong on both counts, of course.'

'I'd imagined your concern was the possibility that he might use your credit cards,' said Merrin. 'It's been obvious, while you've been in town, that you were holding the purse strings.'

'Tony isn't very bright, as you've probably noticed, and when I left the yacht in such a hurry, he was also very drunk. He will have assumed I had all I needed with me – I'm normally very efficient, and I'm pretty confident that he will never think to look in the kitchen cupboard where I'd stored my rucksack. I might as well be honest with you, Merrin, having got this far.' Roxy stared down at the table. 'Before going aboard *Llamedos* that night, I'd, well, I'd joined Max in his bed, so I was a bit all over the place, which explains why I forgot my rucksack.'

'I know,' said Merrin.

'How do you know?' said Roxy, suddenly aggressive.

'Max told me,' said Merrin.

'Max seems to tell you an awful lot about his private life.'

'We're old friends. I have to admit that I was trying to talk him out of having a relationship with you. I can't apologise for that. He's been so much happier and more relaxed since he's been with Poppy. Also, of course, at the time I thought you were married. I assume Max now knows you're not?'

Roxy nodded.

'Well, you've been frank with me, so I will be the same with you,' said Merrin. 'I'm not going to give you any more money because I still don't understand why you can't sort out the situation with your bank. It all seems very odd to me. However, if you change your mind, and decide to return to London, I will pay for your train fare – if, that is, you've exhausted all Max's money.'

'I know you don't think much of me, but there is an alternative,' said Roxy.

'I can assure you there isn't,' said Merrin.

'Just hear me out, Merrin. I popped into your shop this morning looking for you and ended up talking to Joey and Pippa. They're very anxious to set up a website for your crafts, but what with manning the shop and keeping it stocked with their creations, they don't have the time. I know they're going to suggest to you that just for the season, you should employ someone to run the shop two days a week. I could be that person and that would give me a little income, which would mean I wouldn't need to borrow any more money. I'm really good at selling.'

'I'm afraid that's out of the question,' said Merrin.

'Why, don't you trust me?'

'I've made myself quite clear, Roxy. Even though I now know you're not married, I'm still very unhappy about you coming between Max and Poppy. I'm sorry, but I just want you to leave St Ives. If you go back to London and

Tony does come back here, we'll tell you right away and Max and I will try and retrieve your rucksack. Please, just go home.'

'It may have escaped your notice, Merrin, but Max is no longer a schoolboy. You have absolutely no right to interfere with his personal life. It's outrageous. You just don't trust me, do you?'

'No,' Merrin admitted.

CHAPTER EIGHTEEN

On Friday morning, the entire West Cornwall Crafts team met at nine o'clock, an hour before the shop opened, to discuss the pros and cons of a website. The three youngest members were wildly enthusiastic, as secretly was Merrin, but she wanted to see the thought process behind all their excitement.

'Sell it to me,' she said, smiling at them.

Joey was their spokesman. 'An enormous number of people come to Cornwall in the next ten weeks, and a very high percentage of them visit St Ives, as we know. Sales for the rest of the year will be tricky, but much less so if people can buy from our website. Supposing someone buys Lizzie's candles this summer and takes away a postcard with a photograph of our shop and a code offering a small discount on all purchases made before Christmas. Christmas is coming round, the punter remembers our dear little craft shop and Lizzie's splendid candles. The punter digs out the postcard, and hey presto, we have an order!'

'And where do we wrap the goods and despatch?' said Merrin, already knowing the answer.

'We thought you could spare a little bit of space in your studio upstairs, just for a table and a few boxes,' said Joey.

'Who's going to set up the website?' said Merrin.

'Me,' said Pippa. 'I read computer science at uni, and Joey can take the photographs. We just have to decide which items we want to put on the site. Obviously not everything we sell in the shop, at least not to start with. We were wondering whether you could work out all the costings for despatch, and Lizzie says she will do the actual post and packing, with help from the rest of us if we get busy.'

'A very well-thought-out plan,' said Merrin. 'Let's do it. It's not going to cost a lot to set up as we're doing most of the work ourselves, and the benefits could be significant. Exciting, well done, you lot!'

There were whoops of joy all round.

'Did Roxy find you this morning?' Joey asked.

'Yes,' said Merrin. 'I gather you think we'll need extra help in the shop, if we go ahead with the website, so she was touting for the job.'

'You didn't give it to her, did you?' said Pippa, looking horrified.

'No, I didn't. I have my reasons for not wanting her here. What are yours?' Merrin asked.

'We don't trust her,' said Joey.

'That's very reassuring, because neither do I,' said Merrin.

* * *

On Saturday morning, Louis had just brewed himself a pot of coffee when his mobile rang. He didn't recognise the number.

'Louis Peppiatt,' he said a little tersely, assuming it was someone trying to sell him something.

'Chief Inspector, my name's Jeremy Eustace – I don't know if you remember me?'

For a moment the dreadful scene flashed into Louis's mind. The mother terribly injured, blood everywhere and so obviously dead. The terrified little boy crying and trembling in his arms.

'Oh, yes, Jeremy,' he said gently. 'I'll never forget you. How are you?'

'I'm good, thank you. I'm married to Sophie, who's a truly lovely person. What she sees in me I can't imagine, but we're very happy, and we have a baby on the way, a little boy.'

'Congratulations, I'm so pleased for you,' said Louis. 'I've often thought about you over the years and wondered how you were getting on.'

'I'll never forget you either,' said Jeremy. 'You were great, obviously. On that awful day, your kindness was a real comfort. Also afterwards, the way you came round to the house so often and we messed about. Do you remember us playing football?'

'I do,' said Louis. 'I'd recently had a knee operation after some thug had given me a kicking, but I didn't tell you.'

'So, the reason I scored all the goals wasn't because you were being kind – you genuinely were rubbish.'

Both men laughed. 'That's about right,' Louis admitted.

'Louis – can I call you Louis?' Jeremy asked.

'Of course.'

'Louis, I'm calling about Father and my missing stepmother.'

'I rather assumed you were. I'm so sorry I can't help,' said Louis.

'There's been a development,' said Jeremy. 'We've employed a private investigator to try and find her. The police in Newton Abbot weren't much help, and Father is reluctant to go to the Met in case the press get hold of the story. We've recently floated his company on the stock market, and he doesn't want to risk the share price being affected.'

Privately, Louis thought that Hubert Eustace's priorities were somewhat skewed, but then he really wasn't a particularly nice man. To Jeremy he said, 'So, this private investigator is aware of the need for discretion, is he? They're not all as *private* as one would like.'

'Yes, he's been fully briefed by my father, who you may remember is a pretty forceful character. He seems to have made good progress in a very short space of time. We're getting a full report on Monday, but he has already indicated that he believes Annie, my stepmother, may have gone away on holiday to the West Country.' Jeremy paused for a moment. 'Louis, this is slightly awkward. Father asked me to call you because he is aware that he was rather rude to you when you explained you couldn't help us.'

Louis laughed. 'You don't have to worry about that. After all these years in the police force, I have the skin of a rhinoceros. Also – how do I put it – I do remember your dad was never reluctant to share his views.'

'Actually, he has mellowed a little recently,' said Jeremy. 'He has cancer, and has just been told that he only has a few weeks to live. That's why he's so anxious to find his wife.'

'I'm so sorry,' said Louis, 'I didn't mean to be flippant. Actually, although he issued me with a severe reprimand, I did think he sounded very frail. I'm surprised his wife isn't with him – are they separated?'

'No,' said Jeremy. 'She knows he has cancer but not that he's dying. Annie's a lot younger than Father and he's happy for her to go off on jollies, from time to time, but she's never normally away this long. It's bad enough for him being terminally ill, without worrying about the whereabouts of his wife. He's very fond of her and has known her all her life.'

'So, as I understand it, what you're asking me, Jeremy, is this. Since a lot of people who go on holiday to the West Country end up in Cornwall, should you suspect that Annie is on my patch, would I take on the case to help find her?'

'That's about it,' said Jeremy. 'We'd like to be able to tell the private investigator on Monday that you will be involved, if it proves to be necessary. Father feels it would keep him on his toes.'

'It's more likely to irritate the hell out of him, I shouldn't wonder – but yes, of course, I'll help if your stepmother ends up in West Cornwall. However, do bear in mind that even if she does turn up here, it's unlikely to be a police matter.'

'I realise that, if Annie's run away of her own accord,

though I rather doubt she has. Anyway, thanks, Louis – I really appreciate it, and so will Father, although that may not be particularly obvious! The chap we've hired is an ex-copper, so maybe he would like working with you if the need arose.'

'Really,' said Louis, 'what's his name?'

'Len Carter,' said Jeremy. 'Do you know him by any chance?' There was a long silence. 'Louis, are you still there?'

'Yes, I'm here. I've never met Len Carter, but most officers in the police force know of him. You need to watch yourself, Jeremy. He's a very nasty piece of work. He's prone to violence and has a very vicious temper, by all accounts.'

'Are you sure?' said Jeremy. 'Father and I were rather impressed by him. He seemed very professional and polite. He was smartly dressed and turned up on time, asked intelligent questions, and is going to have a report for us within four days of taking on the job.'

'Early on in his career, Len Carter gained a reputation for the use of unnecessary violence,' said Louis. 'Then one night, when he was on duty, a prisoner under his care annoyed him. Len beat him up so badly that the poor sod will spend the rest of his life in a wheelchair. Ironically, he was only in the cells overnight for his own protection. Len received a prison sentence – though, from what you say, he's obviously out now.'

'He certainly didn't mention being in prison, but maybe it taught Len the error of his ways,' suggested Jeremy.

'Most men of Len's type come out of prison tougher and more violent than they went in. Still, it's your call, Jeremy. Make sure the fees are agreed, and then pay them on time or he'll beat the living daylights out of you to get them. I suppose if he's on your side, it'll be alright, but heaven help anyone who crosses him. Please take care.'

'I will, Louis,' said Jeremy, 'and, if I may, I'll send you a copy of his report.'

When the call had ended, Louis poured himself a cup of lukewarm coffee and thought about Jeremy Eustace. Having lost his own mother at a tender age, Louis knew only too well what it felt like, how the pain never completely went away. However, the circumstances in Jeremy's case were particularly dreadful – a mother lying dead in the road was a sight no six-year-old should ever see. Louis's own father had been distant and oddly unemotional, but deep down, Louis felt sure his father cared about him. Hubert Eustace, by contrast, was a bully, used to getting his own way, not an easy man to be a son to, Louis imagined. What about the stepmother, was she kind to Jeremy? Louis wondered. Now, to cap it all, Jeremy had signed up Len Carter to try and find her. That worried Louis a great deal; it was generally believed that Len Carter was barking mad.

Despite his genuine concern for Jeremy, Louis hoped very much that this was not a case in which he needed to become involved.

CHAPTER NINETEEN

Merrin had intended to spend Saturday potting, as her stocks were getting low again, but it was not to be. When taking William for his morning walk, on impulse she knocked on the door of Tristan's Fish Plaice and was greeted by Clara.

'Oh, brilliant – darling Pearl, you're just in time to come and peel potatoes, though I should remind you that dogs are not allowed.'

'We've discussed this many times before – William is not just any old dog, he's William, formerly your aunt's dog – he's family. I'll only help you with the potatoes on condition that William can go and ask Tristan for a sausage, which, as you well know, Tristan keeps especially for him. Agreed?'

'Oh belt up, Pearl, you sound like a lawyer,' said Clara.

'I am a lawyer,' Merrin pointed out, not unreasonably.

The two women settled down with potato peelers, while predictably, William trotted off to the kitchen.

'So, you're here to talk about Max and bloody Roxy again, I assume?' said Clara.

'I am,' Merrin agreed, and then proceeded to bring Clara up to date on her various conversations with Roxy.

'The fact that she's not married is going to make Max even keener, I imagine,' said Clara, gloomily. 'I'm very glad you're not giving her a job. Quite apart from the fact that it would encourage her to stay in St Ives longer, I just don't trust her an inch. Remember she's a liar. We know that.'

'You mean about the tender?' said Merrin.

'Yes, of course, about the tender and the fact that she wasn't on the Wharf when *Llamedos* left the harbour. I'm absolutely sure of that. And now we learn she's been lying about being married.'

'I told Louis about the tender,' said Merrin, 'and he suggested that maybe Roxy took off in the tender just outside the harbour, because the argument had developed as they were leaving.'

'Oh come off it, you're a fisherman's daughter, Pearl. You know perfectly well that as soon as they left the shelter of the harbour, with the boat moving, it would have been very difficult for Roxy to climb out of the yacht and into the tender, and Tony was apparently very drunk so would have been no help at all. Pity she didn't try it though. She might easily have drowned.'

'That's a bit harsh, Clara.'

'Not really, not when you consider what she's doing to Max and poor darling Poppy. Anyway,' Clara looked up from the potatoes and smiled wickedly at Merrin, 'it's very good to hear you quoting our dear chief inspector again. I know you two had a tiff, I could tell, so give me all the details. Have you made up?'

'We have made up,' said Merrin, smiling, 'but I have absolutely no intention of telling you the details.'

'Ooh, that sounds very promising, darling Pearl. Steamy details, not suitable for disclosure. Can I be your bridesmaid?'

Merrin laughed. 'You are incorrigible. The details are not steamy, just private, and I'm afraid you're never going to be a bridesmaid of mine again. What Louis and I want more than anything is to end this speculation about our relationship. We are friends, I hope we will always be friends, but it ends there. So please, Clara, can we stop all this chatter about us being a couple?'

'But Pearl, it's such a waste. He's gorgeous and so are you. you two would be wonderful together. I just don't understand you . . . or him.'

'Clara, you were my bridesmaid when I married Adam, and you know how much I loved him on that day, and how much I loved him until the day he died.' Her voice faltered slightly. 'He's only been dead for just over four years – I'm nowhere near ready for a new relationship, and to be honest, I don't think I ever will be. But that doesn't matter. It doesn't make me sad, because Adam was the love of my life and I was so lucky to be married to such a marvellous chap.'

'I'm sorry,' said Clara, for once actually looking contrite, 'but you're just too young to commit to being alone for the rest of your life.'

'Clara, you are my best friend. I love you to bits, and the fact you care about me so much is marvellous. But while you don't understand how I feel, the important thing is Louis does.'

'I feel a bit teary now,' said Clara.

'Me too,' Merrin admitted.

'I tell you what,' said Clara. 'Let's cheer ourselves up by thinking of all the different ways there are for getting rid of ghastly Roxy!'

By the time Merrin arrived home, Isla was making herself brunch, after a late night out in town.

'Do you want some, Mum?' she asked.

Merrin shook her head. 'No, I'm fine thanks, darling. I was just thinking about tomorrow and lunch with Stephanie. Louis offered to drive over and collect us, but it's ridiculously out of his way so I said we would go under our own steam. You have the directions – how long will it take?'

'About fifty minutes, Stephanie reckons. I'm so glad Cip's coming, and even more glad that you two have obviously made up,' said Isla.

'I do not understand how everyone seems to know that we had a very slight falling out,' said Merrin, exasperated.

'Easy, because you were both miserable and grumpy – absolute pains, the pair of you, to be honest,' said Isla, grinning.

'You should learn to be discreet, like your mother. You will notice that although I am aware you were out very late last night, I have not been so impertinent as to ask how you got on with Joey.'

'How did you know I was with Joey?' Isla asked, aghast.

'See,' said Merrin triumphantly. 'That's what it feels like when the tables are turned, darling girl!'

* * *

With half the day gone, Merrin decided it was not worth starting on her pottery. Instead, she sat down at the kitchen table and began working on the costings for their online business. Isla joined her at the other side of the table with some hefty law books and the two sat in companionable silence, working away. That is, until Merrin's mobile rang. It was Pippa.

'Merrin, I'm so sorry to disturb you, but you know that lovely sea-glass bracelet I brought in yesterday? Well it's gone, stolen. I'm absolutely gutted. It took me hours and hours of work. I can't bear it.' She was obviously crying.

'I'll be with you in five,' said Merrin. 'I'm so sorry, Pippa.' She quickly explained to Isla what had happened and dashed out of the door.

Pippa, normally a stalwart jolly person, was in bits.

'Have you the slightest idea who could have stolen it?' Merrin asked.

Pippa shook her head. 'The shop was very busy earlier and I nearly rang you for help, but it was just a glitch and it's been pretty quiet ever since. The trouble is that when you're stuck behind the till serving, it's impossible to see what's going on at the other end of the shop, from where it's so easy to slip out of the door. I was thinking today about whether there was any way we could move the till to the middle of the shop, but it just wouldn't work.'

'I'll give Jack Eddy a ring and ask him to pop into the shop tomorrow. I won't be here as I'm out to lunch, but do you have a photograph of the bracelet?'

'I do,' said Pippa, beginning to scroll through her phone. 'Shall I send it over to you?'

'Yes, please do, and I will make sure Jack gets it too.'

At that moment, there was a tentative tap on the open door of the shop. A small, slight, elderly woman stood smiling at them. She looked like someone from another age – her grey hair was drawn back into a neat bun, and she wore a pale blue twinset, a string of pearls, a plaid skirt, thick navy tights and sensible lace-up shoes. Miss Marple came to mind.

'Hello,' said Merrin. 'Can I help you?'

'Well, dear, I was rather hoping we could help you. We've just seen your advertisement in the window for shop staff two days a week. That would suit us very well.'

Her appearance was so out of keeping with St Ives that for a moment Merrin could think of nothing to say. Then she rallied. 'When you say *we* can help, what do you mean?'

'Just wait a moment, dear.' She stepped outside into Fore Street. 'Come on, Bea, there's a lady here for you to meet.'

Merrin and Pippa stood transfixed as a second figure stepped into the shop. They were clearly identical twins, but despite their age, they were also dressed identically, too. It would be quite impossible to tell them apart.

Merrin smiled. 'Am I seeing double?' she asked.

'No, dear,' said the first twin, obviously taking the question very seriously. 'I'm Constance Buchanan, known as Connie. This is my sister, Beatrice Buchanan, known as Bea.'

'We're seventy-one and in excellent health,' piped up Bea. 'This is the first time we've been in your shop but it looks lovely. We've just seen your advertisement and we're very excited.'

'We used to live in Berkshire,' Connie continued, before Merrin or Pippa could say a word. 'When Mummy died, we decided to move to St Ives. Our parents used to bring us here for a holiday every summer. We love it so much.'

'We have plenty of shop experience,' said Bea. 'We know how to work a till and a card machine and we're both very friendly, customers seem to like us.'

Merrin decided it was time she got a word in. 'My name is Merrin McKenzie and this is Pippa Meadows. I make the ceramics, Pippa makes the sea-glass jewellery and we have two colleagues, Joey Moon who is an artist and Lizzie Cambridge who makes candles. We're a sort of co-operative.'

'How do you do?' said both twins in chorus, as they stepped forward to shake hands. It was as Bea was shaking hands with Pippa that she stopped and looked into her face.

'Pippa, dear, you've been crying. What's wrong, my poppet?' she asked.

'Someone stole the bracelet I've just finished making. It was only in the shop for a day,' said Pippa. 'I shouldn't be so upset, it wasn't very valuable, but it took me ages to make and I loved it – although I shouldn't say that about my own work.'

'You poor dear,' said Bea.

'It was a beautiful bracelet,' said Merrin. 'The trouble is when the shop is full, it's very easy for people to steal things, because we can't see what they're doing.'

The twins looked at one another. 'Well,' said Bea – or was it Connie? 'We can help with that. When the shop is busy, one of us can be on the till while the other keeps an eye on the customers and tidies up. We wouldn't charge for two if we're both working, because we like being together.'

'Why don't you have a look round the shop while Pippa and I just have a quick chat upstairs,' Merrin suggested. 'Would that be alright?'

'Of course,' they said.

During the summer in St Ives, the hospitality and retail businesses mostly employed young people – the locals, of course, but also university students, mad-keen surfers, sometimes young artists like Joey. Therefore, Merrin's first comment to Pippa was to suggest that they would be stepping outside their comfort zone by employing these two elderly ladies, who couldn't be further from the town's usual types.

'I don't know that it matters,' said Pippa, surprisingly. 'I think they'll be novelty value, and I bet they'll treat customers with good old-fashioned courtesy. I think they could be a big hit.'

'I'm interested you say that, Pippa. I thought, being young, you would think the twins, bless them, weren't at all right for our shop. In any event, I suppose before we make a decision, we should consult Joey and Lizzie first.'

'Why don't we offer them a week's trial?' said Pippa. 'I'm sure the other two won't mind, and after losing my bracelet today, it would be really helpful to have the two of them here when the shop is busy. Two for the price of one – decent!'

'Alright – it's a slightly bizarre decision, but I agree, let's give it a whirl,' said Merrin.

They trooped downstairs to find one of the twins was on the till and the other was busily wrapping up a candle and two of Merrin's mugs while chatting to a slightly bemused customer, who nonetheless, obviously found the pair intriguing.

'A bizarre decision maybe,' whispered Pippa, 'but it looks like a good one to me.'

CHAPTER TWENTY

For the second time in just over two weeks, Merrin felt nervous and definitely outside her comfort zone. She stood staring into her wardrobe, watched by William, who appeared to be wearing a rather critical expression, though Merrin admitted to herself that this could be her fevered imagination at work. Merrin had always assumed that with age came confidence, but this appeared to be a fallacy. Now that she was outside the confines of a legal career, new and uncomfortable challenges kept presenting themselves, or so it seemed.

The contents of her wardrobe were sparse, except for her legal 'uniform'. She possessed three dark suits and four shirts used for court appearances and client meetings. Everything else was decidedly casual and none of it seemed suitable for Sunday lunch with Stephanie and family. There had already been several changes of clothes involving a great deal of sighing.

In the end, Merrin settled on her smartest pair of

trousers, which were not very smart, and a rather jazzy, multicoloured shirt, which she must have bought in a flamboyant mood and was now not at all sure about. Stephanie always looked so elegant, there was no point in trying to compete. She called Isla in for a second opinion.

'You look great,' said Isla, 'and before you say another word, no, I'm not just being kind. Oh, just look at William. He's bored rigid, like all men hanging about while the women in their life try to decide what to wear. Come on, or we'll be late – oh, I meant to say, William is invited too.'

'Is he?' said Merrin. 'Are you sure?'

'The children insisted,' said Isla firmly.

The house surprised Merrin, but then it was Stephanie and Andrew's house now. Somehow, it didn't look like the sort of home that would have suited Louis. It was too modern, too clever somehow, and much too minimalist to be cosy. However, it was both stylish and impressive enough to produce a 'Wow!' from Isla.

Daisy answered the door. 'Everyone's in the garden, come on through. I like your shirt, Mrs McKenzie,' she said. 'Oh, William, come on, boy!'

At the sight of Isla, Edward let out whoops of delight, ran across the lawn and enveloped her in an enormous bear hug. As if following his son's example, Louis stepped forward and gave Merrin a kiss on the cheek. It was their first ever public display of affection and she found it immediately comforting. Thereafter, of course, Louis's attention was entirely usurped by William – it really was a case of mutual adoration.

Stephanie looked wonderful in a pale blue silk kaftan and seemed genuinely pleased to see mother and daughter.

Andrew, too, was warm and welcoming, though it was immediately obvious that he found social gatherings something of a strain. They drank wine in the garden and Merrin saw a table had been laid in a lovely conservatory, where today in the fine weather, the doors were flung wide open.

'You have a beautiful house,' Merrin told Stephanie.

'I love it, though, as you can probably imagine, it is not to Louis's taste,' said Stephanie, without rancour. 'When we parted, I went a bit mad – enlarged the kitchen, built another bathroom, also the conservatory and the swimming pool. The house is nearly always full of the children's friends, which I love, and now there's plenty of room for them all.'

'I wish I'd had more children,' Merrin found herself saying.

'Was it a decision not to have any more?' Stephanie asked. 'Sorry, how presumptuous of me, I didn't mean to pry.'

Merrin smiled. 'I don't mind you asking at all. No, it wasn't a decision either way. It was just that Adam and I were always so busy, we somehow never got round to even considering having any more after Isla.' Her expression clouded. 'I regret it now, though. It would have made things easier for Isla if she'd had a sibling to share her grief at the loss of her father.'

'I'm so sorry about what happened to your husband,' said Stephanie. 'As you probably gather, I was not cut out to be a policeman's wife. The dangers of the job, of course, were an ongoing worry, but also the endless chopping and changing of plans, never knowing when he'd be home or even where he was. It drove me mad.' She laughed. 'Just listen to me – of course, I'm not telling you anything you don't already know.' She took Merrin's arm. 'Come on, I'll show you the house.'

From a distinct disadvantage point – lying on the grass with Edward sitting on his chest and William attempting to lick his face – Louis watched the two women walk into the house, arm in arm, chatting away. It was a pleasure and a relief to see they got on so well. He hadn't been sure they would; they were so different from one another.

'Get off me, both of you,' Louis said amicably.

Isla, spotting his plight, called out, 'Ed, leave your poor father alone and come and play football. William can be in goal.'

Standing up and dusting himself down, Louis saw that Andrew stood alone, looking awkward, as usual. Louis knew it was his own presence which caused Andrew's unease, and nothing he ever said or did seemed to reassure him.

'Come on, old chap, let's go and find another glass of wine,' Louis suggested.

'I'm so sorry, Louis, I should have thought of that. I'm a terrible host,' said Andrew.

'You're not at all,' said Louis kindly.

'I was wondering if you would like to carve. We have roast beef on the rib,' said Andrew. 'I'm sure you'd make a better job of it than me.'

Merrin and Stephanie had just entered the kitchen. 'Steph, remind Andrew about my carving skills,' Louis said.

'They're non-existent, Andrew darling, as I've told you before many times,' she said. 'He hacks away, makes an awful mess of any joint, and then gets angry with himself, by which time the vegetables and gravy are all getting cold and the cook, that's me, is losing the will to live.'

Merrin laughed. 'Is this true?' she asked Louis.

'As I live and breathe, you have been warned,' said Louis.

Lunch proved both delicious and relaxing and, helped by generous amounts of wine, even Andrew became more confident, particularly after being showered with many compliments about his excellent carving. The Peppiatt children clamoured for some more bodyboarding with Isla and this was promised. After lunch, Louis and Merrin took their coffee down to the end of the garden. The view across Falmouth harbour to Flushing was marvellous.

'All that shipping,' said Merrin. 'It's exciting, isn't it, the continual movement – I could watch it all day, it's not like sleepy old St Ives harbour.'

'That reminds me, did the husband of that woman Roxy ever turn up?' Louis asked.

'No, he hasn't yet, but Roxy's now admitted that he's not her husband anyway. It was just a fling. I gather his main attraction was he offered her a sailing holiday to Cornwall. Now she's got her hooks into Max and we're all very worried, because until Roxy turned up, Max, for once, had a lovely girlfriend, who's now presumably in bits. Never a dull moment in St Ives.'

'So, as the disappearing husband isn't Roxy's husband after all, does that mean I'm off the hook, as there's no longer a mystery to solve?' Louis asked.

'I suppose so,' Merrin admitted, 'although she did lie about the tender.'

'Or maybe Clara was mistaken?' Louis suggested.

'Possible. Come on, we'd better rejoin the party. Stephanie has been so kind to me and Isla. She's such a nice person, Louis.'

'She is now she's married to Andrew. Married to me she was always angry and fraught, and that's intended as a criticism of me, not her. Andrew's a decent bloke, a bit boring but solid, and she loves him.'

'And he can carve.'

'Yes, indeed,' said Louis.

CHAPTER TWENTY-ONE

The victim of the St Austell beating had survived. It had now been established that he was both able and willing to testify against his attackers. His story matched Chris Pirie's, who he confirmed had not been involved in the actual beating and had asked the others to stop. Louis had spent a gruelling day in court making sure that the three young men would remain in custody until the trial, which now would not occur until after the August recess. He'd also had to make sure that Chris Pirie was kept at a different detention centre from the other two.

By the time he reached home on Monday evening, Louis was ready for a whisky. He poured himself a modest measure and had just lowered himself into his armchair when there was a ping from his laptop, alerting him to an incoming email. With a heavy sigh, he got up and went to sit down at his desk.

The email was from Jeremy Eustace, enclosing the report from Len Carter. Louis speed-read it and then settled down to carefully read it again. Len Carter might be a nasty piece of work, but he appeared to have been thorough.

From Hubert, Len had obtained the contact details of Annie's best friend, Alice James. Alice had told Len that she and Annie often met for lunch in St Katharine Docks because Annie was mad about boats and loved to watch the yachts coming and going. More recently, she had become friendly with a man who owned a lovely yacht. Alice told Len that she did not know where Annie had gone, but she had mentioned to Alice that her new friend was sailing to the West Country. Alice seemed as bewildered by Annie's unusually lengthy disappearance as everyone else. Hubert had confirmed that Annie loved sailing and had joined her parents on many sailing adventures until their untimely death in a speedboat accident. It did suggest that Annie might have gone for a few days' sailing.

Len had then interviewed staff at restaurants, bars and shops, regular yachtsmen in the docks, the harbour master and the team of dockmasters who managed the operations of the docks. He showed around a photograph of Annie, who was instantly recognised at a number of restaurants and shops. In the restaurants, in particular, a woman friend was mentioned, clearly Alice, but no one remembered seeing Annie with a man. One of the dockmasters recognised the photograph and said he and Annie had spoken at length about the boats coming in and out of the docks. He mentioned that she was very knowledgeable and clearly sailing was her passion.

Len finished the report by saying he was now travelling down to Newton Abbot to talk to the housekeeper. He added that he still believed Annie could be in the West Country and he would be in touch again in a few days, certainly before the end of the week.

Something was niggling in Louis's mind as he re-read the report for the third time. He wondered why Len appeared fixated on St Katharine Docks, when surely Alice and Annie met in other places, and presumably, come to that, Annie had other friends besides Alice. It seemed as if his search had become very confined, very quickly, possibly because he knew more than he was prepared to disclose. Clearly, he believed Annie's love of sailing was in some way relevant.

Louis sat back in his chair and stared out of the window, and then it came to him. It was what Merrin had said yesterday regarding the Roxy woman – something like *the man Roxy was travelling with was not her husband, just a fling. His main attraction being his offer of a sailing holiday to Cornwall.* Could Annie and Roxy be the same person? Louis was not a fan of coincidences, and this one seemed particularly extreme . . . and yet. He picked up his mobile and called Merrin.

'Hello,' she said. 'I've just been speaking to Stephanie to thank her for a lovely day yesterday. We enjoyed it so much, even William, who, as you know, is not normally very social.'

'It's because I was there,' said Louis, confidently.

'Probably true, but annoying that you should be so pleased with yourself. What can I do for you?'

'Are you free for lunch tomorrow? Only there's a mad idea I want to run past you,' said Louis.

'That's intriguing, it's usually me who is accused of

having mad ideas. Do you want to go out or could I tempt you to crab sandwiches at home?'

'Crab sandwiches, please,' said Louis with evident enthusiasm. 'I've got to see Eddy. He's mithering about this spate of thieving that's going on in town. Have you lost anything more?'

'Pippa had a lovely sea-glass bracelet stolen at the weekend. Jack knows about it. However, we now have a secret weapon in the form of identical twin Miss Marples. Today was their first day. They were only supposed to come in for a couple of hours' training but they stayed all day. They clearly love the job and the customers love them. They're working tomorrow as well – you must meet them, they're a hoot!'

'Can't wait. I should be with you at about twelve-thirty. Will that suit?'

'Perfect,' said Merrin.

Beatrice and Constance Buchanan were indeed an immediate big hit – most importantly with Joey and Lizzie, but also with customers. Lizzie had trained them on the workings of the till and card machine, which had taken all of five minutes. They had then insisted on talking to each of the co-operative members, asking searching questions about their products so they would be able to talk knowledgeably to customers.

'I'm in love!' said Joey. 'What a find! How on earth did we ever imagine we could operate our enterprise without the twins?'

There was much discussion as to how the twins could ever be told apart.

‘There is a trick to it,’ said Beatrice, ‘but most people never work it out.’

‘Our father could never tell us apart. Mummy could, but even she struggled sometimes,’ said Constance.

‘So, are you going to tell us the trick?’ Merrin asked.

‘Certainly not,’ said Beatrice, smiling. ‘It will be fun to see which one of you spots it.’

CHAPTER TWENTY-TWO

'Your crab sandwiches are the best in Cornwall,' said Louis, 'which means, of course, that they are the best in the world.' It was a windy day, so they were having lunch at the kitchen table. Horatio was eyeing them from his perch on the wine rack. 'Horatio looks as if he'd like a piece of sandwich. Can I give him any?'

'Only a small piece of crust, and thank you, it's a great feeling to be the creator of a world-class sandwich,' said Merrin. 'Now tell me about your mad idea.'

Louis rose from the table and handed Horatio a small crust. 'There we are,' said Horatio.

'That's his way of saying thank you,' said Merrin. 'If he hadn't wanted it, he would have hurled it on the floor, fluffed up his feathers and turned his back on you.'

'Isn't it about time you taught that bird some manners?' Louis asked.

'I've tried, but it's hopeless, maybe because he has an illustrious name – he thinks normal courtesies don't apply to him. Anyway, enough about Horatio. Tell me all.'

So, Louis told her all about the Eustace family, starting with the hit and run and ending with the disappearance of Annie.

'Some people don't have much luck, do they?' said Merrin, when Louis had finished. 'The business success, the resultant wealth, I assume, and the title don't really compensate for what's been lost, one way and another. All I will say is thank God you were the first policeman at the scene after the accident – that poor little boy.'

'It's because of Jeremy I find I just can't turn my back on their dilemma. He's about to lose his father, he has a baby on the way and his stepmother is missing. Last night, I started reading the private investigator's report and the thing which sticks out a mile is Annie's love of boats and sailing. You'll think I'm mad, but I'll just go ahead and say it anyway. Do you think Roxy could be Annie?'

Merrin was silent for some while. 'You don't hold with coincidences, as I recall,' she said at last.

'I knew you'd say that,' said Louis. 'OK, it was a mad notion, forget it. I dreamt up the idea when I was knackered and the other side of a couple of whiskies.'

'Hang on a moment, Chief Inspector, I actually don't think it is such a crazy thought. Annie knows her husband is ill but not that he's dying. Because of the age difference, he's happy for her to go off on the odd jaunt. She chums up with Tony Barrow and pretends to be his wife to avoid any scandal – you said Hubert was worried about the press getting hold of the story of his missing wife because it might affect the share price. She and Tony row and he goes off with the rucksack full of her important stuff.' Merrin hesitated. 'Oh damn, this is where it breaks down. Surely, then, she would have gone straight back to London and Hubert rather than hang about in St Ives?'

'Maybe she's stayed on because of Max,' Louis suggested.

'You said that Jeremy was worried because although she often goes away on jollies, she always comes back when she says she will. Presumably, she lives in some splendour in Chelsea and Newton Abbot. Would she really give up all that for Max – lovely though he is – and swap for a tiny flat over an estate agency?'

'Unless it really is love,' said Louis.

'You old romantic, you,' said Merrin, smiling. 'If, for a moment, we believe that Roxy is Annie, I suppose she must have an inkling that poor old Hubert is not long for this world, which presumably means she knows she will inherit a stack pretty soon. Maybe that's why she wanted to buy a cottage down here, because she knows she will soon be very wealthy in her own right. Or maybe she was pretending to buy a cottage in order to get her hooks into Max. Hell, I'm going round in circles.'

'I suppose we could ask Max if she's told him anything to suggest she's really Lady Eustace,' suggested Louis.

'I don't think Roxy would tell Max if she really is Annie. She's already told him first that she was married to Tony, and then that she's not married. Yet another lie, admitting that in fact she is married, but to Hubert, wouldn't be popular. Also, if Max knew about Hubert, he would most likely try and persuade her to go back to her sick husband, however much he cares about her.'

'Would he really?' said Louis. 'I thought he had a pretty

dodgy moral compass when it comes to women.'

'It's difficult to explain,' said Merrin. 'He sees his relationships with women as a sort of a game, one with which he never wants to become too involved. However, he does respect other people's marriages. Also, he's a very honest person – in business he is totally reliable. In fact you can absolutely trust him in any scenario because he always tells the truth, even if you don't want to hear it. I went out with him once.'

'Did you?' said Louis. 'I find that surprising. I thought Adam was your first proper boyfriend.'

'He was,' said Merrin. 'I was Max's girl for about two months the summer I was fifteen. It was all very innocent, holding hands in the cinema, that sort of thing. He dumped me, of course, and I was broken-hearted for at least a week!'

'You hussy,' said Louis, with a grin.

'Rude,' said Merrin, returning his smile. 'You know, I still don't understand, if by any chance Roxy is Annie, why she hasn't gone home. Also, there's been something different about Roxy ever since Tony left her. When she first arrived, she was full of confidence, but now she seems nervous, anxious – I don't know, worried too, I suppose. Perhaps I'm imagining it because I'm so cross with her about Max. What are you going to do, Louis, and is there anything I can do to help?'

'Bless you. Just keep your ear to the ground for the time being. I'm very anxious that the private investigator, Len Carter, doesn't find Annie before anyone else does. He's a really brutish, violent man – I'm very worried about his involvement, and I have a feeling that he's not telling Jeremy everything he knows.'

'Oh my God,' said Merrin, suddenly. 'I've only just realised something, how stupid not to have thought of it before! Roxy's full name is Roxanne. Think of the last four letters of her name – *anne*. Annie could be her nickname, which she's only changed to Roxy because she doesn't want to be found. That increases the odds a bit, doesn't it?'

'I suppose it does,' said Louis. 'Yes, it definitely does.'

Louis was halfway back to Truro when he had an idea. Rather than wait until he got back to the station, he pulled into a lay-by on the A30 and called Merrin.

'Goodness,' said Merrin. 'You've only just left. Did you leave something behind?'

'No,' said Louis. 'I've had an idea which could resolve the Annie/Roxy mystery.'

'Go on,' said Merrin.

'I need to track down Tony Barrow. He's bound to know who's who in all of this. I just wondered if you happen to know the name of his yacht, which is probably the quickest way of finding him.'

'I do,' said Merrin. 'The yacht's called *Llamedos*, and before you ask, it's *sod-em-all* backwards. Again, before you ask, apparently Tony had difficulty finding a name for his yacht that wasn't already registered.'

'That's very helpful. I imagine it can't be very difficult to track down the yacht with a name like that. It'll certainly be a one-off.'

'If you're going to be looking for Tony, I need to bring you up to date where he's concerned,' said Merrin. 'When Roxy told me that Tony had sailed to the Scillies to meet some friends, I did call the harbour master in St Mary's.

He knew nothing of the yacht but said he would check with the other islands and come back to me if he could track down Tony. I explained Roxy was trying to retrieve her rucksack. He sounded a very reliable sort of chap and I haven't heard a word from him, which is rather odd. It suggests that Tony may have changed his plans and didn't in fact sail to Scilly.'

'What did Roxy make of that?' Louis asked.

'Well, that's another odd thing. For an intelligent woman, she seemed to have made no effort to track down Tony herself when she realised her rucksack was still on board. She was with me when I made contact with the harbour master in St Mary's, yet she didn't seem that interested.'

'Thanks for all that,' said Louis. 'I expect finding Tony Barrow will lead to Roxy, not Annie at all. I'm just terribly anxious about Len Carter. If Annie is with another man or, say, refuses to return to Hubert, he could turn ugly.'

'Have you warned Jeremy about Len Carter?' Merrin asked.

'Yes, I have, but both he and his father seem to think he's the right man for the job. Certainly, they weren't impressed with my concerns.'

The following morning, Merrin was summoned to the shop. Lizzie was in charge but was having difficulty with a very disgruntled Jack Eddy, who had asked to speak to Merrin.

'What's he want?' Merrin asked. 'I'm up to my neck in costings at the moment.'

'It's about the thefts. They're still going on and Jack feels he's not getting enough support,' said Lizzie.

'That's hardly my fault,' said Merrin.

'Please, Merrin.' Lizzie dropped her voice to a whisper. 'He's not going to leave here until he sees you – and he's not good for business.'

'In five,' said Merrin grudgingly.

Jack was indeed in high dudgeon. 'The boss came to see me yesterday. He was only in the station a few minutes, and just said he felt sure I could handle the thefts because I had such a good track record for solving these sorts of crimes. What do you think about that, my maid?'

'I think you should be very flattered, Jack. Louis obviously thinks so highly of you that he feels it's safe to leave the problem in your capable hands.'

'Can't you have a word with him, little Merrin? He'll listen to you. I definitely need some help with this lowlife, whoever he is. Every time I turn my back, he's stolen something else.'

'Jack, be reasonable,' said Merrin. 'I can't start telling Louis how to do his job. You've always handled the thefts in St Ives, and your clean-up rate has been impressive. The shopkeepers know and trust you, and working together with them has turned you all into a serious bunch of crime-busters. What makes you think you need extra help this time?'

'As I said before,' said Jack with a theatrical sigh, 'it's the sheer volume of thefts. You suggested it might be a gang, and I think you could be right. The shopkeepers might have been happy working with me in the past, but now they're starting to get restless because I'm making absolutely no progress. I need some PCs on the ground. I can't be everywhere at once.'

Two things happened, one after the other. Firstly,

Lizzie came downstairs and handed Jack a steaming mug of tea and a plate of digestive biscuits. His frown cleared immediately and was replaced by a look of pure pleasure. Secondly, Pippa came into the shop, walked over to her stall and screamed.

'Oh no, Pippa, don't tell me something else of yours has been stolen?' said Merrin.

Pippa shook her head and pointed to the table. The display of her most precious items was housed in a glass display cabinet. Merrin looked to where she was pointing. In the centre of the display, carefully laid out, was her missing sea-glass bracelet.

'It is the same one that was stolen, isn't it?' Merrin asked.

'Absolutely,' said Pippa. 'I've only made the one since we opened the shop. What on earth is going on, Merrin?'

Jack was engrossed in his tea and biscuits. 'Jack!' said Merrin, sharply. 'Did you see what's happened?'

'No, my maid, I didn't,' he said, helping himself to another biscuit.

'Jack, please concentrate,' said Merrin, clearly exasperated. 'The bracelet of Pippa's that was stolen last week has been returned.'

'Not possible,' said Jack, complacently. He turned to Pippa. 'As I've already said, you must have mislaid it, my maid – put it somewhere safe and forgotten where you left it. That's a relief, I'm so glad you've found it.'

'I didn't mislay it, Sergeant Eddy,' said Pippa, obviously fighting to keep her temper. 'Someone took it and then for some obscure reason, brought it back again.'

'Now, young Pippa, you must realise that is very

unlikely. Have a good think and I'll bet you will suddenly remember where you were keeping it.'

'It was stolen!' said Pippa, through gritted teeth.

Merrin quickly intervened. 'Jack, Pippa is a very organised person. Also, unlike me and Lizzie, she doesn't carry a great deal of stock, so it is easy to keep track of things. If she said it was taken, then that's what happened.'

'Is it valuable?' asked Jack.

'No,' said Pippa, 'but it took weeks to make.'

'Well, valuable or not,' said Jack, stubbornly, 'no one would risk replacing an item they'd stolen, for fear of getting caught. It makes no sense.'

CHAPTER TWENTY-THREE

Chief Inspector Louis Peppiatt made a number of decisions on Wednesday morning. Firstly, he decided that he would track down Tony Barrow. Secondly, he would start at St Katharine Docks because if Tony had links with the docks, it could mean he also had a link with Annie Eustace, which made it more likely that Annie and Roxy were the same person. Thirdly, he was not going to involve his boss, Chief Superintendent John Dent, in his enquiries at this stage, for he knew exactly how John would react. John would dismiss immediately the emotional tie Louis had to Jeremy Eustace; he would say a young woman running away from an elderly sick husband was not a police matter; at the mere mention of Len Carter's name, John would insist Louis kept well clear of the man.

Imagining his boss's reaction to his decision to become involved tempted Louis to rethink the whole idea. Did it matter if Annie and Roxy were the same person? No, of course not, unless fraud was involved, which seemed unlikely. It was absolutely correct that a runaway wife was not a police matter unless a crime had been committed in the process, which was not the case here, as far as anyone knew. He did feel uneasy about Len Carter's involvement, believing him to be unstable, to put it mildly, but maybe prison had straightened him out – he had certainly impressed both Eustaces, father and son. Yet despite the fact that this wasn't a case he should be involved in – indeed, it wasn't a case at all – instinctively he felt something was wrong, something didn't quite add up, without the slightest idea as to what that might be. It was time to trust his policeman's nose and go ahead with the investigation.

Louis immediately struck gold. Having introduced himself, a phone call to the harbour master at St Katharine Docks released the information that Tony Barrow had a permanent mooring there, and his yacht was indeed named *Llamedos*.

'There'll be no other shipping with that name, that's for sure,' said the harbour master, with a chuckle.

'His yacht's not there now, I assume?' said Louis.

'No, he left a while back, two maybe three weeks ago, heading for Cornwall and the Scilly Isles, I believe I heard. He's not in trouble, is he?'

'Absolutely not. I am trying to contact someone who was travelling with him. Did you see anyone on board when he sailed?' Louis asked.

'I didn't see him leave. There's that much craft in and out of the docks. I only know Tony because he's had a mooring here a long time, and I believe it was his dad's before that.'

'Do you happen to know what he does for a living?' Louis asked.

'Not much,' said the harbour master. 'He helps out around the docks doing odd jobs when he's here. He sails over to France a fair bit. I expect he does the same casual work over there, too. His dad had a string of betting shops. When he died, Tony sold the lot. I'm not saying he's loaded but I suspect he doesn't need to work. He's a bit of a drinker but not when he's sailing, I'll say that for him. He's a proper seaman and won't touch a drop when he's got his hand on the tiller.'

Louis thanked the harbour master and sat pondering what he'd learnt. It was back to coincidences again; Merrin was really going to enjoy mocking him, if this particular coincidence proved to be real, which seemed increasingly likely. Annie spent a lot of time at St Katharine Docks, as confirmed by her friend Alice. Tony Barrow had a mooring there, and Alice had confirmed to Len Carter that Annie had spoken to a lone yachtsman while they were lunching. Of course, it might not have been Tony she was talking to. However, it was strange that both Annie and Tony were associated with the docks, and yet it was apparently Roxy who went sailing with Tony.

There was something else niggling away in Louis's thoughts. He got up from his desk and went to make a cup of coffee. It was while he was waiting for the kettle to boil that the thought struck him – the harbour master had been emphatic that Tony never sailed when drunk. Yet, according to Roxy, Tony was very drunk on the night they had argued and, as a result, he had sailed out of St Ives. Roxy had told Merrin that she had started to walk up the hill out of town when she'd remembered her rucksack. So how long would it take her to walk up to, say, the Malakoff, and then hurry back – about half an hour? Certainly, that was not even remotely long enough for Tony to sober up. Had he broken his own golden rule? Had the quarrel with Roxy upset him that much? Louis thought not – as the harbour master had said, Tony was a proper seaman. In which case, Roxy was lying, just as Clara had always maintained.

Louis called Jeremy Eustace. 'I think I might be making some progress,' he said. 'Could you please email me over a recent photograph of Annie?'

'Yes, of course,' said Jeremy. 'What sort of progress?'

'It's very tenuous at the moment,' said Louis, 'but hopefully I will have something for you in the next couple of days.'

The photograph, when it arrived, meant nothing to Louis as he had never met Roxy, so he emailed it straight on to Merrin, and called her.

'It's hard to tell,' said Merrin. 'In the photograph you sent me, Annie is blonde, wears little or no make-up and looks like she dresses simply. Roxanne has dark hair, wears tons of make-up and dresses very stylishly.'

'What about their features?' Louis asked.

'They don't look outlandishly different, but I can't honestly say from the photograph, which isn't very sharp, that they are the same woman. But they could be. For example, comparing their eyes, Annie in the photograph wears no eye make-up. Roxy, by contrast, really piles it on. That's not very helpful, is it?'

'If it is the same woman, I wonder why she changed

her look so drastically. I suppose because she wanted to conceal her identity,' said Louis.

'The same way she gave herself a different nickname, perhaps.'

'Maybe,' agreed Louis. 'I had an interesting conversation with the harbour master at St Katharine Docks. Let me fill you in.'

When Louis had finished, Merrin was silent for several moments. 'It's weird about Tony and the drinking,' she said, at last. 'That's the second inconsistency in Roxy's story.'

'I agree,' said Louis. 'What I've decided to do now is to go to Torquay and ask some questions. I'll stay in Newton Abbot tonight. In any case, there's an old friend I want to see who's just lost his wife – I say a friend, he is absurdly grateful that I nicked him years ago, but he's a good chap and was devoted to his wife.'

'That's very sad. Can I ask why on earth you're going to Torquay?'

'It's the nearest proper harbour to Newton Abbot, where Hubert Eustace has his country estate. Annie stayed a night in Newton Abbot before she disappeared. Maybe she hitched a lift with Tony from Torquay, assuming she really is Roxy.'

'So when are you going?' Merrin asked.

'I thought now,' said Louis. 'I know Len Carter has gone down to Newton Abbot to talk to the Eustaces' housekeeper, but I think I have the trump card, in that I don't see how he can know anything about Tony Barrow and his yacht, *Llamedos*.'

'No, of course not,' agreed Merrin. 'Just one thing while I've got you on the phone – Jack Eddy is in a tizz.

He thinks you should be giving him back-up to track down the thief or thieves in St Ives, and he's also quite cross with me.'

Louis laughed. 'What on earth have you done to upset Jack? He adores you.'

'Two things,' said Merrin. 'Firstly, despite his earnest request, I refused to agree to tell you how to do your job. Secondly, and weirdly, one of the stolen items from our shop – a bracelet – has been returned.'

'That can't be right. Pippa, isn't it? She must have mislaid it,' said Louis.

'Don't you start,' said Merrin. 'That's what Jack said and you're both wrong. It was definitely stolen and now it's back.'

'Tell Jack I will be over tomorrow afternoon, or at worst Friday morning, if the Torquay sleuthing takes longer than expected. So *are* you going to tell me how to do my job?'

'I might, if you persist in believing Pippa's bracelet wasn't stolen.'

Louis checked into his hotel in Newton Abbot late afternoon. He then went in search of an off-licence and picked up a few beers. It was only three weeks since Donald Coleman's wife Freda had died, and Louis suspected Don would not be keen for a trip to the pub just yet. Louis had phoned ahead to ask if it was convenient for him to call on Don, and the response had left Louis in no doubt that Don was already very lonely.

The little man who opened his front door had shrunk even more than Louis remembered. He'd also aged a great deal but despite this, his legendary enthusiasm was still in evidence. He had always been a man whose glass was not just half full, but filled to the very brim.

'Louis Peppiatt, as I live and breathe. Come on in, my dear fellow. How are you?' Don said.

'I'm fine, Don, but it's you I'm worried about. How are you coping without Freda – *are* you coping without Freda?' said Louis.

'Just about,' said Don, glancing towards the chair by the fire where Freda used to sit. 'Gerry, our son, pops in most evenings, though I've given him a night off tonight, as you're here. People have been very kind. Freda was well known and much loved in these parts. I was so lucky to have her in my life.' Don hesitated and then seemed to pull himself together. He suddenly noticed Louis's carrier bag full of beer.

'That's the ticket,' he said, taking the beer. 'Trust you, Louis, to guess that I'm not ready to go to the pub yet. Grab a seat by the fire and we'll break these open.'

The two men sat round the log fire, which was strangely comforting on a wet, windy evening in mid-July. They had first met more years ago than either of them cared to remember. Louis had been a young constable, newly discharged from the army. Don had been a lecturer at Seale-Hayne Agricultural College by day, and by night he'd stolen small pieces of agricultural equipment and machinery from local farms to support his extravagant lifestyle. The location for their first meeting had been a muddy farmyard, as Louis wrestled Don to the ground and then arrested him. When they'd met again, three years ago, Louis had been astonished to discover that although he had been responsible for Don doing a four-year stretch in prison, both Don and Freda saw him as their hero for rescuing Don from his life of crime. Louis, however, saw it quite differently – Don had learnt the error of his ways in prison and had subsequently paid back the farmers for everything he had stolen. A mighty achievement which, in Louis's view, made Don the hero.

They talked a little about Freda. 'You know she had terrible arthritis?' Don said.

Louis nodded. 'I do, yet she seemed so cheerful and brave.'

'She was, bless her,' said Don. 'She had a stroke in the end, and to be honest, after all the pain she'd suffered, it was a merciful release. I miss her so much, but I have to keep cheerful – she'd be furious if I turned into an old misery. Anyway, enough of me. How's your love life, young Louis?'

'Non-existent,' said Louis, smiling.

'That's ridiculous, boy. How long is it since you and your missus split up?'

'Seven years,' admitted Louis.

Don eyed him, speculatively. 'You're not a bad-looking chap – you've still got all your hair, and presumably your own teeth. You look pretty fit and healthy, you have an interesting job, and as I remember, despite being a copper, you have a fondness for both art and literature. Quite a catch, I would have thought. It's time you pulled yourself together, or you'll blink and suddenly find yourself a lonely old codger, like me.'

'I could do a lot worse, Don,' said Louis. 'Shall I fetch some more beers?'

Louis returned with the beers to find Don poking the

fire. 'I've been thinking. It was very kind of you to come and see me, but I must be on the route to some police business you're pursuing locally,' he said, appraising Louis with a shrewd look.

'I don't deny it,' said Louis. 'I'm off to Torquay in the morning.'

'Anything I can help with? I know an awful lot of people hereabouts.'

'Do you know Sir Hubert Eustace, Don?'

'I know *of* him, of course, but I've never met him. He's a bit of a celebrity round here, of course. His factory gives employment to a great many people in the area. What on earth can Sir Hubert have done wrong?'

'Absolutely nothing, Don. He's asked me to find a missing yacht, and it seems possible that the skipper may have stopped off in Torquay harbour, maybe en route to Cornwall.' *Not a complete lie*, thought Louis, *just a modest spin on the truth.*

'Ah, well I can help you there. My cousin is chief mate to the harbour master in Torquay. Do you know the name of the yacht you're looking for?' Louis told him. 'An odd name,' Don remarked.

'It's *sod-em-all* backwards,' said Louis, smiling. 'The skipper had difficulty finding a name when registering the boat, lost his patience, and that was the result!'

'I like it!' said Don, laughing. 'I'll give my cousin a call first thing tomorrow, tell him to expect you and ask him to start searching for the missing yacht. His name's Rory Baker. He'll sort you out. He's a good bloke.'

'That's a huge help, Don. I was planning to be over in the harbour at about nine tomorrow morning. Is that too early?'

'Not at all,' said Don. 'He's an early riser, like me. I'll call him at six and tell him you'll be at the office at about nine. Hopefully, he'll have something for you.'

Louis returned to his hotel in good spirits. It was not the few beers he'd shared with Don that had improved his humour; it was spending time with the man himself. Don always had this effect on him. Don was now in his early eighties. He had just lost his beloved wife, but he still managed to be cheerful company and retain his genuine interest in the world outside of his grief. After all he'd been through – humiliation, prison, penny-pinching for years in order to pay back the farmers he'd stolen from, and now losing Freda – he was still curious, still able to think of others, and was controlling his feelings by reckoning he owed it to Freda not to be a misery. Citing Don as an example, what possible reason was there, Louis thought, for him to be anything but cheerful with his lot?

He was also feeling optimistic about his search for the truth about Annie and her whereabouts. Now, with Don's help, he should be able to establish whether Tony Barrow had stopped off in Torquay harbour, in which case, it was very likely to be where he'd picked up his passenger, whoever she was. Louis felt certain now that he had to be ahead of Len Carter in tracking down Annie. It was hard to see how Len could make much progress without knowing either the name of the yacht, or her skipper.

Louis felt this was a case that he could unravel quickly.

CHAPTER TWENTY-FOUR

At first glance, Len Carter didn't look like a thug. In his new profession as a private investigator, he had taken great care to make sure this was indeed the case. For work, he always wore a dark suit, a crisply ironed white shirt, a sombre tie and highly polished shoes. He was clean-shaven and his hair was neatly cut. He could have passed for an accountant, a solicitor, maybe a bank manager – unless one studied him very closely. In prison, he had worked out every day, and even now, he went to the gym at least four days a week. His physique was powerful and beneath the sleeves of his ultra-conservative suit jacket, his biceps bulged. His eyes, a rich dark brown, seemed harmless enough, even attractive – that is, unless someone crossed him in any way, any way at all. Then his anger, no, his fury, flashed into those brown eyes, his face distorted, his fists clenched. Beneath the apparent calm reassurance of his manner was a seething cauldron of pent-up wrath, always standing by, just waiting to explode.

Len arrived at Sir Hubert Eustace's stunningly-converted farmhouse by appointment at nine o'clock. The appointment was with Margaret Ashley, Sir Hubert's housekeeper, who showed him into a lavishly decorated drawing room and offered him coffee. He accepted graciously, because it gave him time to assess his surroundings before Mrs Ashley returned with the coffee. Certainly, a great deal of money had been thrown at the restoration and enlargement of a traditional Victorian farmhouse. *If I can find this wretched wife, I can definitely raise my fees*, Len thought. *The old boy's half dead anyway, he's not going to need any financial support where he's heading.*

Mrs Ashley arrived with the coffee, and they sat opposite one another in front of an ornate but unlit fireplace.

'Sir Hubert says I am to answer any question you put to me, Mr Carter.' She smiled slightly. 'I hope I'm able to do that.'

'You know why I'm here?' Len asked.

'Yes, of course,' said Mrs Ashley, a little huffily. 'Sir Hubert and Lady Eustace tell me everything. I've worked for the family for many years – they trust me completely and I know everything of significance.'

'But not to the extent that you know where Annie has gone?' remarked Len. 'I'm assuming she didn't tell you?'

'I had imagined Her Ladyship was going to be back for lunch on that day,' said Mrs Ashley, primly. 'She didn't say she was, but neither did she say she wasn't. It's over two weeks ago now – I'm that worried.'

'And did she give any indication as to where she was going?' Len managed to remain patient, but it was a struggle. It would have been so much quicker to shake the information out of this silly old woman.

'Yes, she said she was going to Torquay harbour. I've already told Sir Hubert this,' said Mrs Ashley.

'Mrs Ashley, it's my job to check and recheck all the information I receive from various sources. Did she say why she was going to the harbour?'

'No, but she often goes there. She loves sailing and sometimes goes out on the water with one of her friends. When she didn't turn up for lunch, I wasn't worried. I just assumed she'd met someone who'd suggested a sail and she just forgot to call me, which I admit is unlike her.'

'So, she wasn't meeting anyone in particular, as far as you know?'

'She may well have been, but there was no reason why she should tell me about her social plans. I may be trusted by the family but I'm staff, Mr Carter, not one of them – it's none of my business who they meet and why.'

'That's as maybe, Mrs Ashley, but it is mine. Are you absolutely certain she'd made no forward plans to meet anyone? Can I see her room – does she have a desk, downstairs, in a study, perhaps? I need to establish if she had a date to meet someone.'

'I'm not letting you near her personal possessions without checking with Sir Hubert,' said Mrs Ashley, stoutly, going very red in the face.

'He told you to answer any questions I asked you,' said Len; his anger was at tipping point. 'I think that indicates he expects you to help me in any way you can.'

'I'm perfectly certain that his instructions did not include letting you examine Her Ladyship's things,' said Mrs Ashley, standing up. 'I forbid it and I'm sure Sir Hubert will too.'

Len stood up too and, moving towards Mrs Ashley, took her firmly by the shoulders.

'Let go of me this instant,' said Mrs Ashley.

Len shook her shoulders, none too gently. 'Not until you give me something more. Just take me to where she's likely to keep her diary. Do it or you'll be sorry.'

'I'm going to tell Sir Hubert all about your behaviour. He'll sack you on the spot when he hears you've been threatening me,' said Mrs Ashley, bravely.

'I'm only threatening you because you won't do as you're told, you stupid old bat.'

In all of her sixty-three years, no one had ever spoken to Margaret Ashley in such a manner, and it suddenly occurred to her that she might be in danger from this man – so outwardly respectable, yet behaving in an increasingly frightening way. She racked her brains, then cleared her throat, trying to sound calm.

'When Her Ladyship goes to the harbour, she usually visits her hairdresser first. She says our local hairdresser is better than any of the highly priced celebrity hairdressers in London.'

Len let go of her shoulders. 'What's the name of the hairdresser's and whereabouts is it?'

'It's called Josephine's. It's right by the harbour entrance. I don't know the name of the street, but it's a very well-known place.'

'You could have saved us both a lot of time and trouble if you told me this at the beginning,' Len said, striding towards the door leading out of the drawing room.

'I forgot,' said Mrs Ashley, suddenly feeling a little faint. 'I've only just remembered Josephine's. It was silly of me but if you hadn't started shouting at me, I would probably have remembered sooner.'

'You're lucky that shouting's all I did,' was Len's parting shot as he left the room.

Walking unsteadily over to the house telephone, Mrs Ashley dialled Sir Hubert's number.

CHAPTER TWENTY-FIVE

Josephine's salon was quiet that particular morning. Two of her stylists were at work and her receptionist was busy on the phone, but there was nothing Josephine herself actually needed to do until her next client arrived in half an hour's time. She was about to go into her little back office for a much-needed cup of coffee, when the door opened and a man walked in. Very few men ventured into Josephine's. It was so obviously girly, from the photographs of hairstyles in the window, to the general decor and feel of the place. Most men only entered to collect a wife, girlfriend or daughter, and nearly always looked uncomfortable, as if they didn't belong – which, of course, they didn't. This particular man looked totally at ease, utterly unfazed by his feminine surroundings. Intrigued, she waited outside her office door to see what he wanted – she was also rather taken with his rugged good looks.

'I'd like to talk to the owner, please. I assume that might be Josephine?' He smiled at the young receptionist.

Well trained, she replied, 'I'll have to see if Josephine is available. Can I ask your name, please, and the nature of your business.'

'It's a private matter and an urgent one, so please just tell her I need to speak to her. My name is Len Carter and I'm a private investigator.'

Josephine stepped forward. 'It's alright, Janey, I'll take this.' She turned towards the man who, close to, looked something beyond rugged – tough, even slightly dangerous. Surprisingly, it had the effect of making her even more curious. 'What can I do to help?' she asked, sporting her best smile.

He smiled in return and lowered his voice. 'I need help with some information concerning one of your clients,' he said.

'I'm afraid I can't discuss my clients with anyone.' She tried another smile. 'Hairdressers are rather like the confessional. Clients tell us things that they wouldn't dream of telling anyone else – not husbands, not even best girlfriends.'

'Look, love, I haven't time for this. You're neither a doctor nor a priest, and I'm not even slightly interested in female gossip. We have a client in common who may be in trouble, and I'm just hoping you can help me. Is there somewhere we can talk in private?'

While Josephine wasn't impressed by being called *love*, she did like masterful men. 'Follow me,' she said and led him through to her office.

Josephine indicated a chair beside her desk, but Len showed no interest in sitting down. 'You have a client named Lady Eustace. She's gone missing and her husband is extremely anxious about her. The police are useless and so Sir Hubert has asked me to find her. I understand she came into your salon a couple of weeks ago, actually on the day she disappeared.' He gave Josephine a piercing look. 'Over to you, love.'

Josephine was not intimidated. 'Firstly, Mr Carter, if we're going to have any kind of dialogue, would you please refrain from calling me *love*. I'm not your love, and never will be. Yes, Annie did come to the salon a couple of weeks ago. I'll just call Janey and ask her for the precise date.'

Len waited while Josephine rang Janey. 'Annie came in on 5th July, the first appointment of the morning at eight-thirty,' Josephine confirmed.

'That is indeed the day she disappeared – none of her family have seen or heard from her since. So, what can you tell me about her time here that morning?'

'Well,' said Josephine, 'I always look after Lady Eustace myself. She's been a valuable client for some years, preferring to have her hair looked after by us rather than fancy London salons.'

'Yes, yes,' said Len, impatiently, 'I know all about that, and I don't want this conversation to revolve round the brilliance of your salon. How did she seem? Was she different from normal in any way?'

'She was cheerful. Actually, she was very excited. She was catching up with a friend in the harbour and they were going on a sailing trip together. She loves sailing but her husband is much older than her, as you probably know, and his sailing days are over, though I'm not sure he was ever very keen. Hunting and shooting is more his style, I suspect.'

'Do you know the name of the person she was going sailing with – man or woman?' Len asked.

Josephine shook her head. 'I've no idea, but I do know she goes sailing regularly with friends. She has told me in the past that her husband is very tolerant about her trips away. Her parents were friends of his and so he was well aware that her family had always been enthusiastic sailors.'

'Do you know where she was heading, and have you any idea how long the trip was supposed to be?'

Josephine frowned in concentration. 'She said it was a longer trip than normal. She mentioned sailing round Land's End and up the north coast of Cornwall. I seem to remember that they were planning to visit St Ives as their ultimate destination. I think I've got that right.'

'So, are you not sure about St Ives?' Len said.

'Yes, yes, I'm certain now I think about it. She'd never been to Cornwall before and had heard St Ives was very special – that's how she explained it to me.'

'Right,' said Len, 'you've been very helpful. So, the missing wife is either in St Ives or drowned at sea. Let's hope it's the former.'

'That's an awful thing to say,' said Josephine.

'Just stating facts,' said Len, cheerfully. He opened the office door and made to leave.

'Mr Carter,' Josephine called after him. 'I've just remembered one other thing.'

'Go on,' said Len, stopping in his tracks.

'She has lovely natural blonde hair and yet, on that day, she made me colour it dark brown. It didn't really suit her, but she insisted. It seemed to me to be an extraordinary thing to do.'

'Has she ever dyed her hair before?' Len asked.

'Not in this salon.'

'Not extraordinary at all then – it was an attempt at a disguise. Clearly she's run away and doesn't want to be found, but I think I can put that right,' was Len's parting shot.

CHAPTER TWENTY-SIX

Although Donald Coleman and his cousin Rory Baker were linked to the same gene pool, they couldn't have looked more different. Rory was tall and slender, with a shock of white hair and piercing blue eyes. He cut an imposing figure. The only apparent similarity to his cousin was the same positive, can-do attitude to life.

'A pleasure to meet you, Chief Inspector,' Rory said, extending his hand and shaking Louis's rigorously.

'Louis, please. It's good of you to see me so promptly.'

'No problem, Louis – I have the information dear old Don said you were after. Come into the office. Coffee?'

The two men settled down with steaming mugs of coffee. Louis had watched the comings and goings of the shipping from the window, as Rory was preparing the drinks. Louis nodded towards the view. 'That's quite a job you have on your hands, by the look of things,' he offered.

'Keeps me busy,' Rory agreed. 'Now about that yacht you're after – *Llamedos*. The skipper is one Tony Barrow, who arrived here on 3rd July and booked in for two nights' mooring. From what I've been able to find out, it appears he left the mooring at about lunchtime on 5th July.'

'That makes a lot of sense. Thank you so much,' said Louis. 'Have you any idea if he had any crew with him?'

'I'm afraid not, but the one other piece of information I gleaned was that he was heading down the coast to Land's End, with a view to sailing up Cornwall's north coast. With a yacht of that size, doing that sort of journey, he would have been wise to have had someone with him.'

'Great,' said Louis, 'just what I wanted to hear.'

'How's poor old Don doing?' Rory asked. 'He'll be lost without his Freda.'

'Being Don, he's putting on a brave face, but he must be devastated. They were such a lovely couple.'

'He's something of a hero of mine,' said Rory. 'After a terrible start in life, it was marvellous the way he turned things round, paid back the farmers and built a successful business. It's a real lesson in how to live a life, isn't it? However bleak things are, with determination one can come through. I must go and see him . . . I have next weekend off, so I'll go then.'

'He'd really appreciate it, I know, and I think your feelings are reciprocated. He's definitely very proud of you,' said Louis.

On leaving Rory Baker, Louis headed for the nearest garage, filled up with fuel, and bought a sandwich and a bottle of water. Then, on his way out of Torquay, he called Merrin.

'How's it going?' she asked.

'Good,' said Louis. 'I am quietly confident that Annie and Roxy are the same person. All the timings fit, and *Llamedos* did moor up in Torquay for two nights and left the harbour on the day Annie disappeared, which was 5th July.'

'Sorry to be stupid, but tell me again why Torquay is significant?' said Merrin.

'Because Annie was staying in the family home in Newton Abbot on the night of 4th July. This was confirmed by the housekeeper, according to Jeremy, and Torquay harbour is only about eight miles from Newton Abbot, and the nearest significant harbour from there.'

'But supposing Roxy is a different person from Annie, she might well have joined Tony in St Katharine Docks, or even in Torquay. I don't see how it proves that it was Annie who joined Tony.'

'At the risk of being mocked,' said Louis, 'it seems to me that it's too much of a coincidence. Annie went missing the day Tony set sail for Cornwall. She loved sailing and Torquay was close by her home. Also, she seems to have disappeared off the face of the earth – easily done, if you pretend to be someone else.'

'But why would she pretend to be someone else?' said Merrin. 'What's the point? Hubert told you he was happy for her to go away on her jaunts, so she didn't have to be secretive about what she was doing.'

'I agree. Roxy masqueraded first as someone else's wife and now, apparently, she has taken up with Max, neither of which suggest a happy marriage to Hubert. But I still think the coincidence is compelling.'

'Oh, I wish I was recording this conversation,' said

Merrin. 'I can't wait to tell Isla that you actually said "I think the coincidence is compelling"!'

'I knew you'd mock,' said Louis, smiling to himself. 'I'm on my way to St Ives now. I should be there in a couple of hours. I'll go and see Jack Eddy first and then, if you're about, could I pop in and see you? I'll try and think about the best way to confront Roxy with my suspicions on my way.'

'Of course, I'll be at home. I can't wait to hear what you're going to do next!'

'Will Isla also be at home?' Louis asked suspiciously.

'I think she will be, once I tell her you're building a case on the basis of coincidence!'

'You're a pair of dreadful women,' said Louis.

'I know,' said Merrin, happily.

'One final encouraging thing,' said Louis. 'If Roxy is Annie, I must be way ahead of the odious Len Carter in finding her.'

As Louis headed towards Exeter, Len Carter had just joined the Hayle bypass, only six miles from St Ives.

On the journey to St Ives, Louis stopped in a lay-by on the A30 and called Jeremy Eustace. While he still had no concrete evidence that Roxy and Annie were one and the same, it occurred to him that he at least should update Jeremy with his suspicions. When Jeremy answered the phone, Louis outlined what he'd discovered and his tentative conclusions.

'I'll come down to St Ives right away,' said Jeremy. 'I'm at home at the moment, so I'll just quickly pack a bag and leave. I should be with you, what, in five or six hours?'

'About that,' agreed Louis, 'but honestly, Jeremy, I think you're being a little premature. Why not wait until I've interviewed Roxy and established if she is Annie before making the journey? You could be wasting your time, because the suspicions I've described to you are not only lacking any evidence – they're really little more than a hunch.'

'I'm coming,' said Jeremy, firmly. 'If I come with you to interview this Roxy, I'll be able to identify her right away. If you interview her on her own, and it is Annie, she might be frightened and run away. Then we'd have to start searching for her all over again.'

'Why on earth should she be frightened, Jeremy?' Louis was quick to ask. 'Is there something about this whole business you're not telling me? Did something cause her to go missing? As I understood the situation, from both you and your father, the reason you are so worried about her is because she's normally very conscientious, both about keeping in touch and also coming back when she said she would.'

'It's absolutely true that she's normally very reliable about keeping in touch with Father,' said Jeremy, after a slight pause. 'If she is posing as Roxy, I have absolutely no idea why. I just thought that me being able to identify Annie, if that's who she is, would be less traumatic for her than being interviewed by the police.'

'As a rule, I'm not in the habit of traumatising the people I interview,' said Louis, tersely. 'Still, as you wish. Would you like me to book a hotel? As you're likely to be late, I would suggest Tregenna Castle, where you have parking on-site.'

'Yes, please. I'm sorry, Louis, I didn't mean to imply that you would frighten Annie.'

'Forget it,' said Louis, shortly. 'I'll text you confirmation of the hotel booking.'

Louis made an online hotel booking, emailed Jeremy the details and then continued on his journey. Now, though, the optimism he'd felt earlier had evaporated somewhat. Jeremy was not telling him everything; there was definitely something he was withholding.

In fact, there were two pieces of information Jeremy had not disclosed to Louis. His father had heard from Mrs Ashley, their housekeeper in Devon, that Len Carter had been threatening and almost violent in order to extract information from her. This was exactly what Louis had warned him about, a warning Jeremy had chosen to ignore. This was why he was so anxious to travel to St Ives – if Annie was posing as Roxy, Jeremy didn't want Len to find her and become violent. Also, Louis's hunch was much more plausible than the chief inspector realised, for Jeremy knew his stepmother had been baptised Roxanne.

Louis Peppiatt's despondency was matched by that of his sergeant. Jack Eddy was deeply sunk in gloom.

'I've never known anything like this, boss,' he said. 'We've had three more missing items just this morning, and none of the shopkeepers have a clue as to who is doing it. I need at least a couple of plain-clothes constables milling about Fore Street, if we're to stand a chance of catching whoever is doing this. I can leave the station unmanned for an hour or two, but I can't spend all day away from my desk. Anyway, I'd stand out like a sore thumb, everyone knows who I am. We need police on the ground acting like store detectives if we're going to catch this bastard.'

'I seem to remember you and Mrs McKenzie reckon there is more than one person involved. Is that still the case?'

'Maybe, boss, mainly because of the volume of theft. They're all low-cost items, but it's hard to imagine one person being able to thieve so much in a comparatively short space of time.'

'What sort of items are being taken?' Louis asked.

'All sorts, boss. Small items of clothing like hats and scarves, also books, cards, ceramics, a lot of trinkets, sweeties, chocolate, toys and fudge. That little maid in Merrin's shop reckons she had a bracelet stolen and then returned to her. Obviously, that can't be right. The trouble is with all this thieving going on, it's not surprising that people are starting to imagine things have been stolen when they haven't.'

'Yes, I heard about Pippa's lost and found story. I agree, it seems far more likely that she temporarily mislaid the bracelet.' At this point, Louis made the decision not to tell Jack that he'd already had his head bitten off by Merrin for tending to agree with his sergeant.

'We're never going to solve this one, boss, unless I get some help,' said Jack, plaintively.

'Alright, I take your point, Eddy. This does seem to have gone beyond the usual petty pilfering. I'll have a word with Sergeant Satchel and see if he can spare a couple of constables for a few days. As you say, if they wander around incognito and keep their eyes peeled, we should be able to solve this one pretty quickly.'

'Thanks, boss,' said Jack, looking decidedly more cheerful.

On his way to Merrin's cottage, Louis stopped off at the West Cornwall Crafts Co-operative. On entering the shop, for a moment he thought he was seeing double. Then he remembered Merrin telling him about her new recruits – elderly, slightly eccentric twin sisters. The shop was busy but so were the twins. One was serving on the till, while the other one was flitting about tidying and dusting, and clearly keeping an eye on the customers. Seeing Louis hovering by the door, she came over.

'Can I help you, sir?' she said. 'Is there anything in particular you're looking for?'

Louis smiled. She might be elderly, but she was charming, full of old-world courtesy.

'Actually, I'm looking for Merrin. Is she upstairs in her studio?'

'No, she's at home today. I can give her a call there, sir, if you'd like to make contact.'

'No, but thank you,' said Louis. 'She is expecting me at the cottage. I was passing so I thought I'd just pop in.' He lowered his voice. 'I'm a policeman, so just checking – have you had anything stolen today?'

'Nothing,' said the twin, triumphantly. 'You see, when there's two of us working, one of us can make sure the customers aren't up to no good.' She winked. 'That's me today, we take it in turns. I'm Beatrice – oh look, my sister's free now, come and meet her.'

Louis was introduced to Constance and solemnly shook hands with both twins. 'My name's Louis Peppiatt, I'm a friend of Merrin's. You probably get asked this all the time, but could your mother tell you apart?'

'Sometimes we tricked her,' said Constance, 'but she was a clever lady and seemed to know instinctively who was who.'

'What a lovely name, Peppiatt,' said Beatrice. 'It must be French.'

'You're right. The Peppiatts were originally Huguenots. Some of them managed to escape St Bartholomew's Massacre and came to England – to London, Devon and Cornwall mostly.' Louis grinned. 'And Constance, your poor mother – fancy playing tricks on her, that's terrible!'

'She loved it!' the twins said in unison.

'Tell me,' said Louis, 'do you both think Pippa's bracelet was stolen and then replaced, or do you believe she just put it somewhere safe and forgot? Actually, before you answer the question, Constance, as I've already told your sister, I'm a policeman, though not strictly speaking on duty at the moment.'

'Definitely stolen,' said Constance, with Beatrice nodding alongside. 'Pippa doesn't carry much stock and it's all on display in her glass cabinet. She has nowhere else to keep her jewellery. We know it sounds odd, but it disappeared and then someone put it back, and we're sure it wasn't dear Pippa.'

'Well,' said Louis, as Merrin opened her door to him, 'I'm now totally under the spell of your lovely twins. They're an absolute hoot, but I can see they take their job very seriously and are wonderful with customers. What a find!'

'I know,' said Merrin. 'We all adore them. Come on in, Louis, you look tired. Tea and biscuits coming up. So, what's happened since we spoke?'

'Nothing good, really,' said Louis, making a fuss of William. 'I lie – one, no, two pieces of good news. Jack Eddy is no longer sunk in gloom, as I have authorised for him to have two constables to help beat the current crime wave in Fore Street. Secondly, Beatrice, or was it Constance, assured me that nothing has been taken from your shop today.'

'The thief wouldn't dare with those two in charge!' said Merrin. 'Here's your tea, and remember to give Horatio a piece of your biscuit.' She put a hand on his shoulder and gave it a shake. 'So come on, what's up?'

Louis told her about his conversation with Jeremy Eustace. 'Why would me asking Annie who she really is frighten her so much that she might run away again – if, that is, she really is Annie? I'm not an ogre, am I?'

'Not too often,' said Merrin, smiling. 'All I would say is that the confident woman Roxy appeared to be when she first arrived in St Ives seems to have vanished. She is nervy and defensive, which makes her sound more like Annie.'

'Hmm. I'm tempted to go round to Max's now, find out where Roxy is and confront her. Get the whole thing out in the open, one way or another.'

'But wouldn't it all be so much simpler if you waited for Jeremy?' said Merrin. 'If you interview Roxy this afternoon, she can deny she is Annie and there is nothing you can do about it. Whereas tomorrow morning, if she is Annie, Jeremy will recognise her. There'll be no wriggle room. Honestly, Louis, leave it until tomorrow.'

'Maybe you're right,' said Louis.

'I've just thought of a way to persuade you to hurry home. Isla will be here very soon, longing to crow about the fact that, apparently, you are now taking coincidences seriously. I'd run for it if I were you.'

Louis stood up. 'You've provided me with an irrefutable reason to go home. I'll leave a message at Tregenna to say I'll pick up Jeremy at nine o'clock tomorrow morning.'

At the Sloop Inn, having booked a room for a couple of nights, Len Carter went into the bar. It was a busy evening, but during the course of sinking a couple of pints, he managed to show two of the barmen a photograph of Annie, explaining that she now had dark hair. Neither recognised her, though Len realised they were too preoccupied to concentrate fully. He would have to wait until morning, and then do the rounds of all the bars, restaurants and shops.

He walked out onto the Wharf, went in search of some fish and chips, and then found himself a bench where he could watch the world go by, as he ate. He wasn't expecting to spot Annie amongst the crowds but there was no harm in keeping a lookout. It was a cloudy evening, but mild with only a light breeze. The town looked charming, lights reflecting on the water now dusk was approaching, the boats swaying gently at anchor and the waves murmuring in the background as they reached the shore. *Well*, he thought to himself, *if the wretched woman had to run away, she picked a pretty decent spot. And the pursuit of her is all expenses paid.*

CHAPTER TWENTY-SEVEN

'So, you decided to wait for me before interviewing this woman who might be Annie?' said Jeremy, when Louis picked him up from Tregenna Castle the following morning. 'Look, I'm very sorry if I offended you yesterday by suggesting you might frighten her.'

'Let's not worry about that now,' said Louis. 'Let's just concentrate on establishing the identity of this woman called Roxy. The situation is this. I have absolutely no idea where Roxy is staying at the moment. However, she has chummed up with a chap called Max Richards, who is a local estate agent. We are going to his office now in the hopes he will tell us where she is.'

'This Max fellow, are you suggesting that Roxy is having an affair with him? Because if so, I'm sure she won't be Annie. Annie is devoted to my father.'

'So devoted that she appears to have run away?' asked Louis.

'We don't know for sure that she has run away,' Jeremy

said. 'For all we know, she could be dead in a ditch somewhere. My father is dying and I want to find his wife so that she can be with him at the end. That's all that matters.'

Louis had driven down onto the Wharf and parked in the first loading bay. He turned off the engine, unbuckled his seat belt and turned to Jeremy. 'I don't doubt your motives for wanting to find Annie, Jeremy. I just found it very odd that you thought if I interviewed the lady in question, and she was Annie, she would be frightened and might run away. As I've said, there is no point in discussing this further until we know if we've found your stepmother, but I don't believe you've told me everything about the reason for Annie's disappearance. Now, let's go and find Max.'

The two men walked up to Fore Street in a rather loaded silence. Jeremy was clearly not going to challenge Louis's doubts. They entered Max's agency to find him sitting behind his desk, talking on the phone.

'Hello, Chief Inspector,' he said, pointing to the phone. 'I won't be a moment. Take a seat.'

Louis and Jeremy sat down. Max appeared to be arguing with a surveyor who had clearly submitted a rather unsatisfactory survey on a property Max was trying to sell. At last, Max seemed to convince the surveyor to take another look at his report.

'The trouble with surveyors,' said Max, having finished the call, 'is they feel that in order to justify their fee, they have to find a multitude of things wrong with a property. They don't seem to realise that a satisfactory report is as valuable as an unsatisfactory one – more so, in fact. Nice to see you again, Chief Inspector. What can I do for you? Are you thinking of moving to St Ives?'

Louis stood up. 'No such luck, I'm afraid. I'm here on police business. It concerns a lady named Roxy, with whom I believe you are acquainted. This gentleman here is Jeremy Eustace. We believe that Roxy may in fact be Jeremy's stepmother, who went missing from home over three weeks ago. Can you tell us where we might find her, please? Mr Eustace needs to get in touch with her regarding an urgent family matter.'

Max stared at Louis. 'I don't understand,' he said. 'Why would Roxy pretend to be someone else?'

'She pretended to be Tony Barrow's wife, as I understand it, so it would appear she has something of a track record for claiming to be someone she isn't,' said Louis.

'I'm afraid I can't help you,' said Max; his expression was stony. 'Roxy left St Ives several days ago in order to return to London.' He turned to Jeremy. 'If she is who you say she is, Mr Eustace, then she should be back home with you by now. Have you checked?'

'I only left London yesterday afternoon,' said Jeremy, 'and she certainly hadn't come home when I left. Besides which, my father knows I'm searching for her down here and would have called me immediately if she'd turned up.'

'Then, with respect, Mr Eustace, I would suggest that Roxy is not your missing stepmother,' said Max.

'And with respect, Max,' said Louis, 'Merrin says she saw you and Roxy together in town just two nights ago. Where is she, please?'

'I don't know, Chief Inspector,' said Max.

'Then give me the address of where she was staying.

Please don't pretend you didn't fix her up with some accommodation – you'll only be embarrassing yourself, because I know you did.'

'I found her an Airbnb in Fish Street.' Max returned to his desk and scribbled something down on a business card. 'Here's the address. By all means go and check it out, but you'll find she left several days ago, as I said.'

'Thank you,' said Louis, 'I'll do that. All I would say, Max, is that Jeremy's father is dying and is desperate to see his wife once more before he does. If Roxy is the missing wife, it is unspeakably cruel of you not to tell us of her whereabouts and deny an old man his dying wish. I certainly wouldn't like that on my conscience. Jeremy, please show Mr Richards the photograph.'

Jeremy produced the photograph of Annie and handed it to Max. 'My stepmother,' he said.

'Well?' said Louis.

'This photo looks nothing like Roxy,' Max said to Jeremy, handing back the photograph. 'Your stepmother is clearly fair. Roxy has dark hair. They are certainly not the same person. I'm very sorry about your father, but I'm afraid I can't help you any further.'

Louis and Jeremy made the short walk to Fish Street, again in silence. The landlady, a Mrs Jenkins, was able to confirm that Roxy had stayed with her for three nights and that Max had paid the bill. Roxy had explained to her that she had lost all her vital possessions on a boat she had been unable to trace, and that she was going home soon. 'To London, I think she mentioned,' said Mrs Jenkins.

Louis took Jeremy to the Sloop for a coffee. It was still

early enough for the main bar to be nearly empty. They seated themselves in a quiet corner.

'I'm sorry, Louis,' said Jeremy. 'I should have told you everything I know, but I haven't told my father either, and it seemed disloyal to tell you but not him.'

'Go on,' said Louis.

'My father is not an easy man, as I expect you remember. He always believes himself to be right, and annoyingly, he's usually right about that too.' Jeremy allowed himself a small smile. 'But where Annie is concerned, he's different – softer, kinder. He just adores her.'

'Does that make you jealous of Annie?' Louis asked. 'I wouldn't blame you, given you lost your mother so young.'

'Not at all,' said Jeremy, and Louis could see he meant it. 'Annie brought so much happiness to our miserable family of two. She'd lost her parents as well, so she understood me and I believe loves us both, Father and me. The trouble is that Father gave her everything she ever wanted, and to start with it was fine. However, in reality, she never has joined the real world – she's still a child in most respects, totally untouched by life's ups and downs.'

'Not a reason to run away,' Louis countered.

'She has a friend called Alice. They've been friends since early childhood, and Alice has always been critical of Father. I believe she's jealous of Annie's life. Anyway, Alice has recently had a baby and, as I understand it, this made Annie long for a baby too – the one thing, of course, in his state of health, that my father can no longer give her. Alice told Annie she was being suffocated by my father and that she should go and find herself a younger man who can give her a child.'

'How did you find out about all this?' Louis asked.

'I contacted Alice when we realised that Annie had disappeared. She was quite frank about admitting she told Annie to make a new life for herself, but she has no idea what her plans were. I also sent Len Carter to see Alice and she told him the same thing.'

'Does Len also believe Annie is in St Ives?' Louis asked, anxiously.

'I shouldn't think so for a moment. I can't see how anyone can imagine she's down here, except you, of course.'

'I'm beginning to have doubts myself,' said Louis. 'Maybe Max is right, and Roxy really is nothing to do with Annie.'

'Well, I think she is and for that reason, I'd like to stay on in St Ives for a little longer to continue the search.'

'You do realise that this really isn't a police matter, if Annie is running away from her husband?' said Louis. 'I'm going back to Truro this morning to do some proper police work. Wives and husbands leave one another all the time for a million different reasons. Annie is doing nothing illegal by deserting her husband. Now you've told me about Alice and her probable influence over Annie, it seems increasingly likely that Annie's disappearance does not suggest foul play of any sort. It seems likely that she wants a new life, and that, from where the law stands, is her right.'

'There is one other thing I haven't told you, Louis,' said Jeremy. 'Annie didn't like the name her parents baptised her, so from a very young age, she insisted on being called Annie instead.'

'So in what name was she baptised?' Louis asked.

'Roxanne,' said Jeremy.

So Merrin was right, thought Louis.

CHAPTER TWENTY-EIGHT

Len Carter ate a solitary breakfast later than he'd meant to. A few more beers had followed his fish and chips and his head was paying the price this morning. He'd just finished his coffee and was not looking forward to the thankless task of touring St Ives in search of Annie, when one of the barmen from the previous evening approached him.

'Hi mate, last night you showed me the photo of a woman you're looking for. I've been thinking about it – could I have another look?'

Len delved into his jacket pocket and produced the photograph of Annie. 'I think I mentioned last night that since the photograph was taken, she has dyed her hair, which is now dark brown.'

'It's a shame she did that. I like a blonde. Do you mind if I just take the photo to the light?'

'Be my guest,' said Len.

The young man returned a few moments later. 'I knew I recognised her. She's Max Richards's new squeeze. He brought her in a few nights ago, I can't remember which now, we've been that busy.'

'Never mind about which day,' said Len. 'Where will I find this Max Richards?'

'He's the local estate agent. He has an office halfway up Fore Street, on the right-hand side going from here.' He glanced at his watch. 'He should be open now.'

Len rose to his feet and took a twenty-pound note out of his wallet. 'Thank you so much for your help,' he said, 'have a drink on me.'

'There's no need for that.'

'I'm a private investigator, I can put it on expenses,' Len assured him.

'Thanks a lot. I've just remembered: her name's Roxy. She's not in any trouble, is she?'

'No,' said Len. 'Her old man's not well. I just need to tell her.'

Max was deeply shaken by the visit from Louis and Jeremy. It was true, the photograph did not look much like Roxy, but that was largely because of the different hair colour. In his heart though, he knew there were too many similarities to ignore. There were already several aspects to this woman named Roxy that were concerning him, the most pressing being that she appeared to have no past. She refused to talk about her background or her family. She would not tell him precisely where she lived, other than to say her home was in London. She seemed to have no job and currently no money, since Tony Barrow had inadvertently made off with her bank cards. That again seemed odd – she did not appear anxious to track him down for their return, or to contact her bank. It was as if she was trying to obliterate everything and everyone that had existed before her arrival in St Ives. This somehow made it feel as if the search for the mythical Annie could be linked to Roxy. Then there was Louis Peppiatt. Max had only met him a few times but had liked him immediately and believed him to be someone who could be trusted. Merrin had great faith in him, too. If Louis believed this hunt for Annie could be connected to Roxy, Max was inclined to sit up and take notice.

Max realised he was feeling rather jittery, generally nervous and confused. In his long and impressive list of relationships with women, he had never felt so immediately committed to anyone as he did to Roxy. This unusual sense of devotion made him feel vulnerable and he had developed an overriding desire to protect her – from what, he had no idea. Work now felt out of the question, so he decided he would shut up shop for a few hours. He was walking towards the door, intent on displaying the closed sign and locking up, when a man burst through the door and stood before him.

'Max Richards?' the man barked.

Max stared at him in surprise. He cut an unusual figure. He was neatly and formally dressed, but somehow the clothes looked wrong on him. He was playing a part and to Max, he immediately looked dangerous.

'I am he,' Max replied, with a slightly forced smile. 'How can I help you, sir?'

'My name is Len Carter. I'm a private investigator, hired to find the whereabouts of a certain young woman named Annie Eustace. I have reason to believe that a woman who recently arrived in St Ives and is known as Roxy is, in all probability, Annie. I gather Roxy is a friend of yours, and I urgently need to contact her because, if she is Annie, her husband is dying.'

A husband, another one! Max was shocked into silence, not least because Roxy had promised him she was not married when she told him about her relationship with Tony Barrow. Surely she wouldn't have lied to him twice about something so significant.

'I knew Roxy,' Max said at last, 'but I haven't seen her for days. I believe she has gone home to London.'

'You were seen in the Sloop with Roxy two nights ago,' lied Len.

The lie paid off. 'I'm sure it was longer ago than that,' said Max, lamely.

The veneer of a well-dressed businessman disappeared. 'Look, chum, I haven't come all this way to be messed about. I am certain your Roxy is in fact Lady Annie Eustace, and I need to talk to her now. So cut the crap and tell me where she is, or you'll be very, very sorry.'

Len was shorter than Max, but Max could see the power in his chest and shoulders and could feel the unmistakable sense of menace. He rallied as best he could – Max could be a hard-headed businessman, but physical violence was completely alien to him.

He smiled his best customer smile. 'I'd like to help you, I really would, but you know how it is. I met this woman Roxy just over a week ago. We had a fling. There was absolutely no commitment on either side. When she left, she didn't give me her contact details. Would you believe, I don't even know her surname. We had a lot of fun but that's all it was, and I have to say her behaviour didn't seem much like a *Lady Eustace* to me.'

Len pulled out his photograph and handed it to Max. 'Before you say anything, I know Annie has recently dyed her hair a dark brown, so don't try saying she can't be the lady in the photograph because she's fair. Take a good look, pal.'

The photograph was a lot better quality than the one Louis had shown him. It also looked a lot more recent – if it wasn't Roxy, it was her blonde twin sister. Max tried to keep his expression neutral. 'A lovely-looking girl, but definitely not Roxy,' he managed.

'You're lying,' said Len. 'I know Annie is still in this town, and I also know you know where she is. I'll find her, because you're going to help me. To continue with this farce of yours could prove very dangerous for your health.'

At that moment, a middle-aged couple entered the shop. Max hurriedly turned to them. 'Good morning,' he said. 'How can I help you?'

'Please,' said the lady, 'this gentleman was first.'

'It's alright,' said Max. 'We have concluded this gentleman's business.'

'Until the next time,' said Len, snatching the photograph from Max and barrelling his way out of the door.

'Oh dear,' said the lady. 'I hope we haven't lost you a customer.'

'I think you probably have,' said Max with a faint smile, 'and I'm very grateful.'

Leading out of Max's office was a tiny kitchenette, which he used to serve his potential clients with coffee or tea.

For when a particularly successful sale was concluded, he also had a small fridge in which he kept a supply of decent Cava. Behind the door into the kitchenette was another door, which could not be seen from the street, and which led, via a flight of stairs, to the flat above, where Max lived.

Max quickly got rid of the couple who had saved him from Len Carter – they were a nice pair but, like many visitors, were only really fantasising about moving to live in St Ives. As soon as they'd left, Max walked into Fore Street and checked in both directions to make sure there was no sign of Len. Then he quickly shut and locked the door, put up the closed sign, hurried into the kitchenette, closing this door as well, and ran up the stairs to his flat. Roxy was waiting for him.

She was sitting on his sofa, leafing through a magazine, an empty coffee cup on the table in front of her.

She looked up and smiled. 'There was a lot of shouting going on down there a while back. Has some big bad wolf blown down someone's house?'

For the first time in their brief relationship, Max was irritated. 'Is your real name Lady Annie Eustace, and are you married?' he blurted out, his voice hard.

There was only the slightest of pauses. 'Why would you think that, Max darling?'

'Please don't play games with me, Roxy, or whoever you are. I've had three people in my office in the last half-hour, all asking if you're really Annie Eustace – a chief inspector of police, someone called Jeremy who claims to be your stepson, and a private investigator who has threatened me with grievous bodily harm unless I tell him where you are. I think, in the circumstances, you owe me an explanation – don't you?'

Roxy met his eye. 'Yes, I was Lady Annie Eustace, and I am still technically married to Sir Hubert Eustace. He's not very well at the moment. He has cancer.'

'Your husband is dying,' said Max, brutally. 'They're trying to find you so you can be with him when the poor bugger snuffs it.'

'He's not really dying,' said Roxy. 'He's responding very well to treatment. That private investigator you mentioned – well, Hubert will have employed him to find me and used his illness as the reason for doing so. But I can't go back to my former life, I just can't.'

'Are you going to tell me why?' Max asked.

Roxy patted the sofa beside her. 'Come and sit down and I'll tell you everything. You're right, I owe you that, and a whole lot more. Please, darling, let me explain, or at least try to.'

Reluctantly, Max sat down on the sofa, leaving as much space as possible between himself and Roxy. 'I am prepared to listen,' he said, 'provided there are no more lies. If you can't commit to telling me the absolute truth, then I'd like you to pack your bags now and go back to your poor husband.'

'I promise to tell you the truth,' said Roxy, meeting his eye, 'but I'm never going back to my *poor husband*, as you describe him.'

'Why not? Even if he's not dying, he's certainly not well. Did he beat you, subject you to coercive control? Was he unfaithful to you, or just downright cruel and uncaring?'

'None of those things. He just killed me with kindness,'

said Roxy, now clearly close to tears.

'That doesn't sound like much of a reason for leaving the poor chap to die alone,' said Max.

'Then, darling, let me explain,' said Roxy. 'My parents were great friends with Hubert and his first wife, Cynthia. Tragedy hit both families. Cynthia was killed in a hit and run when their son, Jeremy, was only six years old. Some years later, my parents were killed in a freak speedboat accident. I was nineteen at the time and an only child. Hubert acted as my guardian, sorting out all the financial and legal implications surrounding my parents' deaths. The three remaining members of our two families became close, and then closer still when Hubert and I fell in love. We married when I was twenty, Hubert was forty-five and Jeremy was thirteen. I think all three of us found great comfort in being together, which acted as solace for our respective losses.'

'The age gap between you and Hubert seems a little extreme, but otherwise the arrangement seems ideal,' said Max. 'So what went wrong?'

'Nothing, absolutely nothing,' said Roxy. 'I understand that Hubert was a very tough businessman, but to me, he was kindness itself and he gave me everything I wanted. Whether it was new clothes, a snazzy sports car, an exotic holiday, a party, the best tickets for the theatre, Wimbledon, pop concerts – literally anything I desired, I got.'

She smiled, suddenly. 'I remember in my very early twenties, I decided I wanted to get a job. I'd always loved clothes and fashion and so I went for an interview at a very smart haute couture fashion house in New Bond Street. I was very nervous and instead of explaining I had come for the interview, I panicked and ordered the most marvellous dress for our upcoming Christmas party. It must have cost a fortune. Instead of being angry, Hubert laughed a great deal and then said, "Please, darling, don't go looking for another job – I can't afford it!"'

'So, clearly a kind and generous man, and after all he's done for you, you don't feel the need to be with him now he's so ill? I just don't get it, Roxy.'

'I understand what you're saying. At the beginning of our marriage, everything was marvellous. I was treated like a pampered child, and in most respects, I was still a child. But I'm thirty-eight now and I feel suffocated, forced to live in an unreal world. As we grew older, the age gap between us became more obvious and about five years ago, Hubert was diagnosed with cancer and our sex life became non-existent. After a while, I began having the odd affair. I don't know if Hubert realises but I suppose I'm so used to him giving me everything I want, I assumed, or at least kidded myself, he wouldn't mind.'

'So, a lack of sex is what made you decide to leave Hubert?' said Max, harshly.

'No. I have a friend called Alice, who I've known since we were children. She has nagged me for years, saying I have a good brain, I should be doing something positive with my life, instead of being happy to be treated like a pampered child. Anyway, Alice married only a couple of years ago and now has a baby, a little girl, who's four months old now. I'm going to be her godmother,' Roxy added proudly.

'So now you want a baby, and for the first time, poor old Hubert isn't going to be able to give you what you want. Tell me, was I being eyed up as a prospective father?'

'The odd affairs I've had in the last few years have been meaningless – until, that is, I met you,' said Roxy.

'I'm very glad to hear it,' said Max, 'if Tony Barrow is an example of the sort of man you've been going for.'

'He was a terrible mistake,' Roxy admitted, 'but I couldn't resist his invitation to sail to Cornwall. I do love sailing.'

'It's the same old story: you're so used to getting everything you want, you settled for a relationship with a drunken idiot in order to get a sailing trip. Now you're prepared to saddle yourself with another much older man – Roxy, I'm only four years younger than Hubert – in order to have a baby. Has it ever occurred to you that it's not normal to get everything you've ever wanted? It's not healthy either and after a while, I imagine, not even fun – "*to travel hopefully is a better thing than to arrive*" is a great truth, in my view.'

'Of course I realise all that. It's why I must leave Hubert,' said Roxy. 'So, I've changed my name, changed my hair, changed the way I dress – and it's why I love the idea of being married to an estate agent in St Ives, living a simple life. I've been happier with you since we've been together than I've ever been in my entire life. I love you, Max darling, really, really love you and if we can have a baby, that would be a bonus, but it's you I want, you who I can't bear to be without.'

'But what about Hubert, and how does Jeremy fit in with all this?'

'They'll be fine without me. Jeremy's happily married with a baby on the way, so the Eustace line will continue, which is important for Hubert. I can't involve Hubert in a divorce. He'd hate that, but you and I could live together until, until . . .'

'Until he dies,' said Max, dully.

Roxy stood up. 'Darling, I'm going to have a shower and get dressed. I know what I've told you is a lot to take in but I promised you the truth and that's what you've got, warts and all. Whatever you decide, I'm Roxy now and I'm going to revert to my maiden name, which is Goodenough.' She laughed a little. 'Maybe I'm not *good enough* for you, but please, while you think things through, never doubt for a moment how much I love you.'

Max watched Roxy Goodenough as she walked across his sitting room, stopping as she exited the room to give him a little wave. Over the years, there had been many girls who had wanted their relationship with him to become permanent, and he had always run away. Yet here he was, actually considering a future with Roxy, who was still married, ridiculously spoilt and being pursued by three people, one of whom was a seriously nasty piece of work. He thought, briefly, about talking things over with Merrin, but she was too close to Louis and impeccably honest. If Louis asked her for any information on Roxy, she would feel honour-bound to tell him everything she knew.

No, he knew he would have to work this out for himself.

CHAPTER TWENTY-NINE

Merrin had risen early, walked William and then settled down in her studio for a couple of hours of potting. She had hoped to hear from Louis as to how things had gone with Max, but it was after midday when she finished clearing up her studio and there was still no word from him. On impulse, she detoured past Max's office on her way home. The office was closed, which was very unlike him, particularly as the season was now in full swing. Max might not be disciplined where women were concerned, but he was very dedicated to his work.

Once home, having made a fuss of both William and Horatio, she put the kettle on the Aga. She stood, waiting for it to boil, and was wondering whether she should call Louis when her mobile rang.

'I thought I should bring you up to date with regard to Roxy,' said Louis. 'Are you in the shop? Is this a bad moment?'

'It's perfect,' said Merrin. 'I've just got home and was

wondering whether I dared phone you. I've just walked past Max's office and it's closed, which is very unlike him.'

Louis related the details of his and Jeremy's meeting with Max. 'Did you believe him when he said Roxy had left St Ives?' Merrin asked.

'I'm sorry because I know he's a close friend of yours, but honestly, thinking about it on the way home, I certainly don't believe he was telling me the whole truth. Anyway, I had a coffee with Jeremy afterwards and he pretty much confirmed that Annie has run away from the marriage, egged on by some friend of hers who'd just had a baby.'

'Does that mean that Annie wants a baby too?' Merrin asked.

'I suppose so. Anyway, based on what Jeremy said, I have taken the decision that it is not a police matter. Jeremy still believes that Roxy is Annie and is staying in St Ives for a couple of days to see if he can find her. There was just one odd thing which came up. Annie was baptised Roxanne but didn't like her name, and so the family have always called her Annie. So, Mrs McKenzie, you were absolutely right about the link between the two names.'

'Surely that nails it? Roxy must be Annie. It definitely has to be more than one of your much-despised coincidences, Chief Inspector.'

Louis laughed. 'Yes, but please don't mention that word! Either way, whether Annie is calling herself Roxy or not, it really isn't a police matter, so I'm out.'

'I understand,' said Merrin. 'I wonder what happened to Tony Barrow and whether he will come back to St Ives in search of Roxy.'

'The guy I spoke to at St Katharine Docks said that Tony

often did some work around the docks but also frequently went to France to work. I expect that's where he is now.'

'It's odd,' said Merrin, 'but every time I've spoken to Roxy about Tony, she seems totally unconcerned about his whereabouts, despite the fact he appears to have never arrived in Scilly. I appreciate she's subsequently become besotted with Max, but still . . . if there was a chance that a man in my life might have drowned and was being eaten by crabs, I'd be very concerned.'

'That's good to know. I'm a man and sort of in your life, so you would be anxious if you thought the crabs were nibbling away at me?' Louis asked.

'Oh no, not in your case, you don't count,' said Merrin.

'Charming!' said Louis.

'You don't count because awful things are always happening to you – getting stabbed, shot at and beaten up. The crabs would be just one more thing to worry about. If I concerned myself with your safety, I'd never sleep again.'

'I'm trying to work out if that's reassuring or not. I think you're saying you would care if you could separate the man from the job, but you've got it all wrong. The dangers of the job are nothing compared with being a father. I'm only in really serious danger when Daisy puts me in goal so she can practise her penalty shoot-outs. I never save a single goal. I spend my entire time ducking and diving to try and avoid being taken out by a bloody ball travelling at a hundred miles an hour. Still, I'd better go, but I think this is a conversation worth pursuing.'

'Maybe,' said Merrin. 'Speak soon?'

'Absolutely,' said Louis.

* * *

Louis ended the call and sat at his desk, deep in thought. Merrin had accepted, with apparent ease, that the Roxy affair was no longer a police matter, which had surprised him. Though she was clearly still concerned about Max, it seemed that she too recognised that it was a domestic matter. Obviously Max had not confided in her with regard to Roxy and her whereabouts, so maybe she felt it best to leave Max and his love life well alone. She must be well used to Max's romantic dramas.

Yet despite the fact that it was very much his decision to drop the case, something was niggling away in Louis's brain; but for the life of him, he could not identify what was worrying him. He went through, in his mind, the information he had been told, true and false. He believed now that Jeremy had told him everything he knew, and surely that should be the end to it – a spoilt wife who had left her husband, despite his illness, to start a new life under an assumed new name to avoid her husband tracking her down. A story as old as time – but there were inconsistencies. Opening his notepad, Louis listed them.

Roxy told everyone that she and Tony had argued their last night on board Llamedos *because Tony wanted to go to Scilly and Roxy wanted to go back to London. So why didn't she go back to London when Tony left St Ives?*

With Tony having sailed off with her bank cards, phone and laptop, why did Roxy make so little effort to find him and therefore them?

Why does Clara's story about seeing the tender attached to Llamedos contradict Roxy's version of her rowing ashore in the harbour after the row with Tony?

Louis stared at what he had written down. All of this, all these doubts, he realised, revolved around Tony Barrow, and as Merrin had said, it was odd that Roxy was so unconcerned about his whereabouts. So, where was Tony, and could he perhaps have anything important to say about Roxy?

Decision made, Louis picked up his phone. He would put out a general alert in UK and French waters for a sighting of Tony's yacht. That accomplished, unless Tony turned up, there really was nothing more to be done.

CHAPTER THIRTY

When Roxy re-entered Max's sitting room an hour later, she found him exactly where she'd left him, slumped on the sofa. She had used the hour well – she looked stunning, her dark hair sleek and shining, her make-up startling but impeccable. She wore a black and silver top over black leggings, which accentuated her long legs.

Max could not help himself. 'You look wonderful,' he said.

Roxy smiled and came and sat beside him. 'That was the idea,' she said. 'I wanted to look my best in case you had decided to throw me out into the wicked old world.'

'I'm not going to do that,' said Max, 'but I've had some thoughts. Firstly, we know your stepson Jeremy is in town. I can call Louis Peppiatt, the policeman, and find out where Jeremy is staying. Why not go and see him and talk things through? Your wish to stay here with me is much too impulsive. Maybe you could travel back to London with

Jeremy and sort things out with Hubert, and also check out how bad his health really is.'

'I'm not going back, not ever. If I went back now, I'd never get away again,' said Roxy.

'But why?' said Max. 'Don't tell me your husband would imprison you. He clearly dotes on you, he's not going to hurt you, is he?'

'No, of course not. How do I describe it? I'm like some hothouse plant, who has escaped from the greenhouse and found out that not only is the fresh air outside wonderful, but also survivable. If I go back now, even if poor Hubert dies, I'll still find it impossible to leave the life I've become so used to. I'll never leave, I'm too weak.'

'So, what you're actually saying is that you're afraid to go back because returning to the lap of luxury, having everything you want, when you want it, is like a drug?' said Max.

'You make me sound very shallow, but you're probably right,' said Roxy. 'However, that doesn't mean I don't want to lead a different life, it's why I left. I long for it, and now I know what I want – it's a life with you, here. But I must never risk going back.'

'And as for the baby idea, Roxy, it's madness. I'm far too old to be a father, and to be honest, it's not something I've ever aspired to be.'

'A child would keep you young, darling, and just think what a marvellous life our child would have. You could teach him or her to sail, to fish, to surf – think how much fun that would be.'

'I'd be in my late sixties by then,' said Max, 'older than

Hubert is now. You're just ricocheting about – a few weeks ago, you left Hubert and started a relationship with Tony Barrow. He disappeared, so you immediately transferred your affections to me. You're just moving from one crisis to the next. You can't possibly know whether you want to commit yourself to a life with me, you don't know me. I can be a grumpy old bugger – ask Merrin, she'll tell you what I'm really like.'

'Max, just tell me one thing – do you love me? Or maybe, putting it another way, do you believe you could love me?'

Max shifted in his seat. 'I do want to care for you and protect you.'

'Well, then . . . ?' said Roxy.

Max stood up and smiled. 'I can't think straight any more, not least because I've had no breakfast. A man can't be expected to make life-changing decisions on an empty stomach. I'll go out and find us a couple of pizzas and a bottle of wine. How does that sound?'

'Perfect, darling.'

'And don't go outside or even downstairs into the office. I don't like the look of that private investigator,' said Max.

'He's hardly going to drag me back to London by my hair, is he?' said Roxy.

'Maybe not, but he's a thug, who's already threatened me with violence. Just stay safe until I get back.'

Max collected a couple of pizzas and then walked down to John's Wine Shop, where he dithered over what wine to buy. He finally settled on a light, dry white, as it was the middle of the day, and was just paying for it when he realised his indecision had been caused by the fact that he was not in a hurry to go home. The mess that was Roxy's life, the pressure he felt at apparently being responsible for her fate, was all too much. He was exhausted. On impulse, he bought a glass of wine and sat down at a little table, with a splendid view of the harbour. It was a view he'd known and cherished all his life and instantly, it calmed him.

The tide was way out and, unbidden, flashes of his childhood came back to him. He thought of playing on the sand as a very young boy, with Clara, Merrin and Merrin's brother Jago; of pier jumping, particularly with Jago; and later, when his father bought him a little dinghy, of sailing adventures, all four of them together. He sipped his wine and relaxed a little. What had suddenly made him dredge up those memories? he wondered. It must be Roxy's talk of a baby, he supposed. Was he too old to be a father? He was fairly fit for his age, not overweight; he didn't smoke and drank only moderately. Maybe Roxy was right, and a child would keep him young – and heavens above, wasn't it time he settled down? Financially, he had been cautious and therefore had reasonably good savings, by Cornish standards. Perhaps now, he should think about taking on an assistant so he could spend more time with his family. *His family*! What was he thinking about? He didn't have a family.

He finished his wine, his mind made up. Although he didn't approve, if Roxy was absolutely certain that she didn't want to return to her home and Hubert, he would try and help her realise that decision. They needed to convince the private investigator, Len, and also Jeremy, that she was not going back to Hubert. Hopefully, Louis would lose interest. If not, Max thought, he would have to take Merrin into his confidence and see if she could help him to persuade Louis to drop the case – which was nothing more than a domestic, after all. He would not commit to a permanent relationship with Roxy, and certainly not a baby, until things sorted themselves out. In the meantime, he would care for and protect her, as he had promised he would.

Feeling more confident now a decision was made, Max stepped outside John's and virtually bumped into Len Carter.

'You took your time in there,' said Len, aggressively.

'Are you following me?' Max asked.

'Of course I'm following you,' said Len. 'I know you're hiding Annie somewhere, and I'm going to continue to hound you until you take me to her. Look at you, who do you think you're kidding, pal? Two pizzas and a bottle of wine – don't even try telling me all of that is just for you. It's a meal for two and we both know who you'll be sharing it with.'

Max thought quickly. 'You're wrong,' he said. 'I'm taking this to share with my friend, Merrin, who lives up Bunkers Hill. Come with me, if you don't believe me.'

'I don't believe you, but presumably this Merrin is a good friend and will cover for you. I'm staying in the Sloop, and I'm not leaving St Ives until I can take Annie Eustace back to her husband, however long it takes. I have undertaken to do a job, and I will see it through, despite you.'

Max pushed past Len and headed up Fore Street. Turning off at Bunkers Hill, he glanced over his shoulder to see that Len was following him up the street. He turned the corner and sprinted up the stone steps to Merrin's cottage, aware that Len was blatantly watching him. Max knocked on the door, wondering what he was going to do if Merrin was out. Mercifully, she opened the door.

'Max—' she began.

'Don't say a word, just let me in,' said Max in little more than a whisper.

Merrin didn't need telling twice. She stood back to let Max in and then firmly shut and bolted the door behind him.

Merrin studied Max in silence for a moment, taking in the pizzas, the wine and the wild look in his eyes.

'I imagine the delicious pizzas and wine are not intended to be shared with me,' she said, with a kindly smile.

Max let out a sigh and sat down at Merrin's kitchen table. 'No,' he admitted. 'I'm trying to take them back to Roxy but there's a nasty private investigator following me about, so I've had to pretend I was coming to see you. Sorry.'

'No problem,' said Merrin, cheerfully, 'it's what friends are for. So, Roxy is still in St Ives then? Louis was told she had gone back to London, I believe.'

'I lied,' said Max.

'I know,' said Merrin, 'and so does Louis.'

'Oh Lord, I thought I might not have convinced him. What's he going to do about it?'

'Nothing, I think,' said Merrin, 'he reckons it's not a police matter.'

'I was hoping that might be his conclusion,' said Max.

'So, as I'm going to be given neither a slice of pizza nor a glass of wine, are you going to tell me if Roxy and Annie are one and the same?'

'It's not my secret to tell,' said Max.

'Even if I promise not to tell Louis?'

'That's a promise you can't keep,' said Max. 'I know you wouldn't gossip with anyone, including Louis, but it is possible that this saga may not just fizzle out. If Louis asked you if Roxy was Annie as part of an official police inquiry, you, as a lawyer, would have to tell him everything you knew.'

'That's true,' said Merrin, privately thinking, *Roxy must be Annie or Max wouldn't be making such a fuss about keeping secrets.* 'Well, Max, if you want me to help you evade the nasty private investigator, you're going to have to tell me where you're trying to take your pizzas.'

'I need to get back to the office,' said Max.

'So Roxy's hiding out in your flat?' said Merrin. 'Please don't answer that – let's call it a hypothetical question.'

'I don't see how to get there. The bloody man will either be outside your flat now, or else he'll be waiting outside my office. He comes across as quite a violent sort. I can just imagine him barging into my office and charging upstairs to terrify Roxy.'

'Louis mentioned he was a pretty unpleasant chap,' Merrin said, looking at her watch. 'A thought, Max – it's lunchtime. Do you know where he's staying?'

'Yes, at the Sloop.'

'Stay here a moment,' said Merrin. 'Let me just check the bar and see if he's there. What does he look like?'

'Medium height, forties I would think, but he should

stand out as he's wearing a very traditional dark suit – not normal St Ives gear.'

Merrin disappeared out of the front door and was back within five minutes. 'He's propping up the bar and he's only halfway through his pint. Run for it now, Max, and I'll intercept him if necessary.'

'Bless you, Merrin . . .' Max began.

'Just go, Max, and be careful.'

'Careful of what?'

'Who, not what. Just don't let Roxy take advantage of you – please, Max, please.'

Max had hardly been gone more than a couple of minutes when Merrin's door burst open. It was just Isla returning home, but she found her mother looking white as a sheet and more than a little terrified.

'What's going on, Mum? I've just passed Uncle Max, who refused to stop and talk to me, and you look like you've just seen a ghost.'

'I thought you were someone else – I'll explain later. Come with me, I've got this RNLI collection box that I've ordered for the shop. I want you to stand with it just at the beginning of Fore Street. If a man in a dark suit comes along, I want you to try and get him to put some money in the box. It's a delaying tactic. I'll be there with you and point him out, but you're young and pretty and he's much more likely to stop for you than for me. Come on.'

'For heaven's sake, Mum, you said no more dramas. I'll only do this if you promise me you're not in danger and that you'll tell me everything afterwards.'

'Promise. Quick, Isla.'

Fore Street was busy. 'He was in the Sloop, I just hope we haven't missed him,' Merrin said. 'If he's still there, I'll walk ahead of him as he comes out, and point him out to you as I walk past you. Delay him as long as you can. OK?'

'OK,' said Isla, with a heavy sigh.

They were just in time. As Merrin approached the Sloop, Len Carter came out of the door and made towards Fore Street. Merrin swiftly turned round and walked ahead of him. 'He's just behind me,' she said as she passed Isla.

'Excuse me, sir, could I ask you to make a contribution to the RNLI?' said Isla, sporting her best smile.

'And what is the RNLI, young lady?' Len asked, with a slightly salacious smile.

'The Royal National Lifeboat Institution,' said Isla. 'It's a charity which saves lives at sea.'

'I'd never go to sea,' said Len. 'In fact, I hate boats and water.'

He made to walk past her. 'But sir, we're a small island surrounded by sea. Even if you don't like boating, you may have friends or even family who do. It's such a good cause.'

Len hesitated. 'Very well,' he said, drawing out a five-pound note from his wallet and putting it in Isla's collecting box.

'Thank you very much, sir, very generous of you,' said Isla. 'Enjoy the rest of your day.' She kept up her smile until Len became lost in the crowd. 'Creepy,' she said, as her mother joined her. Unknown to either of them, Len's older brother had joined the Navy at sixteen and died at sea two years later. They couldn't have chosen a better charity.

'Well done, darling,' said Merrin. 'That's definitely given Max enough time to get safely back to his office.'

'*Safely back*? What's going on, Mum?'

Merrin took her daughter's arm. 'Come on back to the cottage and I'll tell you everything.'

CHAPTER THIRTY-ONE

When Max arrived at his office, he hurried through to the back and ran up the stairs. Roxy was now sitting at the kitchen table, one leg propped up on an adjoining chair as she painted her toenails.

'You've been ages. Where have you been?' she asked. 'I'm absolutely starving.'

'I'll put the pizzas in the oven to warm them up. A glass of white?'

'Yes, please. So what took you so long?' Roxy asked, frowning as she concentrated on her nails.

'It took me so long because I had a run-in with that private investigator again,' said Max, tersely. 'Len Carter, his name is. He's staying at the Sloop and says he's not leaving St Ives until he can take you back up to London with him.'

'You didn't tell him where I was, did you?' Toenails abandoned, Roxy suddenly appeared very anxious.

'Of course not, but things can't go on like this. He tried

to follow me but, with Merrin's help, we managed to shake him off. He's not going to give up though, Roxy. No doubt your husband is paying him big bucks to bring you home. I've no clue as to how he knows you're really Annie, but he's certainly very confident as to who you really are. It seems finding you is not enough. Hubert wants you home.'

'I'm not going anywhere, you said this Len was a thug. I'm not going home with anyone, but especially not him. I just won't, not ever.' Roxy was starting to sound like the spoilt child which in many respects she still was.

Max felt his anger mounting. 'This is a ridiculous situation. You can't stay hidden in my flat for ever. Len's not going to give up. Hubert's not going to give up. As I've already suggested, the obvious solution is to make contact with Jeremy. The very least you can do is explain to Jeremy why you've left and then, presumably, the poor sod can pass the news on to his father. Even though, to my mind, that's the coward's way out.'

'What do you mean?' said Roxy angrily. 'The coward's way would be to give in to the pressure and go home, like a good girl. I don't know how many times I have to tell you: I'm not doing that.'

'The honourable way to deal with this situation would be to meet up with Jeremy and go home with him. It won't be easy, but then you can explain to Hubert face to face why you have to leave, rather than creeping away without a word of explanation. Surely, after all he's done for you, you owe him that much?'

'I'm not doing that. I've already told you. I'm staying here in St Ives, with or without you!' shouted Roxy, tears streaming down her face. 'I think you're just fixated on getting rid of me. All this talk of wanting to take care of me and protect me is just a load of old rubbish. You don't really care about me at all, do you, Max?'

'I do care about you,' said Max, wearily. 'Tell me, do you have a solution to your current dilemma?'

'Pay him off,' said Roxy, reaching for some paper towel to wipe her eyes. 'Just pay him off.'

'Who?' asked Max.

'This Len, of course. Jeremy isn't going to stay in St Ives more than a day or two. He has a pregnant wife at home. She's nice, Sophie, but she's quite a tough cookie. If she tells Jeremy to come home, he'll be on the next train. You told me that you thought your policeman friend is unlikely to pursue the matter. That just leaves Len. Just offer him some money to go away and he will. Those sorts of people can always be bought, if the price is right.'

'Roxy, he's not going to come cheap, and where's the money coming from?' Max asked, already knowing the answer.

'I thought you might lend it to me, darling,' said Roxy, anger apparently forgotten as she came and sat down beside Max, snuggling up close to him.

'And how would you propose paying me back?' Max asked. 'Let's face it, Hubert is not going to give you the money to pay off the private investigator he hired, is he?'

'I'll get a job and I can give you all I earn, if I can stay here rent-free for a few months.'

'Working as what?' Max asked.

'I'll find a job. I'm very resourceful. Please, Max, please help me.'

'The pizzas must be ready,' said Max. 'Let's eat them

and drink the wine, in the hopes it will inspire a solution.'

During their meal, Roxy regaled Max with an endless list of all the jobs she thought would suit her. Max concentrated on his pizza and drank most of the wine. He was becoming more and more irritated with Roxy, as it was becoming increasingly obvious that she had no grip on the real world. She had been right in saying she had never really grown up. She was Peter Pan but unlike the lost boy from Neverland, who was prepared to fight his enemy Captain Hook, Roxy was expecting Max to fight her battles for her. How much of his hard-earned cash would Len want? Max wondered.

Finally, he could stand the totally unrealistic chatter no longer. 'Have you ever had a job, Roxy?' he asked.

'Looking after Hubert was a pretty full-time job,' said Roxy, defensively.

'Presumably you had help, though – a cleaner?' Roxy nodded. 'A cook, perhaps?' Roxy nodded again. 'A housekeeper?' Max suggested. Once more Roxy nodded. 'So, what did you do all day?'

'Hubert used to do a great deal of entertaining, and we went out a lot, mostly to dinners, often with important contacts for his business. I had to do a lot of dressing up and chatting to people who were often fearfully dull. Organising parties at home took up a lot of time, and playing the hostess. We were always busy,' she finished, lamely.

'I have decided to go and see Len tonight and try to pay him off, as you suggest,' said Max. 'In my mind I have set a limit as to how much I'm prepared to pay but at this moment, I'm not going to share that information with you, because I suspect you will want to increase the size of the offer. This I will not do. I'll leave here about nine and hopefully I'll find Len propping up the bar in the Sloop.'

'Thank you so much, darling. So masterful, I love that,' said Roxy.

'And now I'm going to bed for a few hours.'

'Oh goody,' said Roxy.

'Alone,' said Max. 'I need to sleep.'

Max left it until nine-fifteen that evening before heading out in search of Len Carter. His siesta had been fitful. He still felt tired and wretched. What on earth was he doing? Trying to pay off a man who was helping a sick husband search for his beloved wife – what sort of moral sense did that make? He knew the answer: none. And yet was it not Roxy's right to be free of a lifestyle she felt she could bear no longer? His mind revolved in ever more confusing circles.

Instead of going straight to the Sloop, he headed up the Digey and turned left at the top of the street so he was soon standing above Porthmeor Beach. He was just in the nick of time to see the sun set. It had been a glorious day and the setting sun put on a show to bring it to a close. The sky was a gorgeous mix of crimson and blue and as the sun slipped below the horizon, Max felt a sudden keen sense of melancholy – a day wasted in futile argument, culminating in, surely, what had to be a shameful decision.

He headed back down the Digey and as he drew near to Merrin's shop, he saw the lights were still on. Maybe he should ask her advice. There really was nothing now to hide. It was obvious that she had guessed Roxy was Annie

Eustace, and she knew that Roxy was staying in his flat. He opened the door to the shop to be confronted by two elderly ladies, so identical that it had to be impossible for anyone to tell them apart.

'Good evening, sir,' they said in unison.

'Good evening, ladies,' he said. 'I'm sorry to disturb you, I can see you're closing up. Is Merrin around?'

'I'm sorry, no,' said one of the twins. 'She was in earlier, but I believe she's having supper with her friends who run Tristan's Fish Plaice.'

'Never mind,' said Max, smiling. 'I'll catch her tomorrow. My name's Max Richards. If you see her before I do, please could you tell her I'd love a quick chat. Enjoy the rest of your evening, ladies.'

'What a handsome man,' said Bea, as Max closed the door behind him.

'Much too young for you, dear,' said Connie.

As anticipated, Len Carter was propping up the bar. Max observed him for a moment or two and came to the conclusion that the man had already downed a number of pints. If Len was drunk, would that make his intended proposal more interesting, or less so? Hard to tell.

Max approached him. 'Good evening, Len,' he said. 'I'd like to have a chat with you.'

Len looked him up and down. 'So, pal, you're ready to confess that you're bonking Lady Annie Eustace?' His voice was loud and several heads turned in their direction.

'We can't talk here,' said Max. 'I suggest we walk and find somewhere quiet.'

'Not until I've finished my pint,' said Len belligerently.

It wasn't a problem; he downed it in seconds.

The two men exited the pub. 'Let's walk up to Smeaton's Pier,' suggested Max. 'It'll be quiet there at this time of the evening.'

'As you wish,' said Len.

As they walked towards the pier, Max began. 'I am prepared to admit that Annie is still in St Ives, though I'm not prepared to tell you where she is staying.'

'I know where she is,' said Len. 'She's in the flat above your estate agent's office.'

Max decided it was best to ignore him. 'Annie doesn't want to go home to Hubert Eustace. It's not that he's been unkind to her, rather the contrary – much too kind, as I understand it. Either way, there is nothing you or I, or anyone else, can do to persuade her to go home.'

'She'll go home in the end. She's a spoilt little bitch who wouldn't last five minutes in the real world, and she's a right scrubber by all accounts.'

They'd reached the start of the pier and stood by the slipway. For a moment, Max was transfixed, watching the fading light over the water – it really was a magical evening. He walked down the slipway for a better view of the open sea and stared at the scene, hoping it would calm him. He was well aware that losing his temper right now would be very counterproductive.

He turned to face Len. 'I think you're being unnecessarily rude. Yes, she's led a charmed life since she married Hubert, and yes there may have been the odd affair, but I strongly object to the word *scrubber*.'

Len walked towards him, laughing. 'You can strongly object as much as you like, pal, but you're the latest in a long line of blokes who've taken her fancy. They never last more than a week or two and then she goes back to Hubert. This time will be no different, whatever she's telling you now. The lifestyle she says she hates is all she knows, and she can't live without it. Her little excursions into *the real world* provide temporary excitement but that's all they are.'

'How come you appear to be so knowledgeable about her lifestyle, and how can you possibly know about her affairs?' said Max. His hands, in his trouser pockets, balled into fists.

'Hubert gave me the contact details of Annie's best friend. She was very helpful and told me Annie's full life story. Look, I've got a job to do. Hubert's offered me a lot of money to find Annie and bring her home. This is not a gig I'm going to give up lightly. I'll come and collect her in the morning and believe me, you'll be well out of it and bloody grateful to me one day.'

'I have an alternative suggestion,' said Max. 'How much would I need to pay you to simply walk away from St Ives and tell Hubert that you were unable to find his wife?'

Len laughed. 'You have to be joking, pal. I know estate agents are not slow to charge impressive fees, but there's no way you could afford to pay me off. And as for Annie, she has no money of her own. She lives entirely on handouts from Hubert. Get real – there's no deal for you here. Just do as I say and walk away.'

'I can't,' said Max. 'There has to be a sum of money that would be large enough to tempt you to abandon the search for Annie. Just tell me how much.'

'That's where you're wrong, pal. Here's a potted version

of my life story. I used to be a copper, not a bad one at that. Then, I beat up a cheeky inmate in one of our cells. He ended up in a wheelchair and I ended up in prison. Prison is not a great place to be if you're an ex-copper, as you can imagine. I'm building a new life for myself as a private investigator, and I'm doing well. I'm good at my job. Sir Hubert Eustace is rich, influential and at the moment, a very vulnerable man. He's going to pay me a lot of money for the return of his wife, and their story will be great for my CV. So, I'm not going to put a foot wrong.'

'I don't believe you,' said Max.

'Believe what you like,' said Len, 'but I'll tell you this for free: she's not worth it. Not only is she a scrubber, she's cruel and ungrateful, disloyal, greedy, entitled – oh, and don't let us forget, a serial liar.'

'How dare you speak about Roxy like that!' shouted Max. Stepping forward, this man who had never been violent in his whole life aimed a punch at Len. With considerable experience of violence, Len blocked the punch with ease and followed it with one of his own.

Max reeled backwards, losing his footing. As he fell, his head hit the rocks that bordered the right-hand side of the slipway. The sound of the crack was so sickening, it even made Len flinch.

Max came to rest at the bottom of the slipway. Len cautiously edged down to where Max's body lay, holding on to the granite wall as he went so as not to slip – the sea frightened him. Max was clearly unconscious. Len stared down into the water, then back at Max's body. It was high tide and the waves were breaking over the slipway, close to where Max lay. Len looked around him. There was no one in sight. So no witnesses, then. He weighed up his options; he was a quick thinker. With only a moment's hesitation, decision made, he knelt down and with surprising ease, rolled Max's body into the sea.

Len stood up, drying his hands on his jacket. He looked around; there was still no one to be seen. He needed to get away fast, not just from the pier, but from St Ives. There was no time to lose.

Just for a moment, as he turned to leave, Len stopped and stared down into the water, now inky black as night descended. Already, there was no sign of Max Richards – all his thoughts and feelings now gone for ever. The sea had claimed him.

CHAPTER THIRTY-TWO

Merrin McKenzie had always been an early riser. Her mother blamed her father for this trait. Harry Tripconey had been up before dawn most days of the year – for a fisherman, early rising was pretty much obligatory. While she was still a very little girl, Harry often took his daughter with him, wrapping her up in a thick blanket and placing her in her very own chair in his cabin. But before long, Merrin would be up, discarding the blanket, and standing beside her father at the tiller, enjoying, like him, the beginning of a new day. Years later, as a lawyer, she always felt her preparation work was best done between five and nine in the morning – it was her most productive time of the day.

William also appreciated an early start; it was one of many other aspects of their lives together which made Merrin and William so compatible. This particular morning, they set off just before dawn, crossed Porthmeor Beach and headed up the cliff path towards Zennor. For a while they sat on a rock until the sun rose, and then they made their way home via the Island and Porthgwidden Beach. It was only as they were about to climb up the steps beside Bamaluz Beach that Merrin spotted three men standing close together on the small piece of sand from which the tide had recently receded. She recognised the harbour master and also Fran Pascoe, the fisherman son of one of her late father's great friends. They seemed to be staring intently at the ground. *Oh dear*, thought Merrin, *a dead seal or maybe a beached dolphin.* She whistled to William and began to climb down the steps onto the beach.

On seeing Merrin, Fran hastily detached himself from the group and ran towards her. 'Please, Merrin, stop right there. You don't want to see this,' he said.

'Why, what is it, what's wrong?'

'I'm afraid it's a body, my maid, a dead body,' said Fran, gripping Merrin's arm tightly to stop her going any further.

'Oh! How awful! Is it anyone we know?' Merrin asked.

Fran hesitated. 'There's no easy way of saying this . . . I'm afraid it's Max Richards.'

Merrin stared at Fran as if he were mad. 'No,' she shouted, 'it can't be!' Shaking herself free from Fran, she ran across the sand.

Fran caught her just as she reached the body. 'Don't, Merrin, please,' he begged.

'Let go of me! He's my friend!' Merrin shouted.

'Do as she asks, Fran,' said the harbour master. 'She should see him, if that's what she wants.'

Max was lying on his back. Merrin fell to her knees beside him. Max's face was partially covered in sand; his eyes were open though glassy and unfocused. Nonetheless, the body lying on the sand was indisputably Max. 'Oh, Max!' Merrin looked wildly around at the three men hovering awkwardly above her. 'Why's he dead? What's happened to him?'

'We found him lying on his front, half out of the sea,' said the harbour master. 'The tide must have brought him in. I'm sorry his face is covered in sand, but we knew immediately that he was dead and the pathologist would go mad if we tried to brush it off. I'm so sorry, Merrin, I know you two were good friends.'

'We've been friends all our lives,' she said in a voice barely above a whisper. 'Why has he drowned? He's an excellent swimmer.'

'It looks like some sort of accident,' said Fran. 'He has an injury to the back of his head. Maybe he fell, knocked himself out and then went into the sea.'

While they were talking, William had inched forward and was now lying beside Max with his head on Max's leg. 'Get that dog away,' said Fran.

'No,' said Merrin. 'He's my dog and a friend of Max's too. Please let him say goodbye.' Kneeling beside Max with William felt almost comforting. She seemed quite unable to cry but suddenly felt very, very cold. Fran, seeing her shaking, took off his jacket and helped her put it on. 'It's the shock that's making you feel so cold,' he said, kindly.

'The police and pathologist shouldn't be long now, Merrin,' said the harbour master. 'Why not come and wait in my office, it'll be warmer there.'

'I'd like to stay with him until they arrive,' she said. As she spoke, the words seemed unreal. How could Max possibly be dead? Just yesterday, they'd successfully avoided the private investigator. Max had been stressed but so very much alive. Could Roxy have anything to do with his death, or the private investigator – what was his name – Len? Her shocked brain couldn't seem to compute any sensible ideas. Max was dead; why or how seemed unimportant compared with the knowledge that he was gone from her life for ever.

An uneasy silence fell among the group round Max's body. Minutes had passed when suddenly a voice called out from the steps leading down to the beach.

'Merrin Trip, little Merrin Trip, what are you doing? Come here, my maid.' It was Jack Eddy, stumbling down the steps and making a brave attempt at running across the sand, his arms outstretched.

Merrin stood up, stiffly – cold and damp from the wet sand, she walked towards Jack. He enveloped her in his arms, and only then did she begin to cry. 'There, there, little Merrin Trip,' said Jack, rubbing her back, 'you have a good cry on old Jack. Poor Max, what a dreadful thing to happen. Still, the boss will be here very soon. He'll sort things out, he always does.'

'The only thing he could do to make things better,' Merrin murmured into Jack's tear-stained shoulder, 'is bring Max back to life, and that's not going to happen, is it?'

Louis Peppiatt joined the A30. Firstly, he had been dragged out of bed to be told there was a dead body on Bamaluz Beach and that the circumstances could be suspicious, due to a head injury. He was still getting dressed, after the quickest of showers, when he received a second call to inform him that the deceased was Max Richards.

His immediate reaction, as a policeman, was to wonder who could have been responsible for Max's death. A head injury suggested someone else might well be involved, and could that person be Roxy? Or maybe the stress of his current circumstances had caused Max to drink too much and it really was an accident. It flashed through his mind that it was only yesterday morning that he had interviewed Max. As a normally honest man, had the pressure of lying to the police tipped him over the edge in some way? An awful idea, but there was no point in further speculation until he reached the scene.

So immediately, his thoughts turned to Merrin. Did she know yet that Max was dead, and how on earth would she react once she knew? With her brother Jago living in Australia, Max had always looked out for her like a second brother, particularly since she'd returned to St Ives. He was also Isla's godfather, another important role now her own father was dead. Merrin was going to be devastated. He put his foot down and pulled into the outside lane, blue lights flashing.

Stuck in roadwork traffic lights as he approached St Ives, Louis called Jack Eddy but there was no reply. If anyone had already told Merrin what had happened, Louis just hoped it was Eddy – he would know just how much of a loss Max would be to her. Free of the traffic at last, Louis drove along the Wharf and passed Bamaluz, parking up by the museum beside an ambulance and a car he knew belonged to Dr Graham Bennett, a very talented but grumpy forensic pathologist. He jumped out of the car and headed down to the beach.

Seeing his boss arrive, Jack Eddy hurried over. 'Boss, it's Max Richards. Did you know?' he said.

Louis could see Graham Bennett beckoning to him. 'Does Merrin know yet?' he asked Jack hurriedly.

'Yes, boss. She arrived soon after Max was found. I've taken her back to her cottage and Clara is with her.'

'What about Isla?' Louis asked.

'She's in Polzeath with friends. Merrin was going to contact her.'

'Well done, Sergeant. I better go and pacify Dr Bennett. How is his mood this morning?'

Jack grimaced. 'The usual, I'm afraid, boss.'

Dr Graham Bennett was indeed in his usual mood. Louis often wondered whether it was Graham's constant exposure to dead bodies that made him almost permanently angry. Yet in his time, Louis had worked with several jolly pathologists, albeit usually possessed of a dark sense of humour. This morning, Graham's wild red hair, subjected to wind and salt spray, was even more extreme than usual, but the glare he was giving Louis was all too familiar.

'So what time of day do you call this, Peppiatt?' he said. 'I was ready to have the body removed half an hour ago but, of course, we had to wait for you to cast your pearls of wisdom upon the scene.'

Louis ignored him; it was the best way. 'So what have we got, Graham, a murder or an accident?'

'How should I know? That's your job, Peppiatt,' he said with relish.

'For God's sake, just give me something. Time of death for a start.'

'About ten o'clock last night. The harbour master reckons the deceased fell off the slipway by the pier about then, was swept out by the falling tide and then presented himself back on Bamaluz Beach this morning on the incoming tide.'

'How does he know Max fell off the slipway?' Louis asked.

'Oh, so you know the deceased? Dear me, Peppiatt, I must be more tactful. In answer to your question, there's a blood stain on the rocks beside the slipway and what looks like another trace on the slipway itself, close to the high water mark. Obviously, we'll need to match the blood to your chum's, but it seems very likely that it's his. Assuming he wasn't dead when he entered the water, if he was unconscious, for even a few minutes, it would cause him to drown.'

'Who found the body?' Louis asked. 'And incidentally, he's not my chum, but I did interview him yesterday.'

'Poor fellow, that's not a good way to spend one's last day on earth, being bullied by the fuzz. Two fishermen pulled him clear of the water – the man who spotted him is called Fran Pascoe, and both he and his companion are waiting to be interviewed in the harbour master's office. I have the deceased's wallet and mobile. I'll get someone trawling through his calls. Oh, and there's one extra interesting little titbit.'

'Go on,' said Louis, with a sigh.

'That woman, Merrin McKenzie, who found the boy in the bed a few years back. Well, she was also on the scene soon after the body was discovered. Maybe she's your culprit, Peppiatt!'

‘I need some answers quickly, Graham. This case could be linked to another one I was working on,’ said Louis, determined not to rise to the bait.

‘Say four o’clock this afternoon. I’ll text you as soon as I’m ready.’

‘Right, thanks,’ said Louis. ‘I’ll just take a look at the body before it’s moved.’

Louis had seen more dead bodies over his years as a policeman than he could possibly count. Children, of course, were the worst; those were the ones who stayed in your mind for ever. Then young people, dying senselessly through knife crime, or driving at ridiculous speeds on a motorbike or in a car, and at the top of that group were young women, raped and murdered by some madman. Max’s was certainly not the first dead body Louis had seen of someone he’d known, but the sight of Max made him feel unexpectedly sad. Yes, Max had lied to him yesterday, but he’d hated doing it and indeed had been very bad at it – a rather endearing trait for a policeman to witness, when he was so used to being competently lied to by hardened criminals. Jack Eddy joined him.

‘A decent bloke, boss. Hopeless with women, of course, but that applies to most of us.’

Louis smiled. ‘Speak for yourself, Sergeant.’

‘Oh, I do, boss, I really do,’ said Jack, with much feeling. Mrs Eddy’s reputation as a tyrant was the stuff of legend in St Ives.

‘Eddy, I’d like you to interview both the fishermen who found the body and the harbour master. It would appear from the blood on the slipway that it’s pretty obvious where and how Max fell into the water, but get as much detail as you can about the tide and why his body ended up on Bamaluz. When you've done that, could you start asking around to see if anyone saw Max in town last night. Get your station calls put through to Camborne.'

'Yes, boss.'

'Oh, and Eddy, have those constables turned up, the ones Ben Satchel was going to organise for you to help with the thefts?'

'Yes, boss.'

'Right, take them off thieving duty and get them also asking around town for sightings of Max. And have you met the woman called Roxy, who he had taken up with apparently?'

'No, boss, but I've heard all about her, spending money like water when she first arrived.'

'Max told me yesterday that she had left town, but I didn't believe him.'

'It's not good to speak ill of the dead, boss,' said Eddy.

'Unless it helps us find out who killed him, assuming it wasn't an accident.'

'Where are you to, boss?' Jack asked.

'I'm going to see Merrin,' said Louis. 'I'll catch you later.'

'Have you two quite finished gawping at the body?' shouted Graham. 'If you want some results, I need to be able to remove Mr Richards now.'

CHAPTER THIRTY-THREE

Louis hesitated at the bottom of the stone steps leading up to Merrin's cottage. Helping people come to terms with their grief was not something Louis believed he was very good at. The trouble was, there were no words that could bring any real comfort. Merrin had just lost a lifelong friend, who had died far too young. What possible spin could he put on the event to make it seem anything other than dreadful – which it was. Added to that, it was only just over four years since Merrin's husband Adam had died. The death of someone close always dredged up losses from the past. He suspected that as well as mourning Max, she would also be revisiting the loss of Adam.

He took a deep breath and walked up the steps. The front door was ajar. He pushed it open to find Merrin sitting at the kitchen table, staring into space. On seeing him, William rushed across the room, tail wagging, and immediately lay on his back for a tummy rub.

'That's nice to see,' said Merrin. Her voice was

uncharacteristically flat. 'I had an awful job getting him away from Max's body, and he's been lying in a dejected heap ever since.'

'I'm so sorry,' said Louis. 'I think I know just how much Max meant to you.'

'That's enough,' said Merrin, standing up and coming round the table towards him. 'There are no words, are there, in this situation, but I could really do with a hug.'

Louis took her in his arms and held her close. 'It's strange,' he murmured, 'but before coming in just now, I was trying to think of what to say to you, and I had exactly the same thought. There are no words.'

They held each other in silence for several moments and then Merrin gently drew away. 'Actually, we do have a lot to talk about – some of it is quite important, I think. You'll be pleased to know that I've done all my blubbing for now, as you can probably tell from the state of me.'

'As you Cornish would say, you look *bleddy handsome* to me,' said Louis, trying to lighten the mood.

Merrin smiled at him. 'You know it's very bad form for a policeman to lie. Sit down and I'll make us a coffee. A good idea?'

'Yes, please.' Louis drew out a chair and sat down at the kitchen table. William immediately jumped on his lap.

Coffee made, Merrin sat down opposite Louis. 'I think you're going to have to shove that dog off your lap, because there's stuff I'm going to tell you which probably needs writing down.'

Louis did as he was told and drew out of his pocket an ancient and battered leather notebook. 'Fire away,' he said.

'I saw Max yesterday. Roxy is living in the flat over Max's office, and he more or less admitted to me that she is Annie Eustace. I was tempted to go and see her just now – heaven knows what she's made of the fact that Max didn't come home last night. Then I thought it was something I should leave to you.'

'I agree. Before you go on, where is everyone? I thought Clara was with you and Isla was coming home?'

'Clara's had to go back to work and I've only just spoken to Isla. She's been in the sea all morning. She said she is coming home today, so I didn't tell her about Max. She'll be dreadfully upset and I didn't want her driving in a state.'

'I was thinking on my way to you just now that Max's death was bound to conjure up thoughts of Adam's,' said Louis.

'You're right, of course, and that will apply to Isla as well. Max was like a second father to her in many respects. You know, for a man, Chief Inspector, you're surprisingly sensitive.' She smiled at him.

'You shouldn't be alone,' Louis insisted.

'I'm not alone,' said Merrin, briskly. 'I've got you. Now, the really important thing is that a private investigator is in town and he was really threatening towards Max. Isla and I had to cause a diversion so Max could sneak back to his flat, without being seen by the chap. He sounds a horrible man and I think he could be responsible for Max's death. Certainly, he'd got hold of the idea, rightly I believe, that Roxy really is Annie.'

'Do you know the name of this private investigator?' Louis asked, suddenly full of trepidation.

'Len someone,' said Merrin.

'Len Carter?' Louis supplied.

'Yes, that sounds about right. I've no idea what Max was planning to do about the situation. We were only together for a few minutes before he dashed home.' Merrin went silent, tracing, with her finger, a knot in the woodwork of her table. 'As he left, I told him to be careful. He didn't take much notice, did he?'

'No, he didn't,' said Louis, heavily. 'I don't suppose you know where Len Carter is staying?'

'I do,' said Merrin. 'He's staying at the Sloop.'

'This is awful, but I need to leave you right now – firstly to go to the Sloop and then to go in search of Roxy,' said Louis.

'Of course, you must go,' said Merrin. 'There's nothing we can do to help Max now, but if someone was responsible for his death, then we need to find him . . . or her. They mustn't get away with killing such a lovely person. I'll be fine, Isla will be home soon.'

'I won't leave St Ives without coming back to see you.' Louis stood up and kissed the top of her head. 'William, Horatio, look after her – that's an order.'

It was still early morning so the Sloop Inn was quiet. There were a few people eating breakfast outside; some already accompanied their meal with a pint of beer, which made Louis's stomach churn. He went inside and flashed his warrant card at the barman.

'Do you have a Len Carter staying with you?' Louis asked.

'We did have,' said the barman. 'He paid up front for

staying two nights, but he didn't stay the second night. He was in and out of the bar during yesterday until he finally left at about nine-thirty. When I checked his room this morning, his luggage had gone and the bed hadn't been slept in.'

'Was he talking to anyone at the time he left the bar?' Louis asked.

'Yes, he was talking to Max Richards. Actually, they had a bit of an altercation, though I don't know what about, the bar was that busy. Do you think Len Carter killed poor Max then?'

'So you know about Max's death?' said Louis.

'The whole town knows – such a nice fella and a bit of a ladies' man, despite his age.'

Louis was slightly affronted on Max's behalf about the reference to his age, but looking at the barman, Louis realised he couldn't be much older than twenty. Max and indeed Louis himself were old men to a twenty-year-old.

'Two things then: could I have your name and contact details, and do you have an address for Len Carter?'

'Yes to both, give me a minute – my name's Ian, by the way. When I'd finished my shift, I was going to tell Jack Eddy about seeing Max with Len Carter.'

'I'm sure you were, Ian, and I'm grateful for the information,' said Louis.

Ian returned with a piece of paper. 'All the details you want are here,' he said, handing it over.

'We'll need a statement from you, Ian. Jack Eddy will be taking that. You are absolutely certain that it was Max talking to Len and that they left together?'

'Certain,' said Ian.

'And the time, how sure are you about that?'

'I was knackered. When the two of them started arguing, I looked at the clock to see how long it was until closing time. In my job, it gets very tiring when drunk people start shouting at one another.'

'I can believe it,' said Louis. 'Thanks again, Ian. You've been a great help.'

On leaving the Sloop, Louis headed straight for the police station. Len Carter's address was in Peckham. He would need to ring the Met and get them to pick up Len as quickly as possible, in case he went to ground. Ian had given them sufficient evidence to take Len in for questioning, and Len's track record of violence made his involvement with Max's death more than a little feasible.

As he hurried across town, Louis started to wonder if he could have done something to prevent Max's death. During his interview with Max yesterday, Louis had known that he was lying, so why hadn't he pressed him harder until he was forced to take them upstairs to see Roxy/Annie? He knew the reason for his reluctance. It had become increasingly obvious that the case was a domestic issue, not a missing person. 'It was not a police matter – until now,' he muttered to himself, as he strode along.

The more he thought about it though, the more Louis realised that failing to bully Max into a confession was not where he had made a major mistake. His serious blunder lay in the fact he had badly underestimated Len Carter's detective skills. Setting aside for a moment his reputation for violence, by all accounts Len had been an excellent detective. Believing that there was no way Len could have known about Roxy and her trip to St Ives with Tony Barrow, Louis had been confident that Len could not be in town. Heaven knew how Len had made the connection, but made the connection he had; and Louis realised, with a heavy heart, that he should have anticipated that possibility.

At the station, which was empty as Jack was out and about, Louis called the Met, who were only too pleased to have an excuse to arrest Len Carter. Although during his time as a policeman he'd brought about some impressive results, Len had not been popular with his colleagues – another example of a rogue policeman damaging their reputation. That done, Louis decided telling Jack Eddy about taking Ian's statement could wait. His next, and very urgent, job was to try and find Roxy.

Jeremy Eustace was essentially a nice man. However, he was also a weak one – though almost certainly through no fault of his own. He'd been bullied by his father all his life and once his mother had died, there'd been no one to help moderate his father's behaviour. He had also been bullied at boarding school, and it hadn't been until he went to university to read English Literature that he'd begun to blossom and gain confidence. He was a good-looking young man and had soon caught the eye of Sophie Williams, a strong-minded woman, who became his wife. She loved him but found it all too easy to get her own way.

Since he had failed so far to find Annie, Sophie was now demanding that her husband should return home. Jeremy had tried to contact the private investigator, Len Carter, but he was not picking up his calls. Jeremy paid his bill at Tregenna Castle, but before leaving for London, he decided to drive down into town for one more look around for Annie. He parked up in the Sloop car park and went in search of a pasty to eat on the journey home. The pasty shop was full; there was much excited chatter and within moments, Jeremy learnt that a body had been found on the beach.

'Poor old Max,' said an elderly man, standing by the counter. 'Mind you, if it is murder, there's probably plenty of cuckolded husbands seeking revenge for the police to choose from.'

Some good-humoured laughter followed.

Jeremy cleared his throat nervously. 'You're not talking about Max Richards, are you?'

'Yes, m'dear,' said a lady behind the counter. 'Do you know him?'

Jeremy shook his head. 'Only very slightly. Has he really been murdered? That's just awful.'

'We don't know yet,' said the elderly man. 'It looks like he fell down the slipway at Smeaton's. Old Max was not a big drinker and he'd been swimming like a fish since he was a little tacker. It seems a bit odd, so maybe someone else was involved.'

General conversation returned and Jeremy slipped out of the shop, having completely forgotten about his pasty. If Louis Peppiatt was right and Max had not been telling the truth, then maybe Annie was still in town. How would she feel if she learnt Max was dead? Despite serious reservations concerning her recent behaviour, Jeremy was fond of his stepmother. Their relationship was more like that of brother and sister, given how close they were in age, and Jeremy knew, for certain, that if it really was Annie, not Roxy, who'd been living with Max, she would be devastated.

On impulse, Jeremy walked round to Max's office. As yet, there were no policemen in evidence and his office was in darkness – there was nothing he could do. If he didn't get on the road soon, he would be late for dinner, and that would not make Sophie happy. He turned to leave, crossed Fore Street and looked back at the building. In the window on the floor above the office, a tiny light was shining through a gap in the curtains. *Of course*, thought Jeremy. *Max must live in a flat above his work and that's where Annie would be hiding.*

He raced back across the street and knocked loudly on the office door, shouting her name. He stood back in the middle of the road so she could see him from the upstairs windows. 'Annie, it's Jeremy, let me in. It's important!' he yelled. Several passers-by eyed him with interest. 'Please, Annie!' he shouted again.

The curtain twitched, then the window opened a fraction. 'Is that really you, Jeremy?' said a voice he recognised.

'Yes,' said Jeremy. 'Come down and let me in. It's really vital I talk to you.'

Moments later, a figure flitted across the office and opened the door. 'Heavens, Annie, what on earth have you done to your hair?' were Jeremy's first words.

'Never mind that, and I'm not Annie any more. I'm Roxy Goodenough. Come on up. I'm so worried. Max left the flat just after nine last night and he hasn't come home. I'm frightened something awful has happened to him, but I daren't go outside because there's a beastly investigator in town who is threatening to take me home. Do you know where Max is, Jeremy?'

Jeremy had opened his mouth to speak when the doorbell rang. 'I better see who that is. I'll explain why in a minute.' Jeremy hurried downstairs, and instead of a crowd of policemen wanting to search the flat as he'd imagined, he was relieved to see only Chief Inspector Louis Peppiatt standing outside the door.

'Louis,' said Jeremy, quietly, as he opened the door. 'Roxy and Annie are one and the same person, and she's upstairs now. I haven't had a chance yet to explain about Max.'

'We'd better go upstairs and tell her, then,' said Louis, grimly.

CHAPTER THIRTY-FOUR

It took nearly half an hour to get any sense out of Annie Eustace, who now refused to be called anything but Roxy. She screamed on being told of Max's death and then sobbed uncontrollably. When Louis suggested that he needed to ask her some questions, she rounded on him hysterically, calling him cruel and unfeeling. Roxy continued to sob in Jeremy's arms while Louis made some tea, thinking all the while about how brave and controlled Merrin had been. She had known Max all her life, and here was this drama queen making such a fuss when she'd only known Max for a couple of weeks. When the tea was drunk, Louis decided to get tough.

'Roxy, unless you agree to answer questions now, I'm afraid I will have to take you into Camborne Police Station for questioning. Your choice.'

'Please, Louis, you can see how upset she is,' said Jeremy.

'I can and I'm sorry, but this could be a murder inquiry and I need answers now. Your stepmother is a key witness.'

'Alright, I'll try,' Roxy said, tearfully.

'I need to know everything you and Max did yesterday, where you went, who you saw, and timings where possible.'

'Well, it started with you, didn't it, you and Jeremy? You came to the office and bullied Max, trying to get him to tell you about me and where I was. Bless him, he protected me.' There was another burst of sobbing.

'What happened next?'

'Len Carter turned up and Max had to go through the whole thing again, saying I had gone back to London.'

'What time was that?' Louis asked.

'Len arrived only about five minutes after you and Jeremy had left – he was horrible, Max said, quite threatening. I heard them shouting.'

'So, Len must have arrived at about nine-thirty. What happened after that?'

'Max closed the office and then he and I talked about the situation, and I told him that I was married to Hubert but that I could never go back to him again.' She turned to Jeremy. 'I'm sorry, Jeremy, but I just can't. Max thought I should go home with you, but I knew if I did, I would never be able to leave again.' More sobbing followed.

'And then?' Louis asked, starting to lose patience.

'Max went out to get us some pizzas and a bottle of wine. He told me not to go outside, or even downstairs, in case the Len chap was hanging around. I could tell Max was a bit frightened of him. He was ages coming back. Apparently, he had met up with Len again but with the help of Merrin, he had given him the slip. Then we ate the pizzas and drank the wine, and Max went for a sleep. On his own,' she added, somewhat bitterly.

'And why did he go out late yesterday evening? Was he intending to see Len again?'

'Yes,' said Roxy. 'We had decided to try and pay him off, get him to tell Hubert that he couldn't find me. Max went to the Sloop because he knew Len was staying there and thought he'd probably be in the bar.'

'That's ridiculous!' exploded Jeremy. 'There's no way you and Max could have raised enough money to compete with Father's resources. The fee Father offered Len to find you was huge. Len would never have turned that down, particularly as he believed he'd found you.' Jeremy turned to Louis. 'Do we know how Len tracked down Annie?'

'Not yet,' said Louis. Just then his mobile rang. 'Excuse me, it's my sergeant. I'll take the call in the office. Roxy, I need you to pack a bag and Jeremy, could you book her into Tregenna, at any rate, for one night. Can you stay with her?' Jeremy nodded. 'Good, thanks. Roxy, I need the key to this flat and you are not to leave St Ives until I say so. Clear?'

Louis went downstairs to Max's office, closing the door behind him. 'How's it going, Eddy?' he asked.

'Quite well, I think, boss,' said Jack. 'Several people saw Max by the Tate, watching the sun go down.' Jack hesitated. 'His last sunset, as it turned out, poor bugger.'

'Yes, indeed,' agreed Louis, sombrely.

'Then Merrin's twins had a chat with him. Have you met them, boss? Bea and Connie they're called.'

'I have indeed,' said Louis.

'Max went into Merrin's shop just as the twins were closing up. They say it was just after nine. He asked for Merrin, but they explained she'd gone out for supper at

Tristan's. The twins were very taken with Max and thought him very good-looking. They were devastated to hear he was dead. Did you have any luck at the Sloop, boss?'

'Yes,' said Louis. 'I need you to take a statement from a barman there, as detailed as you can make it, as it's key to the case.' Louis then told Jack about Ian and added that it was now established that Roxy was indeed Annie.

'It's looking more than likely that this Len Carter is responsible for Max's death,' Jack concluded.

'The trouble is the evidence is all circumstantial,' said Louis. 'Unless forensics can come up with something, we can't prove Len Carter had anything to do with Max's death. I agree that it's very likely he was involved. But there is no way he will ever confess, he knows how the police force works. I'm just going to call in on Merrin, and then I'll go and see our cheerful Dr Bennett. I'll leave the keys to Max's office and home on your desk. Could you get the PCs to do a search, say in about an hour. I'm not expecting them to find anything but it's worth a shot, and tell them to leave the place exactly as they found it – Max deserves some respect.'

Louis found Merrin and Isla sitting at the kitchen table chopping vegetables. Isla had obviously been crying.

Louis put a hand on her shoulder. 'I'm so sorry, Isla, so very sorry for you both,' he said.

'Please don't be kind to me, Cip, or you'll start me off again,' said Isla, wiping her eyes with the back of her hand like a child.

'How's the investigation going?' Merrin asked. 'And can I get you anything?'

'No, I'm fine, thanks. Roxy has owned up to being Annie but is insisting on being called Roxy Goodenough. Goodenough was her maiden name, apparently.'

'Rather appropriate,' said Merrin. 'Nothing is ever quite good enough for Roxy. Sorry, that's bitchy, but oh so true.'

Louis smiled. 'No comment,' he said firmly.

'So, have you decided that it's the private investigator who killed Max? It has to be, doesn't it?' said Isla.

'He's certainly in the frame as being the most likely candidate. However, it is still possible that Max's death could just be an accident.'

'No, surely not,' said Isla, hotly. 'Max would never have done something so stupid as fall down the slipway, and if he did, it would have been no problem for him to swim ashore. Honestly, Cip, it must be murder.'

'Don't hound the poor man, Isla,' said Merrin. 'I presume until you get the forensics report, you're stuck.'

'Very true,' said Louis. 'I'm on my way to see the pathologist now, hopefully he'll have something we can work with.'

'You're not seeing that awfully rude, grumpy man who handled the James Allnut case?' Merrin asked.

'As a matter of fact, I am,' said Louis, grinning. 'I don't know why you two get on each other's nerves so much. He suggested that since you found James and then were on the scene so soon after Max was found, I should probably treat you as a suspect. As a serial killer is what he had in mind, I imagine!'

'I hope you put him straight,' said Merrin.

'Actually, I didn't dignify his outrageous allegation with

a response,' said Louis. 'And I do admit that Dr Graham Bennett is not blessed with so much as a modicum of charm.'

Actually, Graham Bennett turned out not to be as abrasive as usual – largely because his undoubted skills had not produced anything particularly useful.

'I don't have much to tell you, Peppiatt, but here it is for what it's worth. The blood, both on the rocks and on the slipway, matched that of our victim, as we imagined it would. This means that Richards was not clobbered with a blunt instrument. His head wound is consistent with falling onto the rocks. The damage to his skull is nasty, and after he fell and struck his head, it is just possible that he could have rolled down the slipway into the sea. The severity of the head injury could suggest he was pushed with force, rather than just tripping and falling, but that's something I couldn't swear to in court, I'm afraid.'

'That's a great pity,' said Louis.

'Yes, I can imagine it is, but I'm not prepared to perjure myself, even for you, Peppiatt. His lungs were full of water, so he was alive when he entered the sea. I've recorded cause of death as drowning, which is accurate. If, however, he had not ended up in the sea, it's likely that he would have made a full recovery from the head injury. The blood on the slipway suggests that either he rolled into the sea as a result of his fall, or someone pushed him in. I'm afraid we have no evidence to indicate which was the case.'

'And now you're going to tell me that since the body was in the sea for nearly twelve hours, there is no evidence, no DNA, no sodding clue of any sort to link Max to the person who could have been involved in his death?'

'You are entirely correct, Chief Inspector,' said Graham, 'and before you ask, there are no discernible footprints – it was a granite surface, awash with sea water.'

'And time of death is still around ten last night?'

'Yes, that's about right. So, as the harbour master suggested, the victim must have gone out on the tide and then come back to Bamaluz Beach in the morning. Apart from his head injury, there are just a number of bruises and abrasions, but only what one would expect in the circumstances.'

'Damn it,' said Louis. 'Confidentially, Graham, my likely suspect is an ex-policeman with a history of violence. He's certainly bright enough to know we will have nothing on him so far as forensics are concerned, and he'll also know how the system works. From where I'm standing, it's going to be almost impossible to nail him.'

'Well, as it's you, I will take another look at our friend Richards, in case I've missed something, but I wouldn't hold your breath.'

'Thanks, Graham,' said Louis, as he walked towards the door. 'Oh, just one thing. I mentioned to Mrs McKenzie that you had marked her card as a serial killer since she turns up every time there's a dead body in St Ives. I think her description of you was along the lines of *that awfully rude, grumpy man*!'

Graham almost smiled. 'I'm starting to like this woman. You must introduce me properly to her sometime, Peppiatt.'

'I wouldn't count on her enthusiasm for that suggestion!'

* * *

Sally, John Dent's redoubtable secretary, was obviously relieved to see Louis walk into her office.

'We've been calling you all morning, Louis dear. Why didn't you pick up? It's not as if you're some dozy teenager. People call you because they need to talk to you, and three – or was it four – missed calls should have alerted you to the fact that sir urgently wanted to speak to you.'

'I'm sorry, Sal, but I've been dashing about all day collecting answers to the questions I know sir will ask. If I'd spoken to him any earlier, all my answers would have been the same – *I don't have that information yet, sir*. You will admit, I'm sure, sir would have been far angrier with that response than with a few missed calls.'

'You're probably right, Louis, but don't expect much of a welcome from sir. I'll tell him you're here at last.'

'You look beautiful when you're angry, Sal,' said Louis, with a grin.

'Now you really are in trouble, my boy,' said Sally, trying not to laugh, as she shooed him into Chief Superintendent John Dent's office.

'When a senior officer calls someone junior to himself, and says the matter is urgent, I do expect that call to be answered,' said Dent, his eyebrows bristling to attention, displaying the depth of his anger.

'I'm very sorry, sir. I assume you were enquiring about the drowning in St Ives,' said Louis.

'Yes, of course I was. Most unfortunate, most unfortunate indeed, particularly at the beginning of the summer season.'

Louis couldn't resist it. 'It was also most unfortunate for Max Richards, the man who died.'

'This is not a moment in which to be flippant, Peppiatt. So what progress have you made?'

Louis then outlined the saga of Annie Eustace and the subsequent involvement of Max Richards, a private investigator, and Annie's husband Hubert and stepson Jeremy.

'Len Carter – a dreadful case, I remember it well,' said Dent. 'So he's out of prison now and you believe he may be responsible for Max Richards's death?'

'Possibly, sir. I have asked the Met to pick him up – he fled St Ives in some hurry, so I imagine he headed for home, which is in Peckham.'

'The Met have got him,' said Dent. 'I received a call about half an hour ago. Without any communication from you, however, they don't know what to charge him with.'

'I don't think we can charge him with anything, sir. I suggested the Met should simply bring him in for questioning. My sergeant is sending over to them the interviews we've conducted with regard to Max Richards's last hours. Included in those is an important one from a barman at the Sloop Inn, who saw Richards and Len Carter meet up and then get involved in an altercation while still in the pub. This occurred about half an hour before Richards's estimated time of death. There were no witnesses on the pier at the time he fell or was pushed into the sea, so at the moment we have no proof that the two men were even by the pier at the same time.'

'A tricky one, I can see that. Of course, while I personally wouldn't mind seeing Len Carter back behind bars, at this time of year an accident is preferable. A murder is not good for tourism, but an accident would serve as a reminder to visitors not to mess around near the sea. Anyway, keep digging, Peppiatt. You're good at that.'

'Thank you, sir. Also, Graham Bennett is going to have another look at the body, in case he missed anything.'

Sally was waiting in her office.

'He paid me a compliment, Sal, can you believe that?' said Louis.

'I heard,' said Sally, who was a committed, unrepentant eavesdropper. 'It's more than you deserve for ignoring my calls. I met Max Richards at Mrs McKenzie's private view party. A charming man. When Mrs McKenzie introduced us, his first question was to ask how successful I was at keeping you under control and obeying orders.'

'Really? Cheeky bugger. What did you say, Sal?'

'I'm afraid I'm not at liberty to divulge my reply,' said Sally, primly.

'Max was a lifelong friend of Merrin's and godfather to her daughter. She's very upset, but held it together long enough to tell me some important information. It was from her that I discovered that Len Carter was in St Ives.'

'She's a lovely person and clearly very smart,' said Sally, 'but I've learnt my lesson and that's all I will say about her.'

Louis had just walked through his front door when his mobile rang. It had been a long day. Now he just wanted to sit down with a large piece of paper and try and plot the timeline leading up to Max's death, in the hopes that his poor, tired old brain could conjure up a breakthrough. Still, at the back of his mind there was the unpleasant thought he just couldn't shed. If he'd realised that Len Carter was in town, he could have perhaps saved Max.

He picked up his mobile. 'Peppiatt,' he said wearily.

'Oh dear, I can tell I've clearly chosen the wrong moment to call. It's Peter Carew, Louis. I can easily call back.'

'No, sorry, Peter, I've just got home after rather a long day. How are you and how are the boys?'

'All well,' said Peter. 'Billy told me he met you the other day at a party to open Merrin's shop. He said you were very nice to him. After his ordeal in juvie, I think he's been left rather fearful of policemen, which is probably no bad thing. Look, I'll be brief – Samantha and Jessie Young are coming back to Cornwall tomorrow for a few days.' There was a significant pause. 'You don't know who I'm talking about, do you?'

'Give me a moment,' said Louis. 'Got it, little Jessie who took your marvellous seal painting.'

'The same. Jessie sent me a thank-you letter, but then you know that, because you sent it on to me. I wrote back because her letter to me was so touching. Then she wrote again and asked whether I would reconsider meeting her and her mum. Old fool that I am, I said yes. They're staying at the Gurnard's Head in Zennor, and as well as seeing me, they wondered if they could meet you again. Samantha told me you were a very unusual policeman.'

'Heavens,' said Louis, 'I wonder if that was intended as a compliment. I would like to see them again, but we've had a dead body washed up on Bamaluz Beach and it may not have been an accident. I expect you've heard all about it.'

'Not a whisper. Remember, I am still a recluse, despite your friend Merrin's best efforts. Anyway, I'm glad I don't listen, watch or read the news – so depressing, and I certainly don't want to learn about dead bodies floating about on Bamaluz.'

'By missing the bad bits, you're also missing the good ones, too,' suggested Louis.

'Like what?' Peter challenged.

'I don't know – blind kitten rescued from apple tree finds home with lonely pensioner and they both live happily ever after.'

'A blind kitten up an apple tree? Really, Chief Inspector!'

'Scrub the kitten story, sorry – just trying to lighten the mood after a difficult day,' said Louis, clearly embarrassed.

'Samantha's quite right, you really are an unusual policeman,' said Peter.

CHAPTER THIRTY-FIVE

Yesterday had been a day of shock and terrible sadness for Merrin, but she had not been required to do anything at all practical. After leaving Max's body on the beach, she had been with either Clara or Isla for most of the day. In the evening, Tristan had closed the restaurant and he and Clara had come up to Merrin's cottage. They had talked and cried and as the evening progressed, got mildly drunk. Max had no living relatives, and much to Clara and Merrin's relief, Tristan had offered to go to Truro to formally identify the body.

Today was different. Firstly, she'd had to ring her brother Jago in Australia to tell him his best friend was dead. She'd blurted out the words, haltingly, in her view making a complete hash of it and causing it to be even more painful for Jago as a result. Jago was a man of infinite kindness and it seemed, in retrospect, that he had spent more time comforting her than the other way round. He assured her that he would discuss arrangements with his family and he and his wife, Gemma, would be travelling to the UK in the next couple of days.

'Don't worry, sis,' he'd said. 'I'll help organise the funeral. We'll give the dear old boy the send-off he deserves.'

The next challenge was Poppy. Merrin had not seen her since her private view party – how long ago that seemed now. She waited until early evening, when she imagined Poppy would be at home, and walked round to her cottage on Back Road West.

When Poppy came to the door, Merrin was shocked by her appearance. She looked gaunt and pale, her eyes red-ringed, and she appeared to be wearing pyjamas. On seeing Merrin, she immediately burst into tears.

'Oh, Merrin, I'm so glad you came,' she said. 'I've no one to talk to about Max. He was such a lovely man, I just can't believe he's dead. Please come in, I'll make some coffee.'

Merrin was surprised by Poppy's reaction. Max had apparently left her for Roxy, or Annie, more correctly. It was impressive that Poppy still thought he was *a lovely man*.

Poppy's cottage was charming, containing rag rugs, lots of colour, mismatched furniture and crazy throws. She showed Merrin to a very comfortable armchair and poured her a mug of coffee.

Poppy sat down on the edge of her chair, back rigid, hands tightly clasping her mug. 'He really is dead, isn't he? You were there, you saw him, so town gossip says. Did he look in pain? Was he frightened? I just can't bear the idea of him dying alone.'

'Yes, Poppy, he really is dead, but I don't think he

would have been frightened, or even in pain for more than a second. I don't know what the rumours are saying, but he fell over, hit his head and rolled into the sea. Once in the water, he would have been unconscious. He would have drowned without knowing he was drowning.'

'That's good to know, I suppose. He had so much living still to do. How did it happen? No one seems to know.'

'No one does as yet. It could have been an accident, or maybe someone else was involved. The police are working on it,' said Merrin, trying to sound as vague as possible.

'Is Roxy involved?' Poppy asked, in a small voice.

'I don't know,' said Merrin, truthfully.

'I understood about Roxy,' said Poppy, 'because I understood Max. I knew he had always been serially unfaithful to the women in his life, and I knew I would be no exception. But it didn't matter.'

'Really?' said Merrin. 'That's very generous of you.'

'I absolutely loved him for who he was. People so often make the mistake of thinking they can change their proposed partner. None of us really change – we go on making the same mistakes, over and over, and rarely learn from them. Honestly, I was entirely realistic about Max. I believed our relationship was for keeps but I didn't think, for one moment, he wouldn't stray from time to time.' Unexpectedly, she grinned. 'I guess I just thought he would stray less often as he got older.'

'So, you thought him being a naughty boy was just part of his charm?' said Merrin.

'No, that's not it,' said Poppy. 'I loved him for his kindness, his humour, because we felt the same about so many things. I found him massively attractive, of course –

who wouldn't? – but sometimes he was quite vulnerable, not nearly as confident as he appeared. For example, he hated the idea of getting old. It really frightened him. No, Max being, as you put it, a naughty boy was the price I was willing to pay to have the rest of him. Does that make sense?'

'Completely,' said Merrin. 'You're a very special person, Poppy.'

'So, what happens now?' Poppy asked. 'I know he has no relatives left.'

'My brother Jago was his best chum. He lives in Australia but will be with us in a few days. We're hoping – that's me and Jago, plus Clara and Tristan – you will join us in planning Max's funeral, as my brother said, to give him the send-off he deserves.'

'Do you really mean that?' said Poppy, her eyes brimming with tears again. 'What about Roxy?'

'Not relevant,' said Merrin, firmly. 'I expect she'll go back to her husband now.'

'She's married?' said Poppy.

'Oh yes,' said Merrin, 'and she has absolutely nothing to contribute to the celebration of the life of dearest Max. But you do – you made him very happy, and you have a central role to play in making sure we get it right for him.'

Louis was just leaving for St Ives when his mobile rang. It was Jeremy Eustace.

'Louis, I've had several long chats with Annie and, at last, she has agreed to come back home. I had to tell her that Father is dying, and she immediately realised that she must be there with him at the end. It appears he doesn't have very long. I spoke to his doctor yesterday, and I think all the stress surrounding Annie's disappearance hasn't helped.'

'I imagine it hasn't,' said Louis.

'So, would it be OK if I took her home today? I know you said you wanted her to stay in St Ives, but she'd be better off at home, and obviously, it would be best for Father, too.'

'How do I know she won't abscond again?' said Louis. 'I presume she's now no longer Roxy Goodenough, but there has to be a risk that she will run away again and pretend to be someone else? I certainly don't want to be chasing all over the country again looking for her. She is a material witness in the events leading up to Max Richards' death.'

'I guarantee I will look after her and make sure she stays at my father's house in Chelsea. If you need her back in St Ives, I will be personally responsible for bringing her back down to you.'

'But you can't keep an eye on her all the time. You have a pregnant wife to consider and your job, I assume.'

'I've already spoken to Sophie, and she and I are going to stay in Chelsea with Annie and Father, until, well, until he dies. So far as the job is concerned, I can work from home. You know I owe you, Louis. The boy I once was has never forgotten your kindness. I won't let you down, I promise. Annie will be going nowhere.'

'Alright, Jeremy, I agree, but call me every few days and let me know how things are going.'

Louis pocketed his phone and headed for his car. Driving out of Truro, he realised he was not comfortable with the decision he'd just made, though why, he wasn't sure. The chances of proving anyone else was involved in Max's death were now extremely unlikely, so Annie Eustace and her erratic behaviour were surely no longer his concern.

CHAPTER THIRTY-SIX

Louis and Jack Eddy spent a frustrating half-hour studying the timeline Louis had put together the previous evening. Disturbingly, it felt like closure. There really was nothing more they could do to establish how Max Richards had died, unless new evidence came to light.

'And as far as I can see,' said Louis, 'only Graham Bennett stands a chance, a remote one at that, of coming up with anything new. We know what Max did after he left his flat until he had the brief altercation with Len Carter in the Sloop. After that, it appears we have no witnesses. We could have one more sweep of the town this evening to see if we can jog anyone's memory. I think we owe it to Max to have one more go.'

'OK, boss. I'll get the PCs on it and join in myself. I suppose we could set up a reconstruction of the walk from the Sloop to Smeaton's Pier and maybe get it on the telly.'

'Two problems there, Eddy,' said Louis. 'By the time we set it up, it will be the weekend and most of the visitors who were in St Ives this week will have gone home. Also, we don't know whether Max walked to the pier alone or with Len. Surely, if anyone had seen two men on the pier, arguing or having a fight, they would have come forward by now? I'm a damn fool – I should have checked to see if Len Carter was in town, I shouldn't have underestimated him.'

'Don't fret, boss. We'll have another go this evening and maybe something will turn up.'

At that moment, Louis's mobile rang. It was the harbour master.

'Chief Inspector, there is something in my office which I think you need to see right away. Are you in St Ives?'

'Yes, I'm at the station. What is it?'

'I'd rather you came and had a look, if you can spare the time. It's a bit odd.'

'I'm on my way.'

Louis arrived at the harbour's office and was directed to the remains of a slimy, discoloured lifebelt.

'What am I looking at here?' Louis asked.

'It's what's left of a lifebelt off a yacht. It ended up on Porth Kidney Beach, as much rubbish does. A couple of lads found it and took it home. Their dad only saw it in their garden this morning and brought it straight down to me.'

'Sorry,' said Louis, 'I don't get the significance.'

'Take a look at the name on the lifebelt. It spells out *L-L-A-M* and what looks like an *S* on the end. The bloke who brought his yacht into St Ives with that Roxy on board, the woman who took up with poor Max, his boat was called *Llamedos*.'

Louis frowned. 'His name was Tony Barrow?'

'That's right, sir. A cocky sod, drank a lot, but a good seaman.'

'Tell me,' said Louis, 'do you think he would have taken his yacht out of the harbour if he was drunk?'

'I would have thought it very unlikely. As I say, he was a good seaman and he worshipped that yacht, which was not surprising. A great-looking craft, despite its age and stupid name. It was his home, too, and he was forever polishing and cleaning her. No, he would never have risked taking her out to sea when drunk, I'm sure of it.'

'Interestingly, one of the harbour masters at St Katharine Docks said exactly the same thing. That's where Barrow has his permanent mooring.'

'So you've been checking up on him, sir? You don't think he had anything to do with poor Max's death, do you?'

'Not directly,' said Louis, 'the only link is Roxy. However, there are a number of inconsistencies regarding the timing of Tony Barrow's departure from St Ives. Do you have a record of shipping in and out? The date he is supposed to have left here is 11th July.'

'Yes, of course,' said the harbour master, disappearing into his office.

While he waited, Louis walked across the pier to the slipway where Max had apparently entered the water. There was still a police cordon round the area and a young constable keeping the public away.

Louis introduced himself. 'I'd have thought forensics would have finished with this by now?' he asked.

'They had finished, sir, and then we got a call asking for it to remain sealed off for another twenty-four hours.'

Good old Graham, thought Louis. Despite his truculent ways, he was meticulous and professional when it came to doing his job. He was obviously going to revisit the scene.

The harbour master returned. 'Nothing unusual,' he said. 'Barrow said he would be leaving at around high tide on the night of 11th July. Technically, that would probably have been the early hours of the 12th. Certainly, there was no sign of *Llamedos* when I arrived at work the following morning, so it would seem he left on time.' He hesitated. 'Before you ask, when something like this lifebelt turns up, it is of concern. The fishermen have been alerted to look out for signs of any wreckage, and I have asked the coastguards to do searches of Porth Kidney at low tide during the next few days.'

'Thank you, that's most helpful,' said Louis. 'This lifebelt concerns me, too. Tony Barrow left St Ives to go to the Scilly Isles. It appears he never arrived there. As a result, a couple of days ago, I set up an alert for sightings of *Llamedos* at all UK and French ports – apparently, Barrow often takes on temporary work over in France. As of this morning, there have been no sightings. It would seem that the yacht has completely disappeared.'

Louis left the harbour master's office and began walking back towards the centre of town. From a procedural point of view, he knew he should first double-check with Clara concerning her insistence that *Llamedos* had left the harbour trailing the tender. However, time was not on his side. He hesitated for a moment and then took out his mobile and called Jeremy Eustace.

'Where are you?' Louis asked when Jeremy answered.

'We've just left. We're driving through Lelant now,' said Jeremy.

'I'm sorry, Jeremy, you'll have to turn round and come back to St Ives.'

'Why?' protested Jeremy. 'Annie has told you everything she knows and, truly, she never left Max's flat the night he died. There's nothing else she can contribute, you know that.'

'This is not about Max – at least not directly,' said Louis, 'and my request for Annie to return to St Ives is not up for discussion. I need her back here for questioning now. Please go back to Tregenna Castle and I will arrange somewhere quiet there for us to talk.'

'Louis, surely you can speak to Annie on the phone when we get home. Is it really necessary to be so dramatic?' said Jeremy.

'I'm sorry, but you have a straight choice,' said Louis, his voice chilly. 'You can do as I ask and come back to Tregenna, or I can send a police car to intercept you. Either way, Annie has to come back to St Ives immediately.'

'Alright,' said Jeremy, with a heavy sigh, 'we're on our way.'

CHAPTER THIRTY-SEVEN

Louis hurried back along the Wharf to Tristan's Fish Plaice. It was too early for the lunchtime trade, so the restaurant was quiet except for a few people having coffee. Mercifully, Clara was standing behind the till.

Louis rushed up to her. 'Clara, sorry, a quick question. Have you a moment?'

Clara gave him her best and naughtiest smile. 'I always have a moment for you, Chief Inspector.' Then the smile suddenly vanished. 'Is this about poor darling Max?' she asked.

'No, it's about another matter. Clara, are you one hundred per cent sure that when *Llamedos*, Tony Barrow's yacht, sailed out of St Ives harbour on 11th July, it was definitely trailing the tender?'

'I can't remember the exact date, Louis, but when Tony Barrow left St Ives, the tender was definitely attached to the yacht, which would be impossible if you believe the story Roxy told Merrin. What's going on?'

'I can't stop now, I'll catch you later.'

Louis secured the use of a small conference room at Tregenna Castle and alerted reception to send Jeremy and Annie straight in when they arrived. He was glad of a few minutes to himself. Annie Eustace was going to be a difficult person to interview, and he decided it would be best if Jeremy was not present. Normally reasonably good at assessing people, Louis realised that Annie confused him. She was a loose cannon, for sure. She had taken up with Tony Barrow on a whim because she fancied a sail and then when he'd disappeared, she'd immediately transferred her affections to Max. Her relationships appeared entirely self-centred. She took what she wanted with little regard for other people's feelings. At least, that's how it seemed to Louis. He wished he'd had the time to talk to Merrin and hear again from her exactly what *Roxy* had said about her reasons for staying behind in St Ives.

His thoughts were interrupted by their arrival – first impressions suggested that Annie was seriously displeased and Jeremy confused and worried.

Louis stood up. 'Thank you for coming back to St Ives,' he said. 'Jeremy, would you mind waiting for us in the bar. We won't be long, but I would like to talk to Annie alone.'

'I want him to stay,' said Annie.

'And I want to speak to you alone,' said Louis, firmly. 'If you were a child, it would be different, you would need to be accompanied by an appropriate adult. But you're not a child, Annie, and the only way you can have someone with you is if we arrange for a solicitor to be present. This is not a formal interview, it is not being recorded, but you are still entitled to have a solicitor present, if you so wish.'

'I don't want a solicitor,' said Annie, truculently. 'Go away then, Jeremy, so we can get this over with and get back to London.'

'This isn't like you, Louis,' said Jeremy, as he left the room, his face creased with concern.

'So, what's this all about?' said Annie.

Louis watched her closely. 'I want to talk to you about Tony Barrow,' he said.

Annie looked startled and immediately Louis could see the anger had left her. 'What about him?' she said, dismissively.

'There are inconsistencies between the story you told everyone about what happened on the night of 11th July, and what actually did happen.'

Annie rallied a little. 'That's rubbish. I know what happened. I was there.'

'Then tell me about the events of that night, please,' said Louis.

Annie hesitated. 'Early that evening, I had a drink with Max. I was thinking of buying a cottage down here. Then I went to the harbour and rowed the tender out to *Llamedos*. Sorry, I forgot to say, before the drink with Max, Tony and I had rowed out to the yacht with some stuff for supper, so the second time I rowed up, Tony was already on board.'

'OK,' said Louis, 'I've got that.'

'I could see, as soon as I got on board, that Tony was very drunk. I started to prepare supper, but we quickly became involved in an argument. Tony wanted to go to the Scilly Isles, I wanted to go back to London. In the end, I'd had enough of him and his drunkenness. I told him I was leaving him, climbed into the tender and rowed ashore. The tender is still moored up in the harbour.'

'I know,' said Louis. 'So, what happened next?'

'It was late, after midnight. The town was quiet. I decided to walk up towards the hotels and see if one of them had a room. I was struggling up the hill when I suddenly remembered I had left my rucksack behind, with everything in it – credit cards, phone, laptop, passport – my whole world. I quickly turned round and ran back, just in time to see *Llamedos* motoring out of the harbour.'

'Did you try to row after the yacht?' Louis asked.

'Of course not, I'd never have caught up.'

'And then you went back to Max's and stayed the night. Is that correct?'

'Yes,' said Annie, plaintively. 'I didn't know what else to do.'

Louis was silent for a few moments. 'I have been informed by two harbour masters that Tony Barrow is an excellent seaman and would never take his yacht out to sea if he was drunk. Any thoughts on that?'

'Maybe that's true normally,' said Annie, swiftly, 'but that night he was particularly upset because I told him I was leaving him. I expect he just wanted to get away from St Ives. We all break our own rules sometimes, don't we?'

Annie was starting to feel confident, Louis thought, which was good since she was more likely to slip up. 'We have a very reliable witness who says that when *Llamedos* left the harbour, the tender was being towed. That doesn't seem to fit in with the events you've just described.'

'Well, you know that's not true,' said Annie, 'because the tender is moored up in the harbour.'

'It is now,' Louis agreed, 'but I think you motored the yacht out of the harbour yourself and then rowed back once the yacht was out at sea. By all accounts, the sea was flat calm that night, so it wouldn't have been difficult for someone as used to boats and boating as you are.'

'Why would I do that?' said Annie.

'I don't know, you tell me. All I would say is that you taking the yacht out to sea is consistent with what the witness saw, and also ties in with the fact that Tony would never have gone to sea when drunk.'

'I'm afraid your witness must be wrong,' said Annie.

'My witness also confirmed that the harbour was deserted at the time *Llamedos* left the harbour. There was no one else watching her leave.'

'Then your witness needs to visit an optician,' said Annie.

Annie's flippant tone was too much for Louis. 'You may be interested to know that *Llamedos* never arrived in the Scillies. I have therefore alerted the UK and French ports to look out for the yacht. There have been no sightings, thus far.'

'There's no point asking me where he's gone,' said Annie, belligerently. 'We split up that night, if you remember, and in any case, I only knew him for a few weeks. He could have sailed anywhere.'

'Except that a damaged lifebelt from *Llamedos* arrived on Porth Kidney Beach a couple of days ago. It seems possible that something may have happened to Tony Barrow and his yacht somewhere close to our shores.'

CHAPTER THIRTY-EIGHT

By late morning, Louis found himself sitting at Merrin's kitchen table, nursing a black coffee. On his lap was William, and Louis was being forced to share his biscuit with Horatio, who was strutting about on the table shouting, 'Nuts!'

'I'll put that noisy bird away,' said Merrin. 'You've got your serious face on, which suggests you need to talk.'

'I actually do,' Louis admitted. He then gave Merrin a detailed account of his interview with Annie. 'The story she told me about that evening is the same as the one she told you, isn't it?' he asked.

'Word for word,' said Merrin.

'Which, of course, contradicts what Clara saw,' said Louis. 'I checked with Clara early this morning before the interview, and she is absolutely certain about what she saw.'

'But we've all known this for some time, Louis. Why are you bringing it up now when, presumably, your priority is to find out what happened to Max?'

Louis then explained to Merrin that *Llamedos* seemed to have disappeared, and the appearance of the lifebelt suggested that something could have happened to the yacht close to St Ives. 'I believe that Clara's a totally reliable witness, and now both you and I have been told a very different story by Annie. Why would she lie unless she was covering something up?' Louis said.

'So what's happening to Annie now?' Merrin asked.

'There's nothing to charge her with, obviously, but I've told her she can't leave St Ives for at least another couple of days, while we see if any more debris turns up from *Llamedos*. She obviously offered no explanation for the appearance of the lifebelt. She was just very cross, and Jeremy, her stepson, was very upset. I'm afraid I'd had more than enough of her by the end of the interview, so I said she had a straight choice – to agree to stay at Tregenna Castle where they are now – or become a resident in one of the cells at Camborne Police Station.'

'I bet that made you popular,' said Merrin, 'but I know what you mean about Roxy – sorry, I mean Annie. She's a difficult person to read, isn't she? To be honest, Louis, I've never really liked her. She's so bound up in herself. I hated the way she moved seamlessly from Tony to poor old Max.' Merrin hesitated. 'I know you think Len Carter was somehow responsible for Max's death and I'm sure you're right. However, in both my heart and my head, I blame Annie. Max wouldn't have ever met Len if he hadn't met Annie. Len may have done the deed but Annie, to my mind, was jointly responsible for Max's death.'

As if on cue, Louis's mobile rang. It was Sally from Chief Superintendent John Dent's office. 'Not particularly good news, I'm afraid, Louis,' she said.

'Go on then, Sal,' said Louis, heavily.

'The Met have just called,' said Sally. 'They interviewed Len Carter but have had to release him without charge.'

'What about the statement from the barman at the Sloop?' said Louis. 'Max and Len were shouting at one another.'

'You know perfectly well, dear boy, it's nothing more than circumstantial evidence. Believe me, the Met are very anxious to nail Len Carter – they're not very keen on one of their own going to the bad. However, sir says that unless Graham comes up with something, we're going to have to accept that we'll never know what happened on that slipway.'

'Jack Eddy and two PCs are going to have one last sweep of the town tonight, just in case anyone remembers seeing anything we've missed so far,' said Louis. 'Do we know what Len had to say for himself about what happened?'

'Yes – Len confirmed that he and Max had exchanged words in the pub, but once they were outside, they went their separate ways,' said Sally. 'Len maintains he went for a walk along the Wharf and then decided there was nothing more he could do to find Annie Eustace, and so collected his things and headed back up to London. If you're going to do some more asking around tonight, I'd concentrate outside the Sloop. Maybe someone saw them leave together, if that's what they did.'

'Thanks, Sal, I'll pass that on,' said Louis.

'Well, good luck, Louis. So sorry to be the bearer of bad news,' said Sally.

'That doesn't sound like it was a very cheerful call,' said Merrin.

'It wasn't. I can't see any reason why I can't tell you – Len Carter has been questioned and released without charge. As things stand at the moment, I don't see there's much chance of finding any concrete evidence with which to charge him. I'm so sorry, Merrin, I feel we're letting down Max and all those who cared about him.'

'Louis, if the evidence isn't there, it's not your fault. Len is an ex-policeman – presumably he knows just how to play the system, assuming he's even guilty. Except, except . . .' Merrin looked close to tears. 'Except Max would never have fallen down that slipway and rolled into the sea all on his own. I just know it.'

'I understand how you feel,' said Louis, taking Merrin's hand across the table. 'It's all such a mess at the moment. I have one man dead and another man presumed missing, and not a scrap of evidence to suggest what happened to either of them.'

'And the common denominator is Annie Eustace,' said Merrin.

They sat in silence for several minutes and then Merrin removed her hand and stood up. 'More coffee, or a small glass of wine to cheer us up?' she suggested.

'Go on then, a small glass as I'll have to drive later,' said Louis.

Merrin poured the wine and they clinked glasses. 'Let me tell you about something rather charming,' said Louis.

'Oh yes, please do,' said Merrin.

'Peter Carew called me yesterday. He and the little girl, Jessie – you know, the one who, how shall I put it, acquired the seal painting?' Merrin nodded. 'They have been corresponding, and Jessie has persuaded Peter to let her and her mother come down to Cornwall and thank him in person for the painting.'

'Goodness, that's progress. How marvellous,' said Merrin. 'When are they arriving?'

'I think they may be here already. They're going to stay at the Gurnard's Head. To be honest, I wasn't really concentrating. I was so tied up with thoughts of Max.'

'I'd love to meet them,' said Merrin. 'They might like to come and see the shop.'

'Why don't you give Peter a call and see if you can catch up with them. I know you'd like them, both mother and daughter are lovely.'

'I'll do that,' said Merrin, 'but you ought to see them too, if you can. After all, it was you who salvaged the situation.'

'Actually, they did ask if they could meet me as well, but I can't really commit to anything at the moment. Apparently Samantha, that's the mother, said I was a very unusual policeman.'

Merrin smiled at him and raised her glass in a silent toast. 'Well, she's certainly right about that!' she said.

CHAPTER THIRTY-NINE

When Merrin arrived in the shop the following morning, it felt more like a party than a retail outlet, there was so much chatting going on. Bea and Connie were running the shop, and it emerged that two of the visitors were none other than Samantha and Jessie Young.

When introductions had been made, Samantha said, 'We tried to persuade Peter to come with us but he wouldn't. He says visiting St Ives in late-July is outside his comfort zone.'

Merrin smiled. 'I expect he told you he's a committed recluse, though he's much more outgoing than he used to be.'

'He blames you for that,' said Samantha, 'well, you and Louis Peppiatt. Jessie and I were hoping to see the chief inspector, but I gather he's caught up in some local tragic death.'

'Yes,' said Merrin, 'it was a very close friend of mine – he drowned. Louis's trying to get to the bottom of how it happened.'

'I'm so sorry,' said Samantha.

Merrin's eyes filled with tears. 'Please don't be kind. I'm managing to hold it together pretty well unless someone's kind to me. My daughter's just the same.'

'I know all about that,' said Samantha. 'I don't know if Louis told you, but we lost Leo three years ago when he was only nine – Leo was my son and Jessie's brother.'

'Louis did tell me your story. I'm so sorry, here's me lecturing you about grief when mine is nothing compared with yours. How are you both doing?'

Samantha nodded in the direction of Jessie, who was talking animatedly to the twins. 'Peter's seal painting – you know about that?' Merrin nodded. 'It unlocked something in Jessie, which has helped enormously. After Leo died, she wouldn't talk about him. If someone asked her if she had any siblings, she'd just say no. It was the sensitivity of two remarkable men that changed everything for her, it's why we wanted to come back and thank them both. Listen, she's telling those splendid ladies about Leo and his love of seals right now.'

'I'll tell Louis I've met you. I know he'd love to see you both if possible. When do you leave Cornwall?'

'On Wednesday,' said Samantha, 'so we have two more days here.'

At that moment, Clara walked into the shop. She and Merrin had not met since the morning Max's body had been found, although they'd talked a great deal on the phone. The two women embraced.

'I saw you through the window,' said Clara. 'Have you got time for a coffee? I'm feeling a bit blue so Tristan sent me out for a walk. He suggested my long face was making his hollandaise sauce curdle, the beastly man!'

'Of course I have,' said Merrin. She said her goodbyes to the Youngs and told the twins she'd be back within the hour.

Clara and Merrin picked up takeaway coffees and found a free bench overlooking the harbour. 'Has Tristan been to identify the body yet?' Merrin asked.

'Yes,' said Clara. 'He went into Truro yesterday afternoon. He hasn't said much about it, but then he's a man of few words.'

'That's only because the poor chap is married to you and so can never get a word in edgeways,' said Merrin.

'There we are,' said Clara. 'Dear darling Pearl, you've cheered me up already with one of your customary insults. When are Jago and Gemma arriving?'

'I'm picking them up from Newquay later today. I did explain to Jago that it might be a while before Max's body is released for the funeral, but he seemed to think the sooner they came over the better. I suspect he thinks we're all falling apart.'

'He's not far wrong there,' said Clara. 'Are you finding you still can't quite believe it? I forget about Max for a moment or two and then when I remember what has happened, it seems unreal.'

'I feel exactly the same, but it's only been two days so it's hardly surprising we're struggling – it's such a shock. We thought we still had years of friendship ahead of us with Max, and now we're never going to see him again.'

The thought silenced both women for a while; Clara was wiping her eyes and blowing her nose a great deal. Merrin sat in a stony silence.

'I told you I was going to see Poppy the other day, didn't I?' said Merrin, at last.

'Yes,' said Clara. 'How is she?'

'Not good. I think we all knew how much she loved Max. It was amazing, actually. She seemed to believe that she and Max were for keeps, but she totally recognised that he might stray – in other words, his thing with Roxy didn't really seem to have fazed her that much. I don't think I could ever have been like that with Adam – I would have been heartbroken and jealous as hell.'

'If Tristan took up with another woman, I'd be beyond angry. In fact I'd probably kill him,' said Clara. 'That phrase – *hell hath no fury like a woman scorned* – was written for me!'

'Anyway,' said Merrin, smiling, 'I hope it's OK, but I asked Poppy to join us in planning the funeral.'

'Of course it's fine. Good idea,' said Clara. 'I just hope you haven't asked bloody Roxy, or whatever she's called now, to join in.'

'What do you think?' said Merrin, sarcastically.

Louis was at his desk in Truro when Graham Bennett called.

'I'm afraid I have nothing to report, Peppiatt,' he said. 'I've had another good old root round in the body to no avail. I also sent a team back to the scene of the crime, if that's what it was. There was absolutely nothing there we haven't seen already. It's a pity your suspect didn't do the decent thing and drop a credit card, or something similar. Thoughtless of him.'

'Well, thanks for trying, Graham, I appreciate it,' said Louis.

'The body's now been formally identified, so there's no reason the coroner can't release him for burial or cremation – whatever awaits the poor fellow. I gather there are no living relatives, so into whose name do we release him?'

'Mr and Mrs Tregonning, Clara and Tristan,' said Louis. 'Tristan was the man who identified the body. To the usual St Ives undertakers, and I understand the service will be at St Ia's.'

'Righto, sorry we couldn't do more with this one, Peppiatt.'

Louis had only just finished the call when his mobile rang again. This time, it was Jack Eddy.

'Good morning, Sergeant. Please tell me you have some good news,' said Louis.

'Afraid not, boss. We were very thorough last night but found no one who could help us. Without a doubt, whether old Max was with someone or alone on Smeaton's Pier, there were no witnesses.'

'And Graham Bennett has just called to say he and his team have found nothing new. Barring a miracle, we're not going to be able to nail Len Carter, which means I don't believe we're ever going to know how Max Richards died.'

As Louis finished the call, the harbour master's number flashed up on his phone.

'I thought I should contact you right away. A fisherman's just called in. He's spotted part of a mast and some rigging floating just off Seal Island. It's floating because the mast is made of wood. These days, most modern yachts have fibreglass or metal masts – but *Llamedos* is an old yacht and her mast is wooden.'

CHAPTER FORTY

Louis decided that the time had come to formally interview Annie Eustace. Without any prior warning, he arrived at Tregenna Castle just before midday. Jeremy and Annie were having a drink in the bar, which otherwise was mercifully empty.

'Lady Annie Eustace,' Louis began. 'I'm here to take you into Camborne Police Station for questioning in respect of the missing yacht *Llamedos*, and her owner Tony Barrow.' He followed this with the usual caution, during which both Jeremy and Annie looked increasingly stunned.

'I'm definitely going to be there with her this time, Louis,' said Jeremy. 'It's ridiculous, how can Annie be expected to know the whereabouts of Tony Barrow and his bloody boat?'

'By all means come with Annie in the car, but I will be interviewing her alone except for the duty solicitor, if she so wishes.'

Annie spoke not a word while in the hotel, nor on

the car journey to Camborne. Jeremy began the journey with a long list of protests disputing the need for Annie to be questioned. As none of Louis's answers were at all forthcoming, Jeremy eventually lapsed into silence as well.

In an interview room, armed with a tape recorder, a WPC sitting in and two cups of coffee, Louis began.

'Annie, I believe that Tony Barrow's yacht has sunk out at sea, in an area somewhere between Seal Island and Godrevy Lighthouse. I believe you know how this happened and I'd like you to tell me about it.'

'I know nothing about it,' said Annie.

'Do you realise that failure to disclose information can result in a charge of perverting the course of justice? This is a very serious charge and could even lead to a prison sentence. I urge you to tell me what you know, and again, you might find it helpful to have a solicitor present to advise you.'

'I don't want a solicitor, I've already told you. I just want to go home to my husband, who is terminally ill. I need to be with him – it's outrageous that you're keeping me from him with some trumped-up excuse about a missing yacht.'

'*Llamedos* left St Ives harbour shortly after midnight on 11th July, towing a tender. You must have been on board because the tender is now in St Ives harbour. What happened? Were you in charge of the yacht? Did you hit a rock causing the boat to sink? Did you escape? Did Tony die because he was so drunk? Annie, it will really help you if you just tell me the truth.'

'I told you, I don't know,' said Annie.

'Yesterday,' said Louis, trying another tack, 'you told me that you and Tony had an argument on board when *Llamedos* was still moored up in St Ives harbour. The crux of the argument, you said, was that Tony wanted to go to Scilly, and you wanted to go back to London. So, when you ended up back in St Ives alone, why didn't you go straight back to London, since that was what you wanted to do?'

'Because I'd fallen in love with Max,' said Annie, 'and I hadn't any money.'

'Neither of those facts are true,' said Louis, increasingly exasperated. 'You'd only met Max a couple of times by then, and as for money, I know Max and Merrin both lent you some – plenty to get you back to London. Continuing to lie like this is not helping your case, Annie.'

'Obviously, you've never experienced love at first sight,' said Annie.

Louis ignored her. 'We'll take a short break. Constable Shaw will take you to the bathroom if you so wish and fetch you some more coffee, tea or water. I'll be back in about ten minutes.'

Jeremy was still sitting where Louis had left him. 'Jeremy, let me see if there's a room free – ah yes, there is. Follow me.'

Louis showed Jeremy into a small interview room. 'Do sit down,' he said. 'This is not a formal interview, it's not being taped, I'm just hoping you can help me. Has Annie talked much about Tony Barrow?'

'I don't know what this is all about, Louis, but I can't help you. Annie has not once mentioned Tony Barrow since Max's death. Initially, she was very upset about Max, as you know, but now all she talks about is getting back to her husband. It's unspeakably cruel to keep her from Father in his final days – all because of a missing yacht she knows nothing about.'

'And you maintain that you also have nothing to tell me about Tony Barrow and the missing yacht?' said Louis.

'I know nothing about the yacht, or her skipper, truly,' said Jeremy.

And Louis believed him.

'How long is this all going to take?' Jeremy asked, as Louis stood up to leave the room. 'I had promised my wife I'd be home yesterday. She's pregnant, Louis, as you know. I should be with her.'

'I'm sorry, Jeremy, but this is your call,' said Louis. 'Who needs you most at this moment, your wife or your stepmother? Only you can decide.'

Jeremy let out a sigh. 'I'll stay,' he said.

Louis left the station and walked about outside, trying to clear his mind. His best results when interviewing were usually achieved by gently probing, even offering advice, until he began to gain the suspect's trust. Of course, this didn't always work and he sometimes had to get very tough with hardened villains, when necessary. Shouting at a woman, though, was not his style, but he felt at tether's end where Annie was concerned. He could tell she truly believed she could get away with lying to the police because up to now, she had led a charmed life, always getting her own way about everything. Merrin was right: Annie really wasn't a very nice person.

Of course, what Annie should have done before being questioned was to insist on waiting until Hubert's hotshot lawyer arrived – he was bound to have one. Maybe, though, she didn't want Hubert to know what she'd got herself into. Louis realised he was going to have to play it tough to stand a chance of getting the truth out of Annie, and so he decided to ask the duty solicitor, Robert Pierce, to join them. Annie could refuse his help, of course, that was her right, but Louis hoped she'd change her mind.

Louis briefed Robert Pierce with full details of the possible charges against Annie, and then suggested he went to discuss the situation with his potential client.

'I should mention, Rob, that I'm going to have to be fairly brutal if I'm to make any progress,' said Louis.

Robert grinned. 'Thanks for the warning.'

However, despite their best efforts, Annie once again refused to have a solicitor present, and so Louis returned to the interview room determined to extract at least some sort of confession.

'I had another call from the harbour master in St Ives this morning,' he said. 'A fisherman had spotted part of a wooden mast and some rigging floating in the sea just off Seal Island. As you will no doubt be aware, there are not many yachts around these days with wooden masts – but *Llamedos* has one, doesn't she? By all accounts, Tony Barrow loves his boat and has spent a great deal of time repairing and improving her. *Llamedos* is also his home. He wouldn't be so careless as to shed half a mast and the rigging and do nothing about it.' Louis stood up and pointed a finger at Annie. 'I believe *Llamedos* is on the seabed somewhere near Seal Island, and I believe you know where it is and why.'

Annie began to cry. Louis's natural instincts were to

ease up on the questioning, but he knew he mustn't if he wanted a result.

'The coastguards are picking up the mast even as I speak, and I have asked police divers to start searching the area for the wreck of *Llamedos*. What are they going to find, Annie, besides the yacht itself?' he shouted. 'I believe they're going to find the body of Tony Barrow. I'm right, aren't I?'

'Yes, yes,' sobbed Annie.

'I think she needs a break, sir,' suggested Constable Shaw.

Louis shook his head. 'Right, Annie, so tell me what really did happen and I promise you'll feel better for telling the truth.'

Annie wiped her eyes. 'I'll tell you the truth, but in return will you make sure that I can see my husband before he dies?'

'You may have been able to negotiate your way out of tricky situations in the past, but not this one. Trying to bargain with a police officer is not to be recommended. I will do my best to ensure that your husband sees you before he dies – not for your sake, but for his.'

CHAPTER FORTY-ONE

Sergeant Jack Eddy was in a state, uncertain how to proceed, but primarily confused and upset because he just couldn't believe what he'd just seen happen. Like everyone else along Fore Street, he was captivated by the Buchanan twins. Yes, of course, there was the novelty value. It was unusual to see identical twins of their age also dressed identically. Then there was the way they finished each other's sentences, almost like they were one person, not two. However, their main attraction was their sheer niceness. They were warm, friendly, generous, always willing to help out, and they were funny, too. Jack had got into the habit of popping into the shop on the days Bea and Connie worked. Immediately a cup of coffee and a muffin would appear, and he loved talking to them – they were interesting, knowledgeable, and all-round good company.

So, he could hardly believe what he had seen this morning. It was such a shock and he just didn't know what to do. He called Camborne Police Station in the hopes of being able to talk to the boss. The duty sergeant strongly advised that the chief inspector should not be interrupted. 'There's a lot of shouting going on in the interview room,' Jack was told.

'The boss doesn't usually shout,' protested Jack.

'Well, he's certainly shouting today,' was the response.

Jack paced around his office for some time, getting himself more upset by the minute. Then a thought came to him that was so obvious, he couldn't think why it hadn't occurred to him in the first place. He called Merrin.

When Jack arrived at Merrin's cottage, she could see immediately that he was very upset. So, she made him a coffee and put a plate of biscuits in front of him – both had a calming effect.

'So what can I do for you, Jack?' Merrin asked.

'It's really a police matter,' said Jack, 'but I can't get hold of the boss and I think it's OK to tell you about it because you're sort of involved, and you're a solicitor.'

Merrin smiled. 'You just fire away, Jack, and if I think you're telling me something you shouldn't, I'll stop you.'

Jack leant back in his chair, with a big sigh.

'Thank you, Merrin Trip, you are a good girl. I'd better start at the beginning.' He hesitated. 'Those twins of yours, Bea and Connie, they've become very friendly with the little girl, Jessie, who stole the seal painting. Did you know about the painting?' Jack asked.

'Yes,' said Merrin, 'and I've met them all in the shop. Jessie seemed very taken with the twins and vice versa.'

'The twins told me that Jessie had talked about her dead brother and how he loved seals so much,' said Jack.

'They were very touched by the story and thought Jessie was a very brave little girl.'

'I agree,' said Merrin, wondering where on earth this story was going.

'I was walking along Fore Street this morning when I saw the twins meeting up with Jessie and her mum. There was a lot of excitement because the twins gave Jessie a glass statue of a seal sitting on a rock. Jessie was so pleased with it. She carefully held it high in the air so the sun lit it up.'

'That was very kind of the twins,' said Merrin.

'Yes and no,' said Jack.

'You better explain,' suggested Merrin.

Jack took a deep breath. 'The thing is, my maid, the glass seal was stolen just yesterday from the glass shop at the top end of Fore Street.'

'There may have been more than one seal, Jack,' said Merrin.

'No, I checked. They've only ever displayed the one seal. They don't make the glass themselves, they buy it in. It was quite an expensive item, but they thought it would sell during the summer. They couldn't afford to buy more than one.'

'And are you absolutely sure it is the same seal?' Merrin asked.

'Absolutely. I've seen it often in the shop window when walking past and then, of course, when it was stolen, the shop owner gave me a photograph of it. Look, here it is.'

Merrin studied the photograph Jack had given her. 'It's absolutely beautiful – I can imagine how it catches the light. So, what you're saying is that you believe the twins stole the seal to give to Jessie because of the story about her brother.'

'I can hardly believe it myself,' said Jack, 'but I can't think of another explanation. They are two such lovely ladies, it doesn't bear thinking about.'

'I agree,' said Merrin, 'and, Jack, does this mean you also think the twins are responsible for the spate of thieving which has been going on?'

'It fits in,' said Jack. 'The thieving began about the time they arrived in St Ives, and there are two of them, which would explain the volume of theft. Also, the thefts have dropped off somewhat since the twins started working in your shop, presumably because they have less time. I'm afraid it all fits, little Merrin Trip.'

'It's unbelievably awful if you're right, Jack. What are you going to do?'

'That's just the thing, I don't know. The boss is interviewing that Roxy person, or whatever she's called, and I have been advised not to interrupt him. The trouble is, my maid, I've become very fond of the twins – I often go into your shop and have a chat. I feel too emotionally involved, somehow, to go and arrest them.'

'If Louis is tied up, why not ask Ben Satchel to help you? It's perfectly correct for you to stand down from an investigation that involves people who are friends of yours – it represents a conflict of interest.'

'That's a good idea, I'll give Ben a call,' said Jack.

'He's a good choice,' said Merrin. 'He may be young but he's very sensitive for his age. The twins will be in good hands. Also tell Ben that if they want a solicitor, I'm happy to represent them, pro bono if necessary.'

'Is that a good idea? The shops in Fore Street are not going to like you representing the people who stole from them.'

'If it goes to trial, I'll duck out if necessary. I just thought I might be helpful in the early stages, as they know me. After all, if they are guilty, it's in everyone's interests that we get to the truth of the matter. Goodness, I still can't believe it, Jack.'

'Nor me,' said Jack.

CHAPTER FORTY-TWO

Until Annie began to speak, Louis had not been confident that the true story would emerge. But once she started, the words tumbled out, and it seemed as if it was a relief for her to be able to share it with someone at last.

'I spent early evening with Max, just as I said,' Annie began. 'Afterwards, I rowed out in the tender. I must admit I was much later than I'd told Tony I would be. However, when I went aboard, he was already seriously drunk, shouting and falling about. He was a mess and very angry. I ignored him and went into the galley to start preparing supper.

'He followed me in and started accusing me of having an affair with Max. He said the reason I didn't want to go to Scilly with him was because I had taken up with Max.'

'That was true though, wasn't it?' Louis asked, making sure his voice was gentle and not at all critical.

'Sort of,' Annie agreed. 'I was very attracted to Max, but at that stage in the evening, it was my intention to go home – home to Hubert – but Tony was still dead set on the Scilly Isles. It had been a stupid mistake going on holiday with Tony. I thought he was my escape route, that we could sail round Europe together. It was a pipe dream.' Her voice broke and she wiped away a tear. Louis remained silent.

'This is the difficult part,' Annie said, at last. 'The galley, as you can imagine, was very small. I was chopping up vegetables to make a risotto. I had my back to Tony. He was ranting on about how I'd used him, and I thought it best to just ignore him. Two things happened simultaneously.' Annie took a deep breath. 'I had the knife I was using for chopping the vegetables in my right hand. Tony grabbed my left shoulder and spun me round to face him. At the same moment, the yacht rocked and Tony fell forwards onto the knife.' Annie burst into sobs.

'So you stabbed him?' Louis said, after she'd calmed down.

'No, I didn't. I'd never hurt anyone, I'm not a violent person at all. Ask Jeremy. Looking back at what happened, which, of course, I've thought about over and over, I do vaguely remember the sound of a boat engine in the harbour, and it was that which must have made *Llamedos* rock. Tony was already unstable on his feet from his drinking, and he just toppled forward onto the knife and then onto the floor. I promise you, I absolutely promise you that's what happened.'

'Alright,' said Louis, 'so what happened next?'

'There was blood everywhere. I think the knife must have punctured his heart because it was obvious he was dead from the moment he hit the floor.'

'How did you know he was dead?' Louis asked.

'I felt his pulse. He wasn't breathing, his eyes were open, all fixed and staring, and there was so much blood, so much. I just didn't know what to do.'

'Dial 999?' Louis suggested, still trying hard not to sound critical.

'I couldn't do that because of Hubert's company shares.'

'I'm sorry,' said Louis, 'I'm not following the connection.'

'Hubert's just floated his company on the stock market and the shares are doing really well. When I told him I was going away for a few days, he said he hoped I'd have a lovely time but not to do anything that could get into the press and adversely affect the value of the shares. I promised to be careful.'

'Let me just get this straight,' said Louis. 'I thought you were leaving Hubert, not just going away for a few days.'

'I was intending to leave him. I dyed my hair and changed my name to Roxy and even pretended to be Tony's wife. But, after the week or so with Tony on *Llamedos*, I couldn't wait to get away, and all I could think about was going back home to Hubert and civilisation.'

'OK, let's leave it at that for a moment,' said Louis. 'You're in the galley with Tony dead and the place covered in blood and, as I think I'm understanding it, you didn't want to call for help because of Hubert's share price.'

'If Tony had been alive, I promise I would have called someone, but there was nothing I could do for him, so I had to think what was best for Hubert.'

And yourself, Louis thought.

'Even if I could have moved Tony, which I couldn't because he was too heavy, I couldn't have got rid of all the blood. So I decided to scupper the boat, drown the evidence – it seemed the only way.'

'Go on,' said Louis, incredulous now.

'I went into the cabin and then up on deck and brought everything that was movable and put them in the galley with Tony. I then locked the door. I obviously missed the lifebelt, though. I then motored the yacht out of the harbour, heading to just beyond Seal Island. Then I opened the seacock.'

'I'm not a nautical man – that would cause the yacht to sink?' Louis asked.

'Yes, a yacht of that size would normally take about two hours to sink, and I believe that's about how long it took. I climbed into the tender and cast the yacht adrift and then paddled around for about an hour, until I was sure she really was sinking. I saw no other shipping. It must have been the early hours of the morning by then, and you were right when you said the sea was very calm that night. It was like a millpond, with just the suspicion of a swell. It was beautiful, too – the sky full of stars and a new moon. Then I rowed back into the harbour. I had to row against the tide, but I managed it without any problem.'

'Did you think about Tony at all while all this was going on?' Louis asked, more from curiosity than anything else, just wondering how on earth this woman's mind worked.

'No, not really. I was too concerned about making sure no one knew what had just happened. Luckily I had been wearing a coat – it was covered in blood but the rest of what I was wearing was pretty OK. My shoes, however, were very bloodstained. Before leaving the yacht, I put my shoes and the coat in a bin liner with a heavy casserole dish, and threw them overboard. They sank immediately. When I got ashore, I decided to go to Max's. He had a separate doorbell to his flat, and he let me in. It was as I was explaining that I had left my shoes on the yacht – I suddenly realised that in all the panic, I had left my rucksack in a cupboard in the galley. So that part of the story was true: I did leave all my important possessions on board.'

'So, I'll ask this question once again. Why didn't you then go back to London and your husband? After all, that is what you intended to do, as I understand it.'

'I had to protect Hubert. I started calling myself Roxy Goodenough and I had to wait and see if the wreck was discovered. I was worried that I hadn't scuppered the yacht in deep enough water. However, I decided to give it a couple of weeks and if it hadn't been discovered by then, I thought it would be safe to go home. Of course, I didn't know then that Hubert was dying, and I wasn't expecting you and Jeremy to find me, let alone Len Carter.'

'So, are you saying that you intended to run away again if any part of the yacht had resurfaced?'

'That was the idea,' said Annie, 'so Hubert would not be linked to Tony in any way.'

'Why didn't you run away when I told you the lifebelt had been found?' Louis asked.

'Because Jeremy was watching me like a hawk, as he promised you he would. Also, that was when he told me Hubert was dying, which changed everything. I just have to see him – I can, can't I?' said Annie, her voice anguished.

Louis ignored her, trying his best to keep control of his temper. 'So, what was your relationship with Max all about – just passing the time?' He knew his voice sounded bitter.

'I was really fond of him and it helped having somewhere to stay. I couldn't leave St Ives until I was sure the wreck wouldn't be found, and I kept running out of money. Obviously, I didn't tell Max I was planning to go back to Hubert. In fact, I told him the opposite. I suppose that was wrong. I was taking advantage of him.'

It was too much for Louis. 'If you had told Max you were intending to go back to Hubert,' Louis shouted, 'he wouldn't have gone in search of Len Carter that night, in which case he would still be alive – wouldn't he, Annie?'

There was a long silence. Annie appeared shocked into silence, and Constable Shaw shifted uneasily in her seat.

At last Louis spoke. 'Lady Annie Eustace, I am charging you with perverting the course of justice and for failing to report a death. You will be remanded in custody here in Camborne pending a hearing date, which should be on Wednesday. I will support a bail application in view of your husband's declining health. However, as you seem to have a tendency to abscond, I imagine the bail will be set very high. Hopefully, Jeremy or Hubert will be able to help with this. Do you understand?' Annie hung her head and nodded. 'Two other points – would you be able to pinpoint on a chart, with any accuracy, where the yacht was scuppered? It might impress the judge if you could be seen as being co-operative.'

'Yes, I can do that,' Annie murmured.

'Secondly, when we retrieve Tony's body, I trust the pathologist will be able to tell us whether Tony fell on the knife . . . or was stabbed.'

CHAPTER FORTY-THREE

Jago and Gemma's plane had been delayed, so Merrin and Isla did not leave St Ives until five-thirty to collect them from Newquay Airport. It occurred to Isla that her mother was being unusually quiet as they joined the A30.

'What's up, Mum?' Isla asked. 'Are you brooding about something?'

So, Merrin told her daughter about the twins' theft of the glass seal.

'Are you sure Jack's got this right, Mum? He's such a sweetheart but he does get confused sometimes, and how is his eyesight? Was he sure it was the same glass seal as the one that was stolen?'

Merrin smiled. 'Questions, questions! You're going to make a fine lawyer, darling. I've checked out all the details with him, and he is absolutely certain that the twins gave Jessie the stolen seal.'

'What's going to happen now?' Isla asked.

'Jack has become very friendly with Bea and Connie,

and felt he just couldn't arrest them himself. Legally, that's quite correct, as I'm sure you know – with friends there is a potential conflict of interest. So, the case has been handed over to Ben Satchel. The reason I've been a little preoccupied is because Ben is due at the twins' house in about ten minutes in order to question them – not only about the seal, but also about the other thefts that have taken place in St Ives recently.'

'You think the twins are the phantom thieves who no one has been able to catch? Surely not, Mum. Bea and Connie – no, it's just not possible.'

'That's just the problem,' said Merrin. 'Like you, I just can't believe they would steal anything from anyone.'

Newquay Airport was busier than usual. 'Where are they?' said Isla.

'Jago will be the last off the plane,' said Merrin. 'He always has to wait until everyone else has disembarked. It's a pain.'

'It's more than a pain,' Isla said, indignantly. 'Surely, as a disabled person, he should be allowed off first?'

'It's all about the wheelchair. Don't be so impatient. We're not at Heathrow, he'll be off the plane in another five minutes.'

'Discrimination,' Isla grumbled.

Jago had been partially paralysed in a surfing accident about five years ago. One of life's enthusiasts, he appeared to have never let life in a wheelchair get him down. All he really hated was people trying to help him. With a strong physique, he could manoeuvre himself in and out of his wheelchair with ease.

True to form, Jago appeared at last, wheeling himself

across the airport concourse at great speed despite the large suitcase on his knees. At the sight of his sister and niece, his face split into a huge grin, but the moment brother and sister embraced, they both began to cry. Gemma and Isla exchanged hugs and waited while Jago and Merrin sobbed. They were used to it – the Tripconeys were known to be an emotional bunch on occasion.

On the journey back to St Ives, Jago was anxious for an update on the cause of Max's death. Merrin had to tell him that the sad conclusion was that they would probably never know how or why their dear friend had died.

'It doesn't sound like Louis,' Jago said. 'He always gets the bad guy in the end.'

As usual, Isla was quick to Louis's defence. 'He knows who the bad guy is: it's the private investigator. He just can't prove it because there's no evidence.'

'What about this woman, Roxy?' said Jago. 'Are you sure, is Louis sure, that she had nothing to do with Max's death? She sounds a right weirdo, by all accounts.'

'She wasn't involved in Max's death,' said Merrin. 'She was in his flat when he died. They were both worried about the private investigator, who appeared to be potentially violent and was threatening to take Roxy back to London by force. Max told me himself that he had insisted on Roxy staying in the flat.'

'But someone killed Max,' Jago said, 'and they shouldn't get away with killing such a lovely man. Max would never have killed himself, he wasn't a big drinker – so how come he hit his head and drowned? It makes no sense.'

'Don't upset yourself, darling,' Gemma said to Jago.

'We know, from personal experience, that Louis Peppiatt is a great bloke. If anyone can find out what happened to Max, Louis will.'

The *great bloke* in question was not feeling very great. Not only had the interview with Annie, and the subsequent preparation of a statement, worn him out, but he'd also had to face the wrath of Jeremy.

'You can't keep Annie in custody,' he shouted, after Louis had told him about Annie's confession. 'Supposing my father dies this weekend – how are you going to feel about that, Louis?'

'You told me that your father still has another week or two,' said Louis.

'But all this stress at not being able to find his wife could easily kill him,' Jeremy insisted.

'I'm sorry,' said Louis, 'but the law has to take its course. Your stepmother has confessed to at least two very serious crimes, and we only have her word for it that Tony fell on the knife.'

'Are you suggesting Annie killed Tony?' said Jeremy. 'Because if so, Louis, you must be off your head. She's got her problems, like all of us, but she'd never hurt anyone, let alone kill them. You're barking up the wrong tree, Chief Inspector, by God, you are.'

'I'm not saying she did,' Louis thundered, patience now at a very low ebb. 'Nonetheless, she failed to report Tony's death and then sank him in his yacht. You must see, surely, that the circumstances surrounding the incident have to be thoroughly investigated?'

'Yes, I'm sorry, I do see that,' Jeremy admitted.

'I'm doing my best. I've put in a special request for an immediate hearing, given Hubert's delicate state. Hopefully, it will be on Wednesday. I will support Annie's release on bail, but you need to be prepared for finding a pretty hefty sum, given that she appears to have a tendency to run away. You're free to go and see her now, and I suggested she made a list of things she will need from the hotel for her stay here. Are you going to tell Hubert what has happened?'

'Absolutely not,' said Jeremy. 'I'll be responsible for the bail money and we can tell Father that she lost her rucksack containing her phone, etcetera, hence the silence. I think he's slightly lost the plot so far as time is concerned, and I am determined he should go to his grave never knowing what his wife has been up to.'

Driving home to Truro, Louis thought long and hard about Annie Eustace. Once she had summoned up the courage to tell him what allegedly had happened to Tony and his yacht, while there had been tears, Louis could spot no real sense of remorse. The tears were all for herself – not for Max, not for Tony. The more time he spent with her, the more it seemed to him that she was seriously narcissistic, since she appeared to have little or no empathy for anyone. She seemed completely fixated on herself. He wondered whether this had always been part of her nature – or had Hubert's pampering of her been largely responsible?

Two men were dead, for which she was at least partially responsible. Did she even care?

CHAPTER FORTY-FOUR

On Monday evening, the harbour master arrived at Camborne Police Station, armed with various charts of the seascape immediately beyond St Ives harbour. Annie seemed confident about identifying where she believed *Llamedos* had sunk. Her sailing experience proved useful because, by mid-morning on Saturday, the police divers had found the wreck, and by early afternoon, the body of Tony Barrow had been brought ashore and identified by the harbour master.

Louis was there to meet the body and Graham Bennett arrived shortly afterwards.

'Another body recovered from a watery grave within a week,' said Graham. 'What are you up to, Peppiatt? I have an important golf match this evening, which includes your boss, John Dent. He's not going to be too pleased when I cancel, is he?'

Louis's temper was only just under control. 'I can tell you that the knife sticking out of the victim's chest has been there since about ten o'clock on the evening of 11th July. What interests me is whether he fell on the knife or whether someone stuck it in him. Secondly, I am told he died instantly and it is very important that I know if that is true. Thirdly, I need to know if he was drunk at the time of death, drunk enough to be unsteady on his feet.' Louis glanced at his watch. 'It's only two o'clock now. If you can answer those three questions for me by tonight, Graham, then the rest can wait until tomorrow so you can play your bloody game of golf with sir this evening. I just do not understand this obsession with bashing a little ball about, uphill and down dale, wearing silly clothes.'

'Dear me,' said Graham, 'I can see you're not in the best of moods, Peppiatt. Can I remind you that it's not my fault that you keep presenting me with dead bodies. Having said that, I should be able to give you the answer to your questions this evening, and in a salute to your ridiculous prejudice, I will try not to wear *silly clothes*. Alright?'

Louis waited until the body of Tony Barrow had been removed. He realised he had never asked Annie if she had removed the knife from where it was implanted in Tony's chest. It was rather a shock to see it still there, but hopefully it would make it easier for Graham to work out how it got there. He hadn't mentioned fingerprints to Graham; there was no point. Obviously, Annie's prints would be on the knife handle because she had been chopping vegetables.

Louis thanked all concerned for the parts they had played in finding Tony's body. The future of the wrecked yacht had yet to be determined. He then headed back towards his car. On the way, he phoned the Camborne station and asked the duty sergeant to tell Annie that Tony's body had been found, and to thank her for so accurately calculating where *Llamedos* had sunk. He also asked that the duty solicitor should be informed, in case Annie changed her mind about engaging his services. He noticed there was a missed call from Ben Satchel, but no message left, so clearly it wasn't important.

There was nothing more Louis could do until he heard from Graham Bennett, and the thought of going home to wait for news depressed him. On impulse, instead of reclaiming his car, he climbed the steps to Merrin's cottage and knocked on the door. She opened it immediately.

'Louis, isn't it awful about Tony Barrow? To think he's been lying in *Llamedos* just beyond the harbour all this time. I didn't like him, poor man, but still . . . I suppose Roxy is involved in all this?'

Louis smiled a little wanly. 'This town!' he said. 'Just for once, it would be nice to be able to tell you all something you didn't already know.'

Merrin smiled back. 'It's very unlikely that will ever happen, Louis. You look exhausted – coffee, food, what can I get you?'

'A coffee and one of Horatio's biscuits would be perfect, thank you. You'll understand, I can't tell you anything about what's going on with Tony's death at the moment. There is a hearing on Wednesday morning, and your chum Graham Bennett is hard at work even as we speak. Hopefully, he will have some answers by the end of the day.'

'I totally understand, so to take your mind off Tony Barrow, let me tell you about another case, a very sad one, but at least no one dies.'

'Go on then,' said Louis, accepting his coffee and helping himself to a biscuit; but because he was well trained, he immediately broke off a piece for Horatio. Then, of course, William wanted some biscuit, too. Louis held up what remained. 'Am I entitled to a second biscuit?'

Merrin laughed. 'Just this once,' she said.

She then told him about the Buchanan twins and the theft of the glass seal for Jessie. She explained why Jack felt he couldn't be involved and how Ben Satchel had taken over the case. 'They've confessed to stealing the seal but, on my instructions, have not commented on the other thefts in town. Ben is going to interview them again tomorrow morning, and I will be present to represent them. They haven't been arrested as yet.'

'Even a disillusioned old bugger like me finds it hard to believe those two lovely ladies are thieves,' said Louis.

'I know,' said Merrin. 'No one can believe it. Even Ben said he felt like telling them to shut up when they admitted the theft of the seal, on the grounds that it couldn't be true. And he hadn't even met them before he interviewed them.'

'Oh my God,' said Louis, suddenly. 'Does Jessie know about this? It would be awful for her to find that she was in possession of stolen goods, after the painting episode.'

'Don't worry, I've sorted it,' said Merrin. 'I went to the glass shop, paid for the seal and told them the full story. They aren't going to press charges, so I guess it's now up to the police. If the twins did steal all the other items taken this summer, I suppose the police might want to add the seal to the other charges, but hopefully, Ben can be persuaded out of doing that.'

'You are a marvel,' said Louis. 'So, I assume you're

acting for the twins pro bono as well as buying Jessie a glass seal? If I may say so, Mrs McKenzie, you don't make much money out of your chosen career now you've moved back to St Ives – in fact, it's costing you a fortune. Tell me, can you represent both twins?'

'Yes, I double-checked that, to coin a phrase. If the charges go ahead, they will be charged with the same crime, so yes, I can represent both of them. Also, don't worry about Jessie finding out about the seal. The town is full of what's happened to Tony Barrow at the moment, and the Youngs are going home the day after tomorrow. I don't think the theft of one glass seal is going to make the nationals, do you?'

It was nine o'clock that evening before Graham called Louis with his initial findings concerning the death of Tony Barrow.

'Let me start with your two easy questions first,' said Graham. 'Yes, our victim had consumed a skinful before his untimely death.'

'Enough to make him unsteady on his feet?' Louis asked.

'Well, difficult to be precise – people's resistance to alcohol varies a great deal. He was a big chap and his enlarged liver suggests he was a serious drinker.'

'Oh come, Graham, help me out here,' pleaded Louis.

'I think it is extremely unlikely that he was very steady on his feet,' said Graham, 'and as to the manner of his death, there are no doubts. He would have died almost immediately – the knife severely damaged his aorta, hence the massive blood loss. If his injury had occurred in the car park of a large modern hospital, in theory he might have survived, but moored up in St Ives harbour he had no chance. Immediate medical intervention would have been his only hope of survival, but in my view the damage was too severe for even that to be effective.'

'He was going to die anyway, even with a 999 call or if, by some lucky chance, there was a heart surgeon on the Wharf?' Louis asked.

'Yes, Tony Barrow was going to die anyway,' said Graham. 'Now we come to the tricky one, and the quick answer is I can't tell you if the victim fell on the knife or was stabbed. He clearly fell forwards, face down, if you like, which is why the knife was driven so deep into his body. However, whether he simply fell onto the knife, or fell forwards after being stabbed, I cannot tell you. Whoever was with him turned him onto his back, because that is how the divers found him. The person involved made no attempt to remove the knife but had they done so, it would have made no difference.'

Louis sighed. 'So, once again, I'm never going to know if it was an accident or murder?'

'I'm afraid not. One of us must be losing our touch, Peppiatt. The question is whether it's you or me.'

CHAPTER FORTY-FIVE

One week later

It was Saturday morning. Louis had slept badly the night before and had risen early, since sleep was still eluding him. Before him on his kitchen table was a black coffee and a fried egg on toast. He stared at the egg, which, now he'd cooked it, held no appeal. Reluctantly, he pushed the plate away – he hated food waste; maybe he could reheat it later, though that felt even less appealing.

He hadn't seen or spoken to Merrin for several days. He'd needed time to digest the fact that he had totally failed where Max was concerned. He felt ashamed and reluctant to talk to her, but he knew he needed to make contact. He drank his coffee, rinsed his mug and then picked up his phone.

Merrin was alone in her cottage. Pippa and Joey were manning the shop and Isla was *helping* them – she and Joey had been seeing a great deal of one another, which pleased Merrin enormously. Mercifully, Jago was coming for lunch so cooking for him at least gave her something to do. She had found she needed to keep busy, or thoughts of Max crowded her mind and hurtled her into despair. She was just putting some olive oil in a casserole dish when her phone rang. It was Louis.

'I'm so sorry I haven't been in touch,' Louis said, without preamble.

'That's alright,' said Merrin. 'You've had a really tough couple of weeks. Are you doing anything special today? Only, Jago's coming to lunch and I know he would like to see you, and also we have two hearings to mull over.'

'I'd love that, thank you,' said Louis, with evident relief. 'Merrin, I'm so sorry I didn't do a better job where Max was concerned.'

'Don't fret,' said Merrin. 'Let's talk later. Come about one. Looking forward to seeing you.'

Louis arrived to find Merrin and an empty wheelchair in the kitchen. 'Jago's already gone up to the balcony. It's such a lovely day, we thought drinks up there would be good.'

'Can I help?' Louis asked.

'You take up the bottle and glasses, and I'll be there in a moment with some nibbles.'

Jago was sitting on a chair in the sun, gazing out over the harbour. 'Louis!' he said. 'It's good to see you. How are you?'

'Not bad. It's good to see you too, Jago. How's business?'

'Great, we've moved into clothing now as well, and it's going amazingly well. We're quite a team – me and Gemma, our son, and my brother-in-law Tom Trehearne, who I know you will remember with mixed feelings.

Then there's my original partner, Roger, and his girlfriend, who's a fashion designer and brilliant at it, too – hence the expansion into clothing. Anyway, enough of me, how are you, Louis? Merrin said you sounded frazzled on the phone, and if I may say so, you look a bit knackered. It's been a tough period for you, by all accounts.'

Before Louis could answer, Merrin arrived and Jago opened the wine. 'There's only one possible toast, isn't there?' he said. 'To Max,' they chorused, without hesitation.

'Before we talk about Max,' said Merrin, 'tell us about the hearing concerning Tony Barrow.'

'It's going to trial. Annie has been charged with perverting the course of justice and failing to report a death. A charge of manslaughter was discussed but there's absolutely no evidence to back that up. She's on bail, and a huge sum is involved since she has a habit of disappearing. She's gone back up to London to be with her husband, Hubert, who is dying. She and Jeremy have not told Hubert about Tony's death, and somehow Jeremy has managed to keep Annie's name out of the press. Actually, he's being a star – he's not only put up the bail money, he's paying back to Max's estate the money Max lent Annie, and also, Merrin, the money she borrowed from you. He's a very decent chap.'

'That is good of him,' said Merrin. 'Will Annie go to prison, do you think?'

'Once Hubert has died, I have no doubt they will employ a very fancy lawyer to handle the case. I'm sure he or she will come up with some impressive mitigating circumstances. Annie is not a very likeable character, but I tend to believe her story that it was an accident. So, to answer your question, I think she will avoid a custodial sentence, though I can't help feeling she shouldn't – she's involved, however obliquely, in the death of two men.'

'Has Ben told you about the twins' hearing?' Merrin asked, anxious to change the subject.

'Only that they have been charged with a fair number of thefts, and that the trial is likely to be in the spring. I still can't believe those two ladies could do such a thing.'

'Ah, but did Ben tell you why they steal?' Merrin asked.

'No,' said Louis, intrigued.

'They've been conducting a sort of Robin Hood scenario. They steal stuff to give away to people they consider more deserving.'

'You're kidding?' said Louis.

Merrin smiled. 'I'm absolutely not,' she said. 'They were aware that most of the people living in West Cornwall have a much lower standard of living than the people who visit on holiday. So, they've been trying to redress the balance. Sweets, fudge and toys for local children, clothes and little luxuries for local adults. I don't know if you remember, Louis, but Pippa lost her bracelet and insisted it had been stolen. Then suddenly it turned up again. The twins did steal it before they worked for us. Seeing it was sea glass, they didn't think it was valuable. They stole it to give to a neighbour whose baby had just been stillborn. When they saw how upset Pippa was and realised how much work she had put into making it, they put it back. They made a similar mistake with the seal. They were so touched by Jessie's story, they stole something which was much more expensive than their usual swag and gave it to Jessie in the middle of

Fore Street. They don't keep anything for themselves.'

'And you believe them?' Louis asked.

'I do, and I believe so did the judge. Even he seemed reluctant to send them for trial, such is their charm.'

'Obviously, they can't go on working for you,' Jago said. 'Tell me, do you think this Robin Hood spree was a one-off in St Ives, or do you think it's something they did before moving here?'

Merrin smiled at her brother. 'I didn't ask, didn't dare. I'm just hoping they will be judged on their St Ives high jinks. I still don't know how they got away with it without being spotted, which does suggest it's something they may have done before. Honestly, I still can't believe it. I would like to go on representing them, but I don't want to upset the local shopkeepers, so we'll have to see. Joey, Pippa and Lizzie are absolutely devastated about the twins and are having to work very hard now they don't have them to take up the slack. Also, we've just launched our online business, which is already doing well. The upside is that at least they don't have any time to mope.' She hesitated.

'Changing the subject, Max's will was read yesterday. There are two recipients – he has left his business to Poppy, plus a sum of money to get her started, and the balance of his estate goes to Isla, as his god-daughter. Poppy has always wanted her own business and she'll be brilliant at it. It will, of course, remain known as Max Richards Estate Agents. Isla will now be able to buy a little property of her own, once she knows where she's going to settle.'

'Dear old Max,' said Jago, his voice rough with emotion. 'That's just perfect.'

'On the subject of Max,' said Louis, 'I have already told

Merrin how sorry I am for not handling the case better, but I haven't apologised to you, Jago. I so regret I wasn't able to do more.'

'What could you possibly have done?' said Jago. 'There were no witnesses and no forensic evidence. You may think you know who is responsible, but without evidence, you had no chance. We all understand that, Louis.'

'But that's only part of it. What I should have done is check to see whether Len Carter was in town. He's an ex-copper with a history of violence and I'd already begged Jeremy not to hire him. However, in my arrogance, I thought I was way ahead of him in finding Annie, so I didn't check how he was getting on. Len was a good detective, by all accounts, I should have remembered that. As it turned out, Len told the Met that he had learnt of Annie's whereabouts from her hairdresser, of all people!'

'Oh Louis, you must know that women tell their hairdressers absolutely everything,' said Merrin, smiling.

'I hadn't a clue,' admitted Louis, 'but I certainly know now. The only small crumb of comfort is that Len was unable to claim his fat fee for finding Annie. He didn't even ask for his expenses to be reimbursed, apparently. I suspect he thinks it's prudent to lie low.'

'Louis, it isn't just you who is agonising about missed opportunities. When I helped Max to escape from being followed by Len, I should have realised the danger he could be in,' said Merrin. 'Max was clearly frightened of the man. Why didn't I call you and tell you that Len Carter was on the scene? If you think you're to blame, then you have to accept that I am, too.'

'Enough of this,' said Jago. 'I'm starving and I'm going

to bump myself downstairs.' He lowered himself onto the floor and shuffled forward to the top step. He stopped and turned to face them. 'There is just one thing I'd like to say. You two are driving me nuts. Louis, you are the world's most decent bloke, apart from myself, of course. My sister is just great, in every way. Could I suggest you two start sharing something more meaningful than a mutual sense of guilt. For God's sake, sort yourselves out – if not for me, then do it for Max.'

CHAPTER FORTY-SIX

St Ia's was a very large church for what was essentially a very small town. The current building dated back to the reign of King Henry V, though it had been a place of worship since the 1400s. On the day of Max Richards's funeral, there was not a spare seat to be found and for most, it was standing room only. There were hymns, prayers and readings, and then Jago Tripconey wheeled himself to beside Max's coffin in order to give a brief eulogy.

'Max Richards was my best friend. We knew one another from babyhood, and therefore I feel qualified to say Max didn't have a mean bone in his body. He was kind and generous, and my family and I loved him dearly. Of course, we all know how much he loved the ladies, but he was no misogynist. He just adored the company of women, and over the years, I have come to believe that most of his girlfriends, despite his naughtiness, were pleased to have known him.'

'Too right!' shouted a female voice from the back of

the church, and suddenly everyone was laughing. There were whistles, catcalls, clapping, and stamping of feet. It immediately became clear that there was a disproportionate number of women in the congregation – Max's old girlfriends were out in force. Jago glanced nervously at Poppy but she was laughing and cheering, too.

It took quite a while for Jago to gain the attention of his audience once more.

'An accident put me in this chair – I was showing off my surfing skills when I was far too old to do so. I was nervous coming home to St Ives in a wheelchair for the first time. While a family party was raging, I wheeled myself out onto the Wharf, and looked out over the harbour beach, remembering all the things I used to do, but no longer could. Then Max appeared. He gave me a quick hug, then said, "Race you to the Sloop, the loser pays for the beers." It was the challenge I needed. I kept my chair on the road, wheeling along like a mad creature. Max was on the pavement, having to weave in and out of groups of visitors. So I won and, as I'm sure you can imagine, much beer was drunk. My wife, children and sister have been a marvellous support, but it was Max who made me see my life wasn't over, it was just different and could be just as much fun.

'Thanks, Max – you were a very special person and will be so missed by us all.'

The wake was at Tristan's Fish Plaice, of course. There were so many people that the crowds spilt out onto the Wharf and onto the beach below. The atmosphere was lovely – warm, relaxed and oddly joyful – celebrating a life well lived.

Louis found Merrin in the crowd. 'Are you alright?' he asked.

Merrin looked around her and smiled. 'Yes, it's hard to be sad right now. How Max would have loved this party.'

'I'll get us a couple of glasses of wine – shall we go and sit on the beach? There's something I want to ask you.'

They found a quiet spot in the sun, against the harbour wall. They clinked glasses and murmured Max's name.

'What did you want to ask me?' Merrin said.

'In the last couple of years, a lot of people have suggested we should be in a relationship, and, as you know, for the most part it's annoyed us both on the grounds that it's no one's business but ours. However, what Jago said on the balcony the other day was different. I know he really cares about us, and it made me think that maybe we should be sharing more things together.' He smiled. 'Other than just guilt.'

'I'm not sure I'm ready,' said Merrin. 'It's only just over four years since Adam died.'

'I'm not sure you're ready either, or indeed ever will be,' Louis said, taking her hand. 'And as I have already said, I'm also not at all sure you should involve yourself with another policeman, after losing Adam the way you did.'

'True,' said Merrin.

'But as we agreed at your shop opening party, let's try and spend more time together, take things at our own pace and just see what happens. What do you think?'

'I'd like that very much, Louis,' said Merrin, simply.

They leant back against the harbour wall, not talking but still holding hands, shutting their eyes against the sun, enjoying its warmth and an unexpected sense of peace. So absorbed had they been in their conversation that they hadn't noticed Jago struggling across the sand towards them, helped by Gemma pushing his chair. As Jago approached, he studied the pair. Louis looked a lot less strained than when they'd last met, and Merrin no longer displayed the look of haunted misery caused by Max's death. And they were holding hands.

'Hi,' he said, making them both jump. 'That's more like it!'

EPILOGUE

Since arriving back in their Chelsea home, Annie Eustace had hardly left her husband's side, except to grab a few hours' sleep when he too was sleeping. She had surprised everyone in the household with her depth of devotion to Hubert – all, that is, except Jeremy, who was starting to understand her.

Her past adventures had been just that; there had never been any serious desire to leave Hubert. Her friend Alice had momentarily derailed her commitment to Hubert, but it wouldn't have lasted. Hubert was her security – she could only have her adventures because he was always there for her when she came home. Now he was dying, her confidence was slipping away, along with his life. How she was going to cope with the loss of Hubert and the pending trial, Jeremy could not imagine.

They talked a little about the future. Annie appeared to be very grateful to Jeremy for putting up the bail money so that Hubert did not need to know about the trial, and also for repaying the money she owed. Jeremy asked if he and Sophie could have the Chelsea house, while Annie kept Newton Abbot. She was more than happy for this to happen and immediately wrote to their solicitor to that effect. 'I won't need a house, let alone two, as I'll probably be detained at His Majesty's pleasure,' she said, trying to smile bravely. Bizarrely, she was much nicer, Jeremy realised, now that her world was falling apart – even his wife Sophie, who had never particularly liked Annie, noticed this.

The day came when Hubert's pain required the fitting of a syringe driver to keep his morphine at an acceptable level. Before he lost consciousness, he told Annie he loved her but he had no such words for Jeremy. When he died three days later, Annie was inconsolable, and a doctor had to be called to give her a sedative to calm her down.

By contrast, Jeremy did not shed a tear, which worried his wife.

'Don't bottle up your feelings,' Sophie said. She held out her arms. 'Come here and let me give you a cuddle, you poor old chap.'

Jeremy submitted to the cuddle but remained dry-eyed. 'Aren't you at all sad that your father has just died?' Sophie asked.

'Yes, of course, but it's nothing like when Mother died. That was truly dreadful,' said Jeremy.

'Of course it was, you were only a little boy' – she gave him a squeeze – 'and you didn't have me.'

'Father was never a parent to me, you see. He just wasn't interested. He was too wrapped up in his business – though later, his love for Annie softened him a little. The only person who made me feel safe when my mother died, who behaved like a father should, wasn't my father at all.'

'Who was that?' Sophie asked.

'A young constable in the police force. His name was Louis Peppiatt.'

ACKNOWLEDGEMENTS

For their help and encouragement, I particularly would like to thank Michael Fowler, Diana Palmer, Sally Cuckson, my parrot, Mozart, who continues to provide me with endless material for Horatio's antics – and, of course, the splendid team at Allison & Busby.

DEBORAH FOWLER has published over six hundred short stories, fifteen novels and a number of non-fiction books on subjects such as guides for small businesses and money management. Deborah lives in a small hamlet just outside St Ives.